OFFICIAL STATS

NAME:	Larry Duncan
VITALS:	Age: 36 Height: 6'0" Eye Color: Brown Hair: Dark
OCCUPATION:	Pharmacist
OBJECTIVE:	Protect loved ones, solve medical mystery, save himself from more romantic heartbreak.
ADDITIONAL INFO:	Boy-next-door caregiver type, rescuing baby birds, old folks and damsels in distress.

DANGEROUS
TO
LOVE

DANGEROUS TO LOVE USA

SUZANNE ELLISON
A DANGEROUS LOYALTY

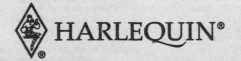

HARLEQUIN®

TORONTO • NEW YORK • LONDON
AMSTERDAM • PARIS • SYDNEY • HAMBURG
STOCKHOLM • ATHENS • TOKYO • MILAN • MADRID
PRAGUE • WARSAW • BUDAPEST • AUCKLAND

For Larry Dunst, creative consultant and real-life hero
of Clough's Pharmacy, Fillmore, California,
and
Frank Dunst, heart of Clough's, who bears no resemblance
to the fictional hero's father...except for his dedication
to his business and his love for his son.

HARLEQUIN BOOKS
225 Duncan Mill Road, Don Mills,
Ontario, Canada M3B 3K9

ISBN 0-373-82313-4

A DANGEROUS LOYALTY

Copyright © 1991 by Suzanne Pierson Ellison

Visit us at www.eHarlequin.com

Printed in U.S.A.

SUZANNE ELLISON

is the author of two dozen novels for adults and young people, including bestselling romances, *Hannah* and *Eagle Knight*. She is also the recipient of the Arizona Library Association's Outstanding Young Adult Author Award for *The Last Warrior*.

A retired schoolteacher with a B.A. in Ethnic Studies and a master's degree in English, Suzanne retains great pride in her two-thousand-book personal-research library, which she affectionately refers to as "Alexandria West." In addition to tracking down unusual aspects of American history, her many interests include dog obedience training, birding, swimming, music and traditional hand-pieced quilting.

She lives in a cozy little house in California with her romantic husband, Brian, her loving daughter, Tara, one terrific dog and a grumpy old cat.

Books by Suzanne Ellison

Harlequin Superromance

Wings of Gold #165
Pinecones and Orchids #258
For All the Right Reasons #283
Words Unspoken #308
Fair Play #315
Candle in the Window #369
With Open Arms #393
Heart of the West #420
Soul of the West #423
Spirit of the West #427
A Dangerous Loyalty #452
Shifting Sands #488

Harlequin Intrigue

Nowhere To Run #46

Harlequin Books

Tyler
Blazing Star
Arrowpoint

Dear Reader,

I used to live in a very small town. One day, my pharmacist, whose family had owned his drugstore for over fifty years, asked me if I had ever written a romance with a pharmacist hero. I told him I had not, but if he would help me come up with a plot with a pharmaceutical twist, I'd try to make him famous.

At first this was merely a joke between us. Each time I came in, we'd bounce around theories of how certain common drugs could be substituted for others—deliberately or inadvertently—causing damage only to those patients with specific conditions. One day my plotting and his proposed medication gaffes clicked, and the whole story snapped instantly into place. The two of us had great fun melding the plot and all the hometown characters together.

Happy Reading,

Suzanne Ellison

Please address questions and book requests to:
Harlequin Reader Service
U.S.: 3010 Walden Ave., P.O. Box 1325, Buffalo, NY 14269
Canadian: P.O. Box 609, Fort Erie, Ont. L2A 5X3

CHAPTER ONE

THERE WAS VERY LITTLE that happened in Porter that Johnnie Sue Rawlings could not see out the front window of the Cornsilk Cafe. From the cash register she could scan Duncan's Drugs, the Curls 'n' Pearls Salon of Beauty and Elwood Hazlett's black-and-white cruiser when it was parked in the back lot, even though the front door of the police station was actually around the corner out of sight. She could study the half-dozen old pickups that normally lined the street, and generally guess where each truck's owner was likely to be wasting time at any given hour of the day. And she could spot the occasional semi rig that strayed off the highway when a driver craved a cup of coffee that wouldn't rust his stomach.

What she couldn't see from her castle, Johnnie Sue heard about within moments after it occurred. Her regulars—the bulk of her business—kept her posted on each day's events and expected her to do the same for them. When something truly out of the ordinary happened—like the time Bernard Bixby's pregnant sow crawled into Elwood's brand-new police car and wedged itself under the steering wheel—some noble soul would call the Cornsilk first thing or come running in to make an announcement to the denim-clad crowd.

But nobody had warned Johnnie Sue that a brunette beauty in a gray-silk businesswoman's suit would show up at the Cornsilk at seven twenty-three on a Tuesday morning in June and settle down in a booth in the dining room, where no local ever dared to set foot until noon. It was obvious that she was not a casual tourist passing by: she had no children, no bulky bag, no travel-worn, headachy look. In fact, she looked as though she'd just walked out of her front door after spending an hour before the mirror. Not a single pin showed through the thick classic bun on the back of her head; not a lock wisped out of place.

For the past ten or twenty years Johnnie Sue had worn her long, thin hair the same way, but she noticed, without envy, that on the stranger the style looked like some radiant new fashion, while on Johnnie Sue it looked like the best way to wring out a shedding, discolored mop. She never thought about her hair when she was working, just as she never thought about her clean, faded jeans, gaudy T-shirts or brilliant aprons adorned with ruffles and her proudly stitched letters that spelled out the words "Cornsilk Cafe."

It had been so long since Johnnie Sue had worn makeup that she would have been hard-pressed to name the ingredients used to paint this perfectly chiseled face, but she could tell that the younger woman had devoted a great deal of time to looking her best this morning. That fact alone was enough to make her stand out like a sore thumb in Porter.

Johnnie Sue headed toward the dining room to tell the outsider she had to move, but when those big eyes flashed up at her—shy as a newborn baby goat's—she took pity on the girl.

"'Mornin'," she declared as genially as she was able, sloshing freshly brewed coffee into a heavy brown mug. "Want a menu?"

The girl licked her slightly mauve lips. "No, thank you. Black coffee will be fine."

Johnnie Sue nodded briskly, not bothering to memorize

the brunette's preference since she did not expect to serve her again. In fact, the reason she'd straggled into the Cornsilk in the first place was puzzling to Johnnie Sue, and Johnnie Sue didn't like puzzles of any kind. Quietly she pondered the possibilities as she headed toward the kitchen to check on the new cook. Sam didn't scramble eggs nearly as well as the last fellow, whose six-year tenure at the Cornsilk had ended abruptly last week when he'd humiliated Hershell Duncan and Johnnie Sue had fired him on the spot.

Her cowboy boots clacked on the linoleum floor as she gave orders to Sam, swiped at a blob of jelly on the nearest table and surveyed her domain. It was, as always, exactly the same, and her greatest goal in life was that it remain unchanged.

A passing trucker had once told Johnnie Sue about the ocean that swept the beach near the California town where he was born. Each wave came and went in moments, he'd said, but each one always looked the same. Johnnie Sue thought of her regulars the same way. It didn't really matter which ones sat on her barstools and filled up her booths; what mattered was that some of them were there at all times, keeping her busy, applauding her bad manners, laughing at her stupid and slightly bawdy jokes. From five in the morning till ten at night she kept the Cornsilk open—later if it was occupied by one man or by twenty. She didn't make a profit on the last few hours or even on the slow afternoons, but that didn't bother Johnnie Sue. After all, she didn't run the Cornsilk just to make a living or to provide a gathering spot for the people of the town. She'd taken it over mainly to keep from losing her mind.

She noticed that the World War II machete Hershell had given her years ago—hanging on the wall above table six—was getting dusty. She made a mental note to spend the afternoon cleaning all the knives in her collection—at least the ones that adorned the Cornsilk walls—before Gert, Maxine and Lotty joined her at three. It was Aggie Duncan, Hershell's late wife, who'd first decided years ago that Johnnie Sue needed a social break during the lonely weekday afternoons, and even though Aggie was gone now, the tradition lingered.

Coffee and donuts at seven comprised another tradition for the men now gathered around Johnnie Sue. To her left, two local merchants jawed with Hershell; to her right, Elwood's chubby young deputy droned on about his do-nothing night. Six other fellows from the surrounding farms lumped together in predictable configurations, and far beyond the barstools—alone—sat the flawlessly sculptured brunette.

Clay Billings, the young deputy, caught Johnnie Sue's eye and lifted his chin in a questioning gesture, and Johnnie Sue shrugged in reply. Quickly she considered the same options she knew Clayboy was turning over in his mind: maybe an out of town lawyer, realtor or insurance agent trying to get her company out from under a claim? But there had been no major arrests in town since that horse-rustling trouble last summer and no insurance problems since Bernard Bixby and the other poor folks who'd used that improperly tested psoriasis drug had died. Aggie Duncan had been one of them, but Johnnie Sue never lumped Aggie in with the rest. In Johnnie Sue's view, when a woman is your best friend for forty-nine years, you don't think of her passing as "an unfortunate drug-related death." In fact, only three years after her funeral, you can't yet think of her as dead.

It was the thought of Aggie, however, that caused Johnnie Sue's meandering mind to take a different tack. Ever since the lawsuit over the psoriasis drug deaths, Larry Duncan—Aggie and Hershell's thirty-six-year-old son—had gotten too big for his britches and started pressing Hershell to retire from the family-owned pharmacy. Hershell, who'd spent his whole life dispensing medication from his tidy little world on the main street of town, insisted that he'd sooner die than stare at the walls eight hours a day now that Aggie was gone. But recently his cataracts had gotten so bad that reading the doctors' scribbles had put him to the test, and a month ago Larry had flat-out forbidden him to fill another prescription until he agreed to the eye surgery he'd been putting off. Johnnie Sue knew that Larry had been desperately trying to hire part-time help since then; the sixty-five-hour weeks were killing him. But neither Larry nor Hershell had ever had much luck getting part-time pharmacists to move to this out-of-the-way spot, and the few they'd hired over the years had never hung on more than a month or two.

Suddenly Johnnie Sue felt sure that this sleek gal had arrived for an interview with Larry, who always checked out his potential employees first thing in the morning before Maxine, his bookkeeper, got to work at nine and ran them off.

Striding across the room with her coffeepot in hand, Johnnie Sue plopped about a teaspoon full of the dark brew into the stranger's virtually untouched cup. "What time's your appointment?" she asked nonchalantly.

The girl looked up. "Eight o'clock." As soon as she fell into the trap, a puzzled expression darkened her green eyes. "How did you know I was here to interview for a job?"

Johnnie Sue tossed her a muted "make the customer happy" smile, perfected after years of diligent practice. "Only got six-thousand souls in Porter," she revealed as though it were a source of pride. "If you aren't one of 'em, you're from out of town."

The brunette tried to smile but failed quite miserably. She looked coiled tight as a spring. *Nervous as a teenager on her first date,* thought Johnnie Sue. And then she realized, *No, it's more than that. This woman is afraid.*

The girl swept back an imaginary lock of loose hair and stared at Johnnie Sue. "Do you know…everyone in town? Or just those people who have lived here forever?"

"Most folks in Porter *have* lived here forever," she clarified. "We're not exactly in the middle of a building boom in this end of Pottawattamie County."

Again, a fragile smile. "No, but isn't that…what makes it nice here?"

The words were right, but they sounded…prerehearsed. "Small-town girl yourself, are you?" Johnnie Sue asked, half hoping to catch the outsider in a lie.

The long, mauve-tipped fingers fluttered against the tabletop. "No, I'm from Des Moines. But I think I've had enough of the big city for a while. It's so much more peaceful here, don't you think?"

"I wouldn't know. I've been here too long to remember what it's like anywhere else."

As though Johnnie Sue had not spoken, the younger woman continued, "I suppose there are…other people who feel the way I do. I mean, people from big cities…like Des Moines…who move to Porter to get away from it all."

"Sure. One or two." With her innate sixth sense honed to a fine edge after thirty-four years in the Cornsilk Cafe, Johnnie Sue knew that the woman wanted information— about somebody in particular?—but couldn't bring herself to ask for it outright. That was understandable if she'd come here for a job. But nobody at Duncan's Drugs— Larry, Hershell or Maxine—could be considered "newcomers from Des Moines." Both Larry and Hershell had been born here, and Maxine, their fervently devoted bookkeeper, had moved to town from back east somewhere when she was thirteen.

She thought about calling Hershell over to meet the stranger, then realized that Larry had deliberately kept the interview from his dad. Hershell was terribly touchy about being "put out to pasture," and Johnnie Sue sympathized with the emptiness of his Aggie-less life. Still, for months she'd watched him squint and squirm when he tried to read her daily specials on the chalkboard. She wouldn't hurt Hershell for all the world, but the last few times she'd gotten her digoxin prescription refilled, she'd made sure to go in to the pharmacy on one of Larry's days. Even a minor dosage error, Larry had warned her, could bring her heart to a quick and irrevocable halt.

"The young fellow who owns Duncan's is a Porter native," Johnnie Sue bragged, getting tired of beating around the bush. "I've known him since he drew his first breath. You won't find a better boss in the whole state of Iowa, take my word."

The big eyes met Johnnie Sue's again, strangely pleading. "Thank you," she said, as though that was what she'd wanted to hear. But the long fingers speeded up their quiet drumming, and the muscles in that long, graceful neck seemed to bunch.

Right about then it struck Johnnie Sue—like a bucket of ice water full in the face—that the classy stranger wasn't fidgeting like some scared young twerp. Those raised hackles looked more like a coyote caught in the henhouse.

The damn girl looks guilty, Johnnie Sue realized with a jolt. *At the very least, ashamed.*

She didn't know what the outsider's story was, but she was damned sure going to find out before she let this slick young woman pull the wool over Larry's eyes. She'd do whatever she had to do to save Aggie's boy from another year in hell.

ALTHOUGH DUNCAN'S DRUGS didn't officially open until nine o'clock, Larry always came in an hour early, rain, snow or shine, to get everything in order without customers buzzing around. Not that it did him much good. Nobody who considered him a "good friend"—roughly half of the town—thought he'd mind being interrupted for one quick purchase. Nonetheless, the one person who never showed up until nine o'clock was Maxine Kensler—or Auntie Max, as he'd been taught to call her as a child. Dowdy, round-faced Maxine had kept the books and bossed the bosses at Duncan's Drugs for forty-four years, which was forty-three years longer than Larry had been running the business, thirty-one years longer than he had been a pharmacist, and eight years longer than he had been alive.

Giving orders to Maxine did not come easily to him, especially now that his mother was dead. Mercifully Maxine was very good at what she did so orders were rarely necessary. Larry left the maintenance of the pharmacy's records—tax documents, drug invoices, permanent prescription files—in Maxine's capable hands. He let her scold the patients who didn't pay their bills and hound those who failed to take their medications; he let her keep a check on inventory. He even let her decide which calls were crucial and which ones would have to wait.

But he did *not* let her arrange his employee interviews.

Fiercely loyal to Larry's father, Maxine insisted that as long as Hershell believed he was still capable of safely dispensing medication, then nobody, least of all his sole surviving son, should tell him he'd grown too old to work. Although Maxine never broke the rules of confidentiality by leaking news to folks outside of the pharmacy, Larry had made little headway convincing her that *he* was running things these days and there were things he'd prefer that she didn't tell his dad. So whenever he wanted to spare Hershell's feelings, he simply kept pertinent facts to himself.

One of those facts was that he'd received a call yesterday afternoon from an old Des Moines College of Pharmacy chum, with news that a young alumna was looking for work out near Porter. Larry, desperate for relief, had been so thrilled that he'd asked his friend to track down Rene Hamilton and set up an interview at once. It was not until several jubilant hours had passed that he began to wonder why this capable woman was interested in a part-time job with no benefits in a thimble-sized town with the worst weather this side of hell.

All he knew about this applicant was that his friend's contacts had reported that she had her pharmacist's license, a cheerful disposition and a quiet kind of efficiency that stemmed in part from the years she'd spent clerking in a pharmacy while she'd worked her way through school. In short, it seemed to Larry, Rene Hamilton was perfect. And that was even *before* she walked in the door.

It was seven-fifty-eight when he heard the string of bells jangle from the back of the store. Bent over a box of yet-to-be sorted pills from a Boston pharmaceutical company, Larry straightened at once and peered out from over the swinging side door that separated the pharmacy section from the rest of the store.

He'd expected a competent-looking woman, sturdy and neatly dressed. Unlike his father, he didn't believe that a female pharmacist was an aberration. He'd never worked with one before, but that was only because he'd never worked anywhere but in this very store, and the pitifully few applicants they'd had over the years had all been men.

Under the circumstances, he would have hired any legally licensed applicant, male or female, who didn't come equipped with horns and a red tail. Larry considered himself an excellent pharmacist, but one thing he'd learned in recent weeks was that an exhausted first-rate pharmacist is a far greater danger to his patients than a well-rested average one. And he was, quite simply, on the verge of collapse.

It was, then, with a sense of heavenly reprieve that he stared at the appealing female who strolled toward him, smiling as though it were her place, not his, to extend a welcome. Rene Hamilton had the rare sort of beauty that thrived even without a flattering fluff of curls. Her hair, a rich, shimmering black, was scrupulously pulled back into a thick classic bun that highlighted her uniquely angular cheekbones. Her striking features were softened by large, luminous eyes and full lips kissed by only a hint of muted pink.

Larry enjoyed female companionship, but he was not a skirt chaser. In fact, ever since Sandra had gone back to her ex, he'd deliberately kept his distance from women. In Porter, most of the women he knew were married anyway, and those who weren't were either too old, too young or divorced. And as far as Larry was concerned, dating another divorcée was out of the question. It was bad enough that he'd been a chump the first time around. Surrendering every inch of his heart to someone who could only loan him half of hers was a mistake he would never make again.

Yet as his vocal chords constricted, he knew, on a nameless, instinctive level, that his sense of surprise—of wonder?—as he stared at Rene Hamilton had nothing to do with her potential for the job he was about to offer her.

"Good morning," she said quietly, the hope in her voice warming him like sunshine slipping through the cracks of a tightly drawn shade. "I'm Rene Hamilton. I'm here to talk to Larry Duncan about a possible opening here for a pharmacist."

Larry nodded and swallowed hard. "I'm Larry. Glad to meet you," he offered, holding out his hand. She had to shift her purse from her right hand to her left in order to take it, and the clumsy gesture seemed to discomfit her. By the time their palms pressed, Larry was feeling silly—his hand had been out there waiting an awfully long time—and surprised, because *her* hand was warm and moist while his own stayed dry and cool.

"I don't know how much you know about Duncan's Drugs, Rene," he said, trying to launch the conversation. "This is probably different from the sort of pharmacy you worked for in Des Moines. My dad opened it right after World War II, and since then it's pretty much stayed the same."

Rene licked her lips, a nervous gesture strangely at odds with her flawlessly sleek appearance. "I understood that your father is retired."

Larry shrugged. "*I* think he is, but I haven't convinced *him* yet."

She tried to smile but didn't quite succeed. "So you...aren't quite sure if you need another pharmacist out here?" she asked, unable to mask her disappointment.

He shook his head. "I'm *positive* we need another pharmacist, Rene. My father has been working part-time for years now, ever since I finished school, actually. But as he's gotten older and more tired, he's worked less and less. And now he's got cataracts, in addition to some...well, some personal problems." He considered telling her that his dad had been nearly broken by his mother's death...and his part in the way she had died. It was public knowledge that Rene could have discovered from almost anyone in

Porter, but it still seemed too private to share with a stranger. "I'm working from eight in the morning to nine at night, five days a week and half a day on Saturday," he told her instead. "I need somebody to share the late-afternoon load and relieve me evenings and Saturdays. I don't mind working nights sometimes, Rene. We can trade shifts every now and then. I just can't keep working sixty-five hours a week. Sooner or later, I'm bound to make a critical mistake."

He could have told her about the wonder drug for psoriasis that had, over several years, killed five Porter natives and one newcomer to the town. The deaths had not occurred because of an error of judgement on the part of overworked Larry or his dad, but in such a small town it was, nonetheless, a lingering scar on the reputation of Duncan's Drugs. And Duncan's would lose all public trust if there were ever any hint of negligence down the road. On top of that, poor Hershell was still an open wound when it came to the amethopterin deaths, and Larry feared that any hint of a similar scandal—whether his unhappy father was exonerated from guilt or not—might push the proud old man right over the edge. As it was, Hershell spent several hours each night wandering through the Duncan cornfields, through the side streets of Porter, in and out of Larry's house, the pharmacy and the Cornsilk Cafe. Johnnie Sue jealously guarded his secrets, of course, but once, when Larry had cornered her after hours and forced her to talk, she'd admitted, "He's not getting better, Lare. Sometimes I think he's just wasting away, day by day."

"Why don't you have a seat, Rene?" Larry offered, suddenly aware that he was handling the interview all wrong. An employer wasn't supposed to beg for help; he was supposed to grill the prospective pharmacist, to weigh her background against that of all the other applicants, to make her scramble to convince him that it was to his advantage to hire her over all other comers. *Hogwash,* he told himself. *The ball's in her court and she knows it.*

He gave Rene Maxine's favorite chair, the one snuggled under her rolltop desk, and perched on the stool he used when he was filling prescriptions after hours. She sat discreetly, not an inch of thigh peeking out from under her smoothly draped skirt. It occurred to him, studying the trim silk suit, that her appearance was more appropriate for a city business than for a country store. She was almost... well, over-dressed, as though she were trying too hard. Again he wondered, *Why is she interested in this job?*

"Tell me about yourself," he suggested. "I'm curious about what brings you to this part of the state."

Again she smiled—that nervous, not-quite-happy smile—as she told him, "I've been working at a pharmacy in Des Moines since I was eighteen. Nine years." The smile grew genuinely pained. "I'm not a slow student, Mr. Duncan. I just had to work my way through school without financial assistance. But it had its advantages, because I did learn a great deal about working in a pharmacy before I started my internship, and now I feel fully qualified to handle any duties you might require of me."

He offered a smile of his own to put her at ease. "I'll require you to call me Larry," he declared, hoping his voice twinkled with friendliness rather than desire. "Everybody else does. This is a *very* small town."

"That's why I want to move here." The words came out in a rush. "I'd like to live where everybody knows each other and everyone feels safe."

Larry was glad she was opening up to him, but her guileless declaration struck him as out of place. It fitted into the conversation—barely—but her vehemence seemed uncalled for. It reminded him vaguely of the time he'd been stuck in a college debate in which the other team took a line of attack for which he was totally unprepared. Desperate, he'd used his researched arguments anyway, painfully aware of the fact that he wasn't answering his opponents' questions but not knowing what else to say. He had the eerie feeling that Rene had memorized this answer to the question he hadn't yet asked…at least not out loud. Now, almost to reach some sense of closure, he said, ''I take it that it's the small-town atmosphere of Porter that draws you most to Duncan's Drugs.''

She nodded quickly, causing one of the clips holding her tightly-wrapped tresses to slip ever so slightly. Vaguely he realized that Johnnie Sue always wore her oyster-colored clump of hair in a similar knot; never, in the lifetime he'd known her, had he seen it any other way. Yet he'd bet his bottom dollar that Rene had straightjacketed her hair just for this occasion. It took little imagination to picture it drifting invitingly around her beguiling face. He wondered if any man had ever found poor Johnnie Sue beguiling. After his father, Larry loved her more than he loved any living soul on earth, but he had never really thought of her as *female*. Yet it was the only way he could think of Rene.

Before she could reply, the back door banged open and Gert Wilson's gawky, high tone rang out a greeting. ''Larry? Larry, are you in here?''

Larry cringed. ''Back at the desk, Gert,'' he called out, turning to meet another of his mother's dear friends. He liked Gert and normally was glad enough to see her. Gert and Maxine had been like sisters for years, which meant that Maxine would hear about his interview before he had a chance to explain it in his own way…to Maxine or his dad.

''Larry, Julie forgot to get her morning-sickness pills

again! I swear that girl would forget her own head if it weren't screwed on. She should have taken them last night but she fell asleep on the couch and Henry didn't think to call me or I would have rushed right down. If you could just—'' she stopped abruptly as she bolted through the double-hinged half door and spotted Rene.

Her bright red hair, once natural but now a shade too brassy, perched in tightly permed rolls all over her head. Johnnie Sue had once privately observed to Larry that Gert was built somewhat like a goose—long, skinny neck, flapping elbows, wide bottom, splayed feet. But Larry would never have pummeled poor Gert with that description, and neither would Johnnie Sue.

"You've got company!" she accused.

Larry stood up, feeling a flush of anger toward all of his mother's old friends. Most of the time he didn't mind having them fuss over him as though he were ten. He knew they did it out of love, so he promised to obey and ignored them anyway. But every now and then—especially with a stranger in a professional situation—he found their busybodiness a bit cloying. This was one of those times.

"This is Rene Hamilton, who may be coming to work for me," he announced, refusing to be cowed. "Rene, Gert Wilson is an old family friend."

"'Old' as in I've known Larry since he was in diapers, not old as in 'one foot in the grave,'" Gert corrected him. She flushed, then said with a winsome grin, "My goodness, I sound like Johnnie Sue! She must be rubbing off on me."

Larry quickly turned toward the current prescription box to hide the curving corners of his mouth. Gert echoed Johnnie Sue about as much as a mouse mimics a catamount! But for timid Gert, the assertion of youth was pretty heavy stuff, and Larry secretly cheered her tiny spark of bravado.

He was pretty sure which drug Doc Swanson had prescribed for Julie Clancy, but he wasn't about to guess. The poor little thing was having one hell of a pregnancy—Gert was filling Rene in on the queasy details—and this wasn't the first time she'd forgotten to get a refill ahead of time. Of course, Julie's recent wedding had done little to change her dependence on her mother, who'd coddled, fussed and fluttered around her all of her life. Widowed young, Gert had lived for her only child, supporting her by cleaning house for half the folks in town. Since Julie's recent marriage—which was not, according to Gert, a particularly happy one—Gert had less to do with her time and a lot more to complain about. As Larry listened to Gert tell Rene, a total stranger, a great deal more about Henry Clancy's shortcomings than even an intimate family member could possibly want to know, he decided to count his blessings that, during his brief marriage, at least his mother-in-law had lived out of town. In fact, the only silver lining in his whole fiasco with Sandra was that none of her family still haunted Porter.

Not even her two precious kids.

"Here you go," he told Gert when he could get a word in edgewise. "Tell Julie to get a new prescription. The original only called for three refills, and this is half of the fourth."

Gert nodded, kissed him on the cheek and called him a lamb, then waddled out the back door.

When he sat down again, Rene's cheeks seemed a little rounder, as though she were desperately trying to conceal a fit of giggles.

Once Gert was out of earshot, Larry didn't try to stay solemn. As his own chuckles broke forth, so did Rene's, and the shared laughter warmed the quiet space between them.

"Is that woman a typical Porterite?" Rene asked, green eyes aglow with amusement.

"Will you still come work for me if I say yes?"

Rene's grin consumed her whole face, transforming it, lighting it, lighting his own heart as well.

Don't let her touch your heart, Larry cautioned himself. *She's just an employee, and if you let her know how eager you are, she might not even be that.*

"I told you I wanted a taste of small-town life," she teased, her chuckle sweetly beguiling. "I guess that's a sample."

He nodded, trying to sober his smile. "There is no such thing as privacy in Porter, Rene," he said simply. "If you come to work here, you better not have any secrets, because you won't be able to hide a thing."

To his surprise, Rene's smile vanished instantly. "I'm not sure what you mean by that, Mr. Duncan."

Regretting his casual comment, Larry waved away her use of the formal name. "*Please* call me Larry. I meant no offense."

"I know you didn't," she said quickly, too quickly, as though she feared that her own faux pas had offended *him.*

"Rene," he tried to explain, "I guess what I'm trying to say is that a pharmacy in Porter isn't quite like a pharmacy in Des Moines. Our customers aren't busy commuters who rush into whatever store they drive by on their way home. They're...well, they're practically family. Gert is a lot more at home at Duncan's Drugs than some folks in town, but she's not exactly an exception to the rule. Did you notice that new shopping center on the highway as you drove in?"

Rene nodded.

"When that discount drug store opens next month, we're going to be hit right between the eyes. Folks are going to drive out there to the grocery—it's only six miles—and sooner or later, they'll drop by Pharmafix for tissues or diapers or bug spray. All we've ever been able to offer our customers is convenience and trust. We're right here—all the time—and they know we'll rush on down and open up if they have some emergency.''

''Do they also know that you'll refill an expired prescription at no charge?''

Her tone was so straightforward that he had a strange sensation that, for the first time since she'd arrived, he was listening to the real Rene.

''I've known Julie for all of her nineteen years, and I've known Doc Swanson even longer,'' he snapped. ''He's up at Eagle Point fishing until next Sunday. Before he left he told me to cover any maintenance drugs that needed refilling in his absence.''

''Maintenance drugs do not include medication for morning sickness,'' Rene corrected him a bit tersely. ''With birth defects so closely tied to prenatal medication, I should think you'd be extraordinarily careful.''

Larry stared at her, wondering, for just a moment, if she knew about the amethopterin scandal and was testing him. And then it occurred to him that maybe she wasn't a pharmacist at all but some sort of industry spy or private eye.

''Are you really here for a job, Rene?'' he asked suddenly. ''Or are you looking for some kind of information?''

Larry watched her face turn pearl-gray, her shoulders slump. Even the flawlessly crossed knees, so delicately concealed by the sober silk skirt, seemed to sprawl a couple of inches. She looked as though she'd just been punched in the mouth. And he knew how a woman looked when she'd been hit, because he'd first met Sandra less than an hour after her ex-husband had purpled her lower lip and cracked her jaw.

"I'm sorry," he murmured, suddenly feeling two inches tall. "I didn't mean to be rude."

Rene blinked rapidly. "And I didn't mean to be critical."

Larry wanted to ask her what, exactly, she'd had in mind if it wasn't criticism, but her anguish—no, that wasn't too strong a word for it—wounded him unbearably. He'd vowed to conquer his marshmallow response to any woman in pain, but so far it was more a dream than a reality.

He gave her a moment to collect herself, then gently explained, "I exercise some discretion with certain patients and certain prescriptions. Maybe I press the edges of the law, but only to save a friend from a weekend of misery or cut down the cost for my fixed-income patients...and only with the prescribing physician's approval. We've got two other doctors here, you know, and one of them is a real stickler for regulations. I never cut corners on his prescriptions. But Phil Lacey and Bob Swanson try to make things easy for their patients. They're of the old school."

Rene nodded, looking a little more composed. But her discomfort was still evident. It made her look younger, somehow. Less competent, but more approachable and...more appealing.

"If I came to work for you, Mr., uh, Larry, would you expect me to bend the rules this way?"

Larry shook his head. "Not if you're uncomfortable doing so. Besides, it's a seat-of-the-pants kind of judgment call that—no offense—a person can't make unless he's lived here most of his life."

Again she nodded, still looking subdued.

He wanted to get off the subject, to nail down her ac-

ceptance of the job. No matter what he thought of Rene
Hamilton or she thought of him, he needed her desperately,
and he couldn't afford to be squeamish about technicalities.
"I think it's important, though, for you to understand the
basic, well, homey way we run things here. Service is all
we can offer; we can't compete with Pharmafix prices."

She said nothing, but she watched him intensely.

"For instance, you asked if I were giving away drugs
to Gert. If I did, I'd have to give them away to everybody
in town and I'd go broke. But Gert knows she doesn't have
to write a check or dig in her purse for cash when she's
in a hurry. I'll put this prescription—" he quickly scribbled
out the details of what he'd given Gert with a note that it
was "pending approval" of the prescribing physician
"—in this little box on Maxine's desk. When she comes
in she'll figure out what Gert owes me and add it to her
running bill. Or, in this case, to Henry Clancy's bill now
that Gert's daughter is married to him. She'll also record
it properly in our register before she files it." He pointed
to the date of the prescription, the date of today's partial
refill, and his own initials, "L.D.," at the bottom of the
four-by-five-inch sheet. "Everything clear and tidy. Maxine has been running things here for half a century, and
she knows how to translate those chicken scratches that
mean I'm the one who filled this particular prescription,
not my father." He tried to smile reassuringly. "He's the
original here at Duncan's, so he doesn't have to sign his
initials at all. Maxine knows that any blank prescription
means the medication was dispensed by Dad."

Rene tried to smile, but she still looked like a puppy
cringing before a rolled-up newspaper. Vaguely he remembered how she'd looked when he'd first seen her—regal,
perfect, cool as ice. He wondered if that image had been

a facade and this easily injured creature was the real Rene Hamilton...or whether it might be the other way around.

"I really am sorry, Mr. Duncan. Larry," she pleaded now. "I'm told that I tend to sound critical when I'm nervous. I've been trained to do everything just right, and I wanted you to realize that I would be...trustworthy. I know what happened out here—I mean, I know about the amethopterin lawsuit a few years ago—and I thought it would be important to you to hire a pharmacist who couldn't possibly do any more damage to your reputation. Please don't think I'm trying to tell you how to run your business. All I want—" she gulped a bit desperately "—is a chance to do my job. I mean...a chance to work here in Porter." Again she swallowed before she corrected herself. "I mean, here at Duncan's Drugs."

Larry didn't know quite what to think about this puzzling, beautiful woman. One minute, self-assured, the next minute, frightened; armed with credentials and enthusiastic recommendations, yet disturbingly desperate to get this obscure part-time position.

"Why?" he asked as gently as he could. "Why are you so eager to come to Porter? It doesn't really matter, Rene, but I...wish you'd level with me."

At once a flush of moisture filmed Rene's beautiful green eyes. "Do you really want to know, Larry? It's actually rather...personal."

Soberly he nodded. It didn't matter what she told him; any reason would do. What mattered was that she told him the truth, that her eyes met his when she told her story. Sandra had always managed to look away when she'd lied to him, concealing her falsehoods with her tears.

For month after month of their year-long marriage, she had deluded him into thinking that he was the happiest man on earth, when all that time she'd been secretly working toward a reconciliation with her former husband…a reconciliation that had ultimately occurred in Larry's bed the afternoon he'd taken off from work to proudly bring home the new Acura Integra he'd bought her for Christmas. The shock of it—not to mention the pain—had left him reeling for months; in fact, he was certain that he would have figured out the cause of the amethopterin deaths sooner if he hadn't been in such a sorry state. He would always wonder whose life he might have saved if he'd been on the ball.

Rene's lips tightened in an odd mixture of fear and determination as she confessed, "Last month there was a holdup in a pharmacy less than a mile from where I live, near downtown Des Moines. I know the pharmacist who was closing up that night. Greg Finch. I went to school with him." She shivered, despite the sunny warmth of the store and her thick suit.

Larry had heard about the attack on Finch, reputedly a first-rate pharmacist. The story had made him glad he worked in a country town. He hadn't thought about how it would strike a woman who worked downtown.

"There were two men in stocking masks," Rene continued, her voice a bit raw. "They cleaned out the cash register, stole five thousand dollars' worth of drugs. They beat Greg senseless and left him for dead."

Larry couldn't meet her eyes. His prior accusations, mercifully unspoken, now shamed him. "I'm sorry," was all he could say.

"I went to see him in the hospital," she whispered. "All wrapped up in white. We talked for about ten minutes before he got tired. On the way out the door Greg said, 'Be careful on your way home, Rene. You never know when trouble's going to come knocking on your door.'"

She brushed away an undignified tear. "You want to know why I want to come to a small town?"

"Rene—"

"I'm afraid. I hate to admit it, but I'm *afraid* to live in a big city anymore. I'm afraid of being hurt while I'm in the pharmacy at night or walking through the parking lot or driving to my apartment alone. Ever since Greg got robbed I've been afraid at work and afraid at home. I want to get out of Des Moines, Larry, just as fast as I can. I've asked every pharmacist I know to tell me about any small-town job available, and the instant I heard that Porter had a population of six thousand, I knew that this was the place for me."

Again she swallowed, then tugged on the hem of her spotless gray skirt. Slowly, then, she straightened, and her expression grew flat and hard. As Larry watched her slip on that other mask, the one she'd been wearing when she had first come through his back door, he noticed that one wisp of that primly draped hair had fought its way free. Despite her distant, almost defiant, pose, she still seemed swathed in strands of sweet helplessness that threatened to enmesh him. He fought the quiet lurch of his heart.

After a moment's silence, Rene said calmly, "Please forgive me for falling apart, Mr. Duncan. *Larry.* I didn't intend to go into all of that. I just wanted to get this job so much that I...well, I guess I got carried away." Now looking quite composed, she met his concerned gaze as she finished, "I think you really need me to help you out, and I'm eager to relocate in a small town."

Larry was still puzzled by her Jekyll and Hyde nature, but at bedrock he believed her story, and he believed that she'd be a strong addition to the store. The fact that he felt...well, *drawn* to her—to her eyes, to her full lips, to her perfectly curved, straightjacketed breasts—was not a function of her suitability for employment at Duncan's Drugs. It might turn out to be a sparkling joy, an irrelevancy or even a difficult complication, but Larry was sure he had the professional poise to handle the situation. No woman at Duncan's Drugs would ever feel pressured into returning a personal interest in the boss. If something should happen between them, well…nice. Very nice. And if it didn't, he'd still get a pharmacist, and at the moment he needed a pharmacist a great deal more than he needed a lover. After Sandra's defection, he wasn't even sure he wanted the latter.

"Rene, the job is yours if you want it," Larry assured her. "I can probably give you twenty-five or thirty hours a week right now. After Pharmafix opens its doors…well, anything could happen. But you don't need a lot of money to make do in Porter, and this is as safe a town as you can find in all of Iowa. We only have two policemen, and most of the time they hang out at the Cornsilk because they've got nothing else to do." He grinned as he remembered the time a drifter had made a lighthearted pass at a young Cornsilk waitress and Johnnie Sue, accusing him of attempted rape, had held him at knife-point until Elwood's first wife could get him out of the shower. "The last time we had a holdup here was in 1965, and that was a Halloween prank by two of my cousins. We have a murder once every decade or so, but the victim and the killer are never strangers." His hand covered hers for just a moment in a gesture of fraternal comfort…at least, he told himself that comfort was the only spirit of his touch. "You won't get rich in Porter, Rene," he assured her with a huskier tone than he'd expected, "but you'll be in no danger here."

A specter of a smile lit Rene's perfect face. "I'd be delighted to work for you, Larry," she told him. "When do you want me to start?"

They spent another ten minutes discussing the pharmacy, the lawsuit and the difficulties Rene might face finding rental housing in Porter. Larry mentioned that Lotty Barrington, one of his late mother's best friends, owned one of the two apartment houses in town and could probably make some sort of arrangements for Rene.

Again she thanked him profusely. After they'd agreed on her starting date and salary, she said goodbye, then tacked on as she was leaving, "Larry Duncan, you are a very kind man."

Larry felt a warm surge of pleasure before he realized that his ex-wife had often said the same thing to him during those early days when he'd devoted himself to binding her emotional wounds. Suddenly he realized that he hadn't asked Rene if she'd ever been married.

For some reason, his oversight troubled him, even though he told Maxine—when she asked him the same question half an hour later—that just because he'd vowed never to marry another divorcée didn't mean he couldn't hire one.

RENE WAS SHAKING by the time she slipped behind the wheel of her cherry-red, twelve-year-old Datsun. *Dear God, what have I done?* she moaned into the steering wheel. *Do I really have the guts to go through with this?*

She had lied to that man. Lied straight out to a man who positively glistened with goodness; all he needed was a halo on his head to prove he manned St. Peter's gate. Even before that crusty old waitress had given her sales pitch, Rene had heard through the pharmacists' grapevine that Larry Duncan was a very nice guy, and the half hour she'd just spent in his company had confirmed his reputation.

In retrospect, Rene wondered if Larry had seen through her act and was just too kind to say so. After all, she'd been counting on chutzpah to carry her through this charade, revving herself up with fresh fury at Fran Bixby. But her anger had lost its power in the face of Larry Duncan's gentleness. Deceit did not come easily to Rene, and she wondered, even now, how she'd stumbled through that unexpectedly personal interview without spilling out her whole seedy plan.

She took a breath of consolation from the fact that at least her tears had been genuine. She hadn't made up the story about the attack on Greg Finch. It was true, it was grisly, and it made her skin crawl every time it crossed her mind. But she'd only learned about it last weekend, a good two weeks after she'd decided to move to Porter. Two weeks after the last time she'd laid eyes on Seth Rafferty.

Rene exhaled heavily, turned on the engine and headed out of town. She'd already studied a local map, so she knew where she was going, even though the rows of cornfields all looked pretty much the same. With the Bixby land only three miles to the south, Rene spotted Fran's inheritance almost immediately.

She wasn't sure how much land Bernard Bixby had left to his only daughter—several hundred acres, based on the distance to the next mailbox—but she could see, as she slowed down to study the old farmhouse, that somebody had looked after the place while Fran had been flitting about in Des Moines. The two-story brick home had freshly painted white shutters, open now that it was summer, and well-tended roses clustered on both sides of the front door. A long concrete walkway from the roadside to the house had obviously recently been swept, and a lawn mower, well-used but unrusted, waited patiently by the toolshed near the garage. The barn, a massive wooden structure that had once most likely been painted red, stood about a hundred yards behind the house. Chickens and ducks squawked from the small attached corral.

It was a lovely, pastoral scene, a near-perfect replica of the sort of country home Rene's ex-husband had always longed for. *Someday we'll get out of the city,* he used to tell her as they lay in bed, his hand buried in her hair, her hand companionably resting on his thigh. *We'll get a place of our own, Rene, where the kids can have a pony and I can plant a vegetable garden every spring.*

As she pulled off the road behind a cottonwood tree a good quarter mile from the house, the ache that rippled through her chest was almost unbearable. *Why couldn't you have waited just a little bit longer?* she cried out to him in her heart. *Once I finished school I would have moved anywhere you wanted. And I'm so ready to give you those babies now!*

She had only intended to drive by today, to take a glance at what had drawn Seth to this obscure corner of Iowa. But now that she'd come this far—knowing he was so close— her urge to see him, even from a distance, was suddenly overwhelming.

Carefully locking her purse and her common sense in the car, Rene snuck back along the road, hoping desperately that there was no one staring at her from the upstairs windows of the house. As she walked, her new heels poked the dry dirt and slipped once or twice in the muddy irrigation runoff, and when a farmer drove by in a pickup and offered her a ride, she quaked as she told him it was a lovely day for a walk. By the time she reached the back of the toolshed—which she hoped would shield her from anyone's view—Rene was sweating inside her suit and feeling like a peeping Tomasina.

Suddenly, from the back of the house, she caught a

flicker of movement. Stifling a gasp, she realized that it was only laundry fluttering on the line.

Only laundry, she told herself. *Only delicate undies, lacy teddies, and that damn red dress of Fran's I found on the floor.* The rest of the clothes were just as familiar—white jockey shorts, worn doubleknits, those leftover, two-for-the-price-of-one men's plaid shirts she used to order from Sears at the end of every season.

Rene was battling a sudden wave of nausea when a mass of dogflesh, half snarling Doberman and half horse-sized mutt, hurled itself through the air, barking spasmodically. Rene gagged—partly out of fear of getting bitten, partly out of fear of getting caught—and turned to run as though the furies were at her back. She'd stumbled a good ten yards before she realized that the dog was on a chain—albeit a long one—and she was now safely beyond its reach.

Still, she didn't slow down until she reached the Datsun, trembling with fear and self-loathing for what she had done.

And what she planned to do as soon as she moved to Porter.

CHAPTER TWO

TWO WEEKS AFTER her interview with Larry Duncan, Rene arrived in Porter driving her bright red Datsun and a small rented trailer full of hand-me-down furnishings: a mended floral couch, a kitchen dinette set with tape over the tears in the vinyl, and the twin bed she'd purchased in a garage sale to replace the double one her co-workers, including Fran Bixby in cosmetics, had given her when she'd married Seth.

Even in hindsight, she couldn't remember anything revealing about Fran's behavior in those days, which should have warned her about the future. She'd always known that Fran was a flirt, of course, but until Rene had married Seth, Fran had never shown much interest in him. Sometimes, she'd gone out to lunch with him at work, but so did anybody else in the store working the same shift. Rene never gave it a thought.

She would never forget the devastating night she found them together; it was seared in her memory with a welding torch. It had been her first semester in pharmacy school, the semester that Seth had made no bones about the fact that—after six years in school already—he thought Rene should have quit college after graduation so they could start a family. He'd already dropped out of college and was trying to launch his own garden-supply business by then, and he sorely needed both her comfort and advice. The business was floundering, but Rene was doing well in

grad school. She wished she could have spent more time
with Seth while he was feeling down, but she made sure
that the time they did share was loving. Until the night
before she left him, Rene truly believed that their marriage
was still strong.

She had a night class on Tuesdays that semester—Phar-
macology 1-A. She'd finished a midterm early and rushed
back home to celebrate. The mood died the instant she
reached her living room. Neither Fran nor Seth—both naked, with limbs intertwined—had noticed Rene while she'd
stared at them, transfixed by the anguish of betrayal, for a
full thirty seconds or more. Nor had they heard her silently
slip into the bedroom to pack a single suitcase and grab
her pharmacy books. She did not look back to see if they
noticed that she slammed the door on her way out of her
husband's life.

Rene never found out how Seth felt when she started
divorce proceedings the next morning. To this day she
didn't know if he was relieved or frightened or angry or if
he just didn't care. All she knew was that when the papers
were served he offered no protest, and on the few occasions
she saw him after that, she was flanked by her lawyer, and
Fran kept Seth on a short leash across the room.

Oh, Seth, how did it ever come to this? she wondered.
But Rene had no good answers to that question or any of
the others that had plagued her for the past two years. *Why
did you betray me? What did you see in Fran? And why
in the name of heaven am I here running after you now?*

As Rene pulled up in front of Lotty Barrington's apartment building, she shook herself, trying to slough off the
harrowing sense of shame. She leaped out of the car before
she got cold feet again, then bounded up the steps just as
the manager's door swung wide open with a bang.

"Oh, my goodness!" rasped an old woman curled up in

a wheelchair on the other side of the sill. Her legs, clad in terry-cloth slipper-socks but otherwise bare, looked thin as twin dowels but surprisingly suntanned. "You really *are* a good-looking girl, aren't you? Larry didn't do you justice! And you *are* just the right age!"

Rene swallowed, a bit unnerved both by the sudden sight of those useless legs and the gleeful sound of the old woman's prattle. Larry had not mentioned that Lotty Barrington—if, indeed, this was Lotty Barrington—was disabled. Nor that she seemed to feel that Rene had answered a "wife-wanted ad" rather than come to town to work as a pharmacist.

"Hello, I'm Rene Hamilton," she greeted the widow formally, glad she'd gone back to her maiden name after the divorce so at least she didn't need to lie about that. "Are you Mrs. Barrington?"

"It's Lotty, little girl!" the old woman gushed as her bony fingers cheerfully crushed Rene's outstretched hand. "Nobody calls me 'Mrs. Barrington' but the doctors up in Des Moines. Didn't Larry tell you that I'm practically his aunt?"

"Well, I—"

"His mama was one of my dearest friends in the whole world. Like to broke my heart when she died. Broke that boy's, too, though he don't like to talk about it much."

"Boy?" repeated Rene. Nobody had mentioned a child. Not that it was any of her business.

"I mean *Larry*, little girl. Now his daddy does his best, don't you know, but Larry won't let him help no more. Hershell's the one we worry about now, so don't you be surprised if he shows up knocking at my door at all hours."

Rene was too bewildered to reply to this unrequested Duncan history lesson. She had a feeling that this woman would prove every bit as nosy as that crusty old bird she'd met at the Cornsilk Cafe, but there was something so warm and well-meaning about Lotty's wide-lipped smile that it was hard to take offense.

"I do appreciate your finding a spot for me on such short notice, uh, Lotty," she managed to reply. "Larry said it was often difficult to find places to rent in Porter."

"Purt nigh impossible," Lotty assured her. "But you won't find a better apartment in the whole town than the one I've got for you." She grinned with untarnished pride. "Follow me, little girl."

Rene considered pointing out that at twenty-seven, she was hardly a little girl, but decided against it. If she wasn't willing to tell these people who she really was, she couldn't very well complain if they formed a mistaken opinion of her. And she'd already painted a picture of herself as a fragile female who feared things that went "boo" in the dark.

Lotty reached up to grab a chain of keys off a nail stuck in the door frame, then wheeled past Rene before she had a chance to offer to push the woman's chair. Instantly Larry's "aunt" glided down the doorsill ramp, across the sidewalk, and around a sharp corner to a door marked eight. Before Rene could catch up with her, the door was unlocked and Lotty had sailed right in.

By this time Rene was profoundly grateful she hadn't had time to offer to help this whiz on wheels. It was obvious that Lotty—though her legs were surely useless—wasn't the least bit handicapped in any meaningful sense of the word and certainly didn't need help. Rene had a hunch that weeks often passed between the times it occurred to Lotty that some people would pity her for living in a wheelchair.

"So, this is it. Not bad for the price, huh?" Lotty asked

proudly as she swept one gnarled hand around the living room.

Quickly Rene glanced at the faded flowered wallpaper and the once-blue rug that was base-brown bare in spots. The old wall heater made her glad she'd be long gone by fall. But there was a fresh, airy smell about the place, and every nook and cranny was spotless. Although there was no furniture, the place had a homey feeling. The shiny-chromed refrigerator hummed, pink-pansy curtains fluttered in the breeze coming through the open windows, and a small vase full of Johnny-jump-ups had been placed near the sink. Obviously Lotty—or whomever she paid to clean the place—had gone to a great deal of trouble to make her feel at home.

Rene fought a lump in her throat that was half guilt, half gratitude. "It's beautiful, Lotty," she declared sincerely. "I'm sure I'll be very happy here."

As Lotty began to talk about the advantages of the location when the snow piled up outside in the winter, Rene had to turn away. She knew it was wrong to take a job or rent a place under false pretenses. Both Larry and Lotty expected her to stay more than a couple of weeks…or however long it would take to do what she'd come to do. With Lotty, of course, she could salve her conscience by paying for an extra month's rent. But poor Larry needed help desperately, and though Rene intended to lighten his load while she stayed in town, she knew he'd stopped looking for another pharmacist when he'd hired her and he'd probably have no advance notice before he had to start beating the drums for one again.

Something about Larry's open-handed decency touched Rene deeply. In their first interview and subsequent telephone calls, he'd struck her as a sensitive, intelligent man who seemed a bit too interested in her well-being, all things considered. Oh, he'd made it clear he was desperate for help at the drugstore, but Rene had a feeling that he would have hired her even if he'd had to lay somebody else off.

It was that suspicion that bothered her the most. She did not expect Larry to give her any trouble, nor did she shirk from the notion of his touch. In fact, the few times he'd touched her, she'd felt...well, she wasn't sure quite *how* she'd felt, but the warmth of his skin had brought to the surface feelings she had long ago buried. Granted, Larry didn't spin her on her ear the way Seth had when they'd first met, but she wasn't a teenager now.

She'd noticed Larry's boyish smile and manly build; enjoyed his warm brown eyes and thick dark hair. Despite his innocent boy-next-door comportment, his bristly mustache hinted at some secret inner rogue. Overall, there was something quite appealing about Larry Duncan that made Rene feel flattered that she'd apparently measured up to his personal standards. In some other time and place, she knew she would have looked forward to getting to know him better. But in *this* time and *this* place, Rene knew that if Larry got involved with her, he could only get hurt. And she wouldn't wish the kind of torment she'd suffered on *anybody*.

Except, perhaps, for Fran.

"DON'T YOU GIVE Max any trouble when she takes you into Des Moines to see that ophthalmologist next week," Johnnie Sue ordered Hersh on Sunday night as he watched her sever a peeled apple into slices with clean clanks of her heavy knife. "You're driving Larry nuts about this eye stuff, Hersh, and he's not going to let you work until you get things right."

"Right? My own son's giving *me* the orders now, and you think things are ever going to be *right?*"

Johnnie Sue dumped the apple slices into a round pan snuggled with crust, then lovingly wove a latticed dough top. "Well, the question is, how bad does it have to be? You can either fix your eyes and work sometimes, or you can go blind and sit like a stump. Seems to me like an easy choice to make," she pointed out, deftly crimping the edges before she sprinkled some sugar on top. She slid the pie—the last of ten—inside the Cornsilk's massive oven and firmly shut the door. "Besides, you know Larry only bosses you around because he loves you."

Hershell knew that Larry loved him. Not quite the way Paulie had loved him; but then again, he'd never loved Larry quite the way he'd loved Paul. Maybe it was because sturdy Paulie, his firstborn, had spent most of his afternoons tagging after his dad at Duncan's, while Larry had crawled around the Cornsilk kitchen, listening to his mother chat with Johnnie Sue. Maybe it was just one of those things. Hershell had learned long ago that family love, like friendship, isn't something you can order in a size you're sure will fit. It almost always needs some sort of alteration.

His love for Larry was in need of some now. It was bad enough that the boy had ordered him—just plain commanded him outright!—not to set foot in Duncan's Drugs until he had his cataracts removed. But now he'd gone and hired a *female*—a little girl, really, not even thirty yet—to do the work he said his own father wasn't good enough to do! And by the time Rene Hamilton started work tomorrow morning, there wouldn't be a soul in town who didn't know how his boy had humiliated him.

He knew that folks in town talked about how old Hershell had been losing it since Aggie had died. Everybody knew that he wandered about at night, drifting in and out of the pharmacy, sitting in the city park, chatting with whichever cop took the graveyard shift on nights when he didn't want to bother Larry or Lotty or Max. Max had trouble explaining his midnight visits to her husband, Larry expected him to talk if he came by to visit, and Lotty fussed at him if he just sat and stared. Only Johnnie Sue let him in at all hours without complaints or platitudes.

Never once, in all the time he'd known her, had Johnnie Sue said something stupid like "You'll get over it in time." She never said, "One day you'll look back on this and laugh," or, "Trust me, it's going to be okay." Johnnie Sue understood that when your heart was shattered you couldn't buy a new one or send the old one into the shop. You just limped along with the crippled one as best you could…except for those days when even limping was more than you could do.

Correctly reading his sullen silence, Johnnie Sue declared, "Come on, now, Hershell. You know that Aggie doesn't like it when you pout."

He couldn't argue with that, or with anything else that Johnnie Sue had shrewdly pointed out, so he sat in silence as she refilled his cup and plopped one big hip down on the edge of the tiny table across from him.

It was an old table from a half-size booth that didn't quite fit out front. Its chrome legs were badly scratched, and cigarette burns riddled the yellow Formica top. A single glance would have convinced any passerby that it was of no account. Yet, Johnnie Sue's table held a mystique for half of the town. To be allowed to pull up a chair beside it was an honor of great magnitude that, over the years, Johnnie Sue had afforded to maybe half a dozen people—three of whom were Duncans. And only the Duncans had the right to barge into the kitchen and sit at the table—anytime, day or night—without an explicit invitation.

But Hershell never sat at Johnnie Sue's table when there were other men in the restaurant. Not because he knew they would have talked about the time he spent with Johnnie Sue—and, had she been any other woman, tried to dirty it by making guesses about what she did with him alone at night—but because he needed their companionship also, and he could always talk to Johnnie Sue when they weren't around.

Of course, Hershell didn't hang around her kitchen after closing just to talk. He often let Johnnie Sue do the chatting while he dozed, slumped over her table, knowing that in the morning he'd find himself covered up with her best hand-pieced quilt. He was always a little stiff from sleeping all hunched over, but sleeping on Johnnie Sue's table beat the socks off staring at the ceiling while he lay in his Aggie-less bed without sleeping at all.

"Larry says he wants to move back home," Hershell declared morosely. Larry had moved off the farm when he'd first come back from graduate school—said he was a man and deserved his own home. He'd lived alone in town for years until he'd married Sandra, and even after she'd left him, he'd never mentioned coming home. Not when his mom was alive and he'd treated his dad like a capable man. "Says he's lonely. Does he think I can't see through that? He's busy all day with Maxine."

Johnnie Sue whipped off her ruffled apron—turquoise, this time—and tossed it across the room to the laundry bin. "Boy gets lonely after hours, Hershell. In the last few years he's lost four different people who meant the world to him. You've only lost one."

Hershell stiffened as he always did when anybody mentioned Larry's wife and kids. Never had he felt more tenderness for his son than the day he'd found out what Sandra had done. In fact, he'd felt a rage so powerful it had shaken him, and he was glad that he'd never seen the young woman again after the news got out. Every time he thought about the way Sandra had betrayed his boy, he ached as though the hurt had been his own.

"You're forgetting Paulie," he chided Johnnie Sue, amazed that she could have left his firstborn off of Larry's list of grave losses.

Johnnie Sue smiled gently, or as near to gently as anybody had ever seen Johnnie Sue smile. None of her regulars—in fact, nobody still alive but Larry and Hersh—knew that there was a tender streak in Johnnie Sue. Of course, nobody knew she'd been pregnant when her husband had left her and she had grieved for the miscarried baby for years. When she'd first arrived at the bus stop thirty-odd years ago, Hershell and Aggie—and even the boys—had tried to pin her heart back together, but for a while there they'd been afraid that the shattered young girl would give up the battle and do herself in. But Johnnie Sue had forged her own armor: she'd swathed herself in burlap, at least on the surface, and never told a soul that she had a heart wrapped in silk. Most of the time she behaved like a pretty odd duck, but in Hershell's opinion, no finer woman lived on the face of the earth.

"I'm not forgetting Paulie," Johnnie Sue answered briskly. "I just got stupid there for a minute. I was talking about the last two or three years as though time made a difference."

Hershell nodded. Paulie had been gone for seventeen years, and the pain had not yet eased. Johnnie Sue's husband had been gone twice as long, and there were still times, after hours, when Hersh would find her staring out the window as though she expected to see him drive up any day.

LARRY TRIED to tell himself that the fluttery feeling in his chest on the Monday morning Rene was due to start work was just relief. After all, he *was* exhausted, and he was worried about his dad. The cataract surgery was scheduled for next month, and when it was over he'd feel a lot better about Hershell's eyes. But he'd still have to deal with the question of whether his father, at seventy-five, was truly competent to come back to work even part-time at the store.

He tugged on a brand new pair of jeans, wondering if the casual clothes might strike Rene Hamilton as unprofessional. He didn't even wear one of those white smocks or a name tag. After all, most of his customers had known him all his life, and if they didn't, they seemed to have no difficulty figuring out who was in charge as soon as they entered Duncan's Drugs. But somehow the red polo shirt he slipped on looked juvenile instead of spunky, and the yellow one looked garish instead of cheerful. In the end he chose a sober gray that Sandra had always said was a terrible color on him.

With your brown hair and brown eyes, a nice rich shade of green would be best, she'd suggested, running her hands over his naked thighs. *Or maybe baby blue, the color of the sky...*

He realized with a start that he hadn't worn blue or green since the day Sandra had left him. Somehow, now it seemed as though he were letting her win. The thought angered him, so he tossed off the gray shirt and pulled on a blue one. Deciding that it was a good cross between attractive and respectable, he kept it on all through breakfast and even afterward, when he went out to check on the kids' rabbits in the backyard. It wasn't until just before he left the house that he traded it for a white button-down-collar shirt and a tie, and replaced his jeans with a pair of double-knit pants.

RENE HAMILTON REPORTED for work at eight o'clock on Monday morning, and by noon, she was beginning to think that the reason Larry couldn't hold on to staff had nothing to do with the location of Porter or the work.

Half of it was the busybodiness of the tiny town.

The other half was Maxine.

Maxine gossiped about everything except pharmacy business, but she made such a big fuss about "confidentiality" that the few secrets Duncan's had seemed far more controversial than they actually were. She seemed to take great pride in keeping nuggets of information from Rene.

When Larry introduced her to his bookkeeper, Maxine smiled tensely, but she could hardly conceal her bitterness as she told Rene that she was certain that Hershell would return to work right after his eye surgery. Rene noticed that Larry did not correct her.

Despite that inauspicious beginning, Maxine retained a veneer of courtesy until Rene found it necessary to intervene when she started giving medical advice to a customer just before lunch. Some fellow named Henry Clancy, who apparently ran the gas station across the street, wandered in complaining about an injury to his shoulder sustained in trying to push a car out of an intersection. First Maxine teased him about his weight, then accused him of neglecting his pregnant wife. As if that weren't bad enough, she started recommending specific painkillers.

Rene waited until she could get a word in edgewise, then said courteously, "It sounds to me as though your condition may warrant a prescription drug, Mr. Clancy. The most effective painkiller would be ibuprofen, or maybe piroxicam, if you have no history of stomach problems.''

''What's my stomach got to do with it?'' Henry griped. ''It's my shoulder that's killing me.''

''If you have an ulcer, the piroxicam will kill you, too, Henry,'' Maxine informed him, raising her chin just a bit as if to prove that she knew her stuff. ''It's wonderful for most people, but it's poison for somebody with ulcers.''

Henry glared at Maxine, then at Rene. ''Outsiders coming in here trying to poison me!'' he mumbled. ''Where the hell is Larry?''

Rene glared at Maxine, then offered Henry a saccharine smile. She decided not to explain that Larry was at lunch. Instead, she tried to keep the conversation professional. ''Piroxicam is an excellent drug, Mr. Clancy, and it most certainly is not poison. Mrs. Kensler is simply pointing out to you what any *licensed pharmacist* or *dispensing physician* would be legally and morally obligated to inform you or any other patient who is considering a drug with known side effects.''

Maxine, whose face flamed as she realized that Rene was warning her not to cross professional boundaries, straightened and focused on Henry. ''You better go see Doc Swanson if it gives you much trouble, Henry. All you can get here is the aspirin on the fourth shelf.''

Henry grabbed some aspirin, plunked it down on the counter in front of Rene, and growled, ''I suppose this stuff can kill me, too?''

''Only if you're taking a blood-thinning agent like warfarin. The two interact in a way that—''

''Oh, the hell with it!'' Henry bellowed as he turned and stomped out. ''I'll just tough it out on my own.''

The instant he was out of earshot, Maxine turned furiously on Rene. "I hope you're satisfied! You got Henry all het up and you cost Larry a sale!"

"If you hadn't interfered, I could have handled it more diplomatically, Maxine. But you are not a licensed pharmacist and you should not be giving out medical recommendations! With the blows to Duncan's reputation in recent years, we can't afford to make any mistakes here."

"*We* can't afford to make any mistakes? I've been working here since before you were *born,* girl! Don't you try to tell me how to do my job!" She puffed up like a courting dove. "I was trained by *Hershell.*"

She said the word as though the man were royalty, and Rene decided not to argue. She would do her best for Larry in the brief time she'd be in Porter, but she couldn't afford to get too tangled up in the underpinnings of Duncan's. He'd have to deal with Maxine as he saw fit. She had enough problems in her own life.

But none of those private problems came to the fore during her first day at work. Although she rubbernecked to watch the street and strained to catch each customer's casual gossip, she didn't pick up a clue about Fran or Seth. She learned about Johnnie Sue's secret purchases of romance novels at the Buck-A-Bag in Washburn and the oft-told tale of silly Gert Wilson punching out the fellow who ran over her little Julie's Easter hat when she was five. She discovered that the sheriff had gone to school with Larry; Maxine's husband had deer heads all over his barn. She even learned that half the town was busy coddling Larry's father, who was often seen at his wife's grave.

And she learned that Larry Duncan was as patient a man as ever walked the face of the earth. He always had time for a friend or a stranger, and he carried half the town on the books. He seemed to be the only one in town without something rotten to say about a woman named Sandra who'd deliberately deceived him.

Rene hated knowing that someday they'd say the same things about her.

"SO HOW'S YOUR new pharmacist working out, Lare?" Johnnie Sue asked as she scrubbed halfheartedly at the Jell-O stain near Larry's left elbow while he sipped a Coke at dinner. Even if Hershell hadn't spent the whole morning bemoaning the fact that it was Rene Hamilton's first day at work, Johnnie Sue would have known that something was up the minute Larry walked in wearing his Sunday "goin' to meetin'" clothes.

Her preliminary backdoor sleuthing in Des Moines had revealed nothing more than the fact that the people Rene worked with, believing Johnnie Sue to be a faithful customer who was sorry to hear she was leaving, "thought the world of the girl" and were broken-hearted to see her up and leave for no apparent reason. Johnnie Sue had heard her "reason"—once from Larry and once from the girl herself—and she wasn't buying it. There *were* folks who chose to leave the big city for the quiet country life— Johnnie Sue had once been one of them—but Rene Hamilton just didn't fit the bill. There was nothing down-home about her, and nothing that looked as though she *wanted* to learn how to be down-home.

"Hey, Larry, wake up!" Johnnie Sue prodded when he did not promptly answer her inquiry about Rene. "I said, how's the new girl working out over there? She getting along okay with Max?" She was preparing a rough-tongued zing to snap him out of his daydreams when something amazing happened that stopped her in her tracks.

Larry smiled.

In the eyes of some other woman, it might have passed

as another way of saying "all right" or "no problem" or even "I guess she's working out okay." But Johnnie Sue had seen Larry Duncan's "all right" smile when she'd asked about his grades when he was ten, his "no problem" smile when she'd hired him to wash her truck at fourteen, and his "I guess she's working out okay" smile when Gert's daughter, Julie, had clerked last summer before Henry Clancy had gotten her pregnant and she'd had to get married right away.

The look on his face right now looked alarmingly similar to the silly grin he'd worn when he'd brought Kathy Jessup by for dessert on the night he'd taken her to the junior prom. In fact, it reminded Johnnie Sue of the sheepish gaze he'd bestowed on that cheating tart, Sandra, while they were exchanging vows.

Dear God, that poor boy has swallowed a baited hook all over again, Johnnie Sue realized with a start. But her sinews grew taut as she vowed. *I'm damn well going to find out what Rene Hamilton is fishing for before she reels him in.*

AT EIGHT FORTY-FIVE, Larry strolled up to the back door of Duncan's Drugs and tried the handle. It was already locked, which did not surprise him. By now, the evening clerk was probably gone and Rene was wrapping things up all alone. As frightened as she was of crime in the workplace, she wasn't likely to leave the back door open downtown after dark, even if "downtown" only consisted of two quiet blocks.

It was for that reason—and that reason only, he told himself—that he'd promised to come back at closing himself instead of sending Maxine. Once Rene got used to the system, she would close alone, but not the first day. Surely after a week or so she'd realize that there was nothing to worry about. The kind of crime she feared had not yet pushed its way this far into the American heartland.

Larry slipped his key into the door, let the bells jangle, then called out, "Rene? It's only me."

There was a surprising silence before he heard her voice. Slightly breathless, but not afraid.

"Mr. Duncan?"

Larry rolled his eyes, glad she was around the corner out of sight. "I thought we were done with that Mr. Duncan stuff, Rene."

He wasn't sure why it bothered him so much. After all, it wasn't as though Rene had become a member of the family. She was just an employee…a brand-new one, at that. One of the many who had come and—sooner or later—would also go.

The hell she is, an urgent voice within him argued. *I can't afford to lose this one. I need top help too badly.*

And then Rene came into view, and Larry found himself gripping the countertop until his fingertips grew white. She hadn't changed since morning, but now her tight tresses were starting to fight their way to freedom and her eaten-off lipstick revealed a vulnerable, compelling mouth. She looked deeply tired, and almost…well, disappointed. To see him? Or was she disappointed for some other reason?

He'd done his best to counteract Maxine's poorly disguised lack of welcome. In fact, he'd probably gone overboard trying to make sure that Rene had a good first day. At dinner he'd called Maxine and read her the riot act. *When push comes to shove, I'm the boss, Aunt Max,* he'd had to tell her. *We can't afford to lose Rene.*

She'd hung up in a snit, but he knew she'd clean up her act in the morning. He also knew what she had against Rene. But Maxine could run off a dozen Renes and it wouldn't change the fact that his father just wasn't fit to keep on working. Nor would it change the fact that this Rene—this beautiful, half-strong, half-fragile creature—would not be easy to replace.

"Hello, er, Larry," she greeted him cautiously. "I think I've got everything wrapped up."

He nodded, trying not to stare at her exquisite emerald eyes. "How was your day?"

She smiled brightly—far too brightly for honesty's sake. "Oh, it was great, Larry. No problems at all."

He didn't smile back. He knew she was trying to act professional, but he wanted her to be real with him. "Maxine was kind of hard on you this morning," he apologized. "I talked to her this evening and I think tomorrow she'll warm up."

Rene's smile seemed to lose its grip. "Oh, that's very kind of you, Larry, but I'm sure I'll have no problems."

She'd denied having problems in two sentences back-to-back, and Larry wondered why she felt it was necessary to convince him that everything was so spectacular.

"The first day's always hard, Rene. Go home and get some sleep. It ought to be easier tomorrow."

The smile eclipsed completely. "Larry, it was easy enough today. You don't need to coddle me."

She sounded the tiniest bit irritated, the way Sandra had during the last month of their marriage…when she'd been seeing her ex-husband but Larry hadn't found out about it yet. He wondered why the comparison had sprung to mind, then realized that the only thing the two situations had in common was that he'd been oblivious to the true feelings of a woman he'd been futilely trying to please.

"I'm sorry if I sound…well, however I sound to you," Rene suddenly declared. "It's just that…you're my boss, and I'm trying to behave professionally. I'm not in the habit of complaining to an employer on the first day. If you were my brother or my landlord or my next-door neighbor, I'd—''

"I get the picture," he cut her off, retreating to safe professional ground. Instantly he cleared his face from any hint of affection or concern as he started to explain Duncan's closing-up procedures. Valiantly he tried to stifle the feeling that she'd just slapped him in the face.

He knew that all she'd done was draw the lines—the appropriate lines—for their relationship. It was Larry who'd been pushing too hard. Not just too hard, he realized with a hot flush at the back of his neck, but pushing in the wrong direction altogether. He'd wanted to get close to Rene, to offer her kindness and security, to offer her… *To offer her what?* he railed at himself. *Whatever the hell it is, it hasn't got a damn thing to do with the pharmacy.*

That's when it all hit him below the belt. He'd hired a woman to replace his dad because he hadn't had any choice. That much was true. But he'd also told himself that if Rene Hamilton had no romantic interest in him, he could turn away from the sensual longing she triggered in his body…and the protective ache she triggered in his heart.

I can ignore her as a woman, he vowed fiercely as Rene slipped the long strap of her purse over her shoulder, the simple gesture drawing his eye to the erotic curve of her enticing breasts. *She's just another employee. Nothing the least bit special to me.*

But as he watched the smooth glide of her hips as she slipped past him—inadvertently brushing his rigid thighs— he knew that it would take a heart of stone to ignore Rene's femininity, and his was made of homespun wool.

CHAPTER THREE

AFTER A FEW WEEKS on the job, Rene began to feel more or less at home at Duncan's Drugs. Day after day, she met the old and young of Porter proper, the neighboring farms, and stragglers from the tiny burgs of Washburn, Raymouth and Sweeton, which were, incredibly, even smaller than Larry's hometown. There were occasions when somebody would come in and ask for a prescription without chatting for five minutes with Larry or Maxine about a new grandchild, an upcoming wedding, or the effect of the weather on this year's crop, but those times were few and far between. Rene quickly came to understand that "service," as it was interpreted at Duncan's, had more to do with how the customers felt when they left the store than how they'd been helped with their purchases.

Health—good health, poor health, past health, anticipated health, dreams of health, despair of ever regaining health—was always a major topic. With some dexterity, Rene observed, both Larry and Maxine could chew the fat regarding almost anybody's health without revealing anything that was confidential. This resulted as far as she could tell, from the simple fact that most of the time, everybody's health was public knowledge long before a given prescription arrived at Duncan's Drugs. They didn't reveal any of their patients' secrets because there were no secrets to reveal.

It was, for instance, no secret that pudgy Clay Billings

had asthma, a condition that might well have precluded his employment on a more sophisticated police force. Poor Julie Wilson Clancy almost had a miscarriage, and Wanda Carmichael, who sang in the church choir with Maxine and Hershell, was recovering slowly but surely from her recent gall bladder surgery despite some scary complications.

Nonmedical gossip found its way to the pharmacy also. Rene learned that Johnnie Sue Rawlings won Sunday's jackpot bulldogging out at the same ranch where she shot skeet on Saturdays; everybody said she was a deadeye shot. Toolie Hibbs's granddaughter was getting married out in California to a man who wore sandals and loud Hawaiian shirts to work. Elwood's ne'er-do-well little brother had finally made good in Arizona selling real estate. About the only local whose name hadn't been mentioned at Duncan's so far was Fran Bixby's. And not once had Rene picked up so much as a ghost of a rumor about Seth. How she ached to learn if he'd grown tired of cotton-candy Frannie and was desperately praying that his wife would take him back!

She reminded herself that she had reason to hope.

After two years of waiting for the pain to subside, Rene had buoyed herself for her graduation ceremony last month, struggling to believe that being a pharmacist was somehow more gratifying than being a wife. But it was an insurmountable task as she sat in her metal folding chair, knowing that she had not one family member in the bleachers to cheer for her success. A fellow classmate had planned a graduation party, but after that, Rene knew she'd be going home alone.

And then, she'd seen him. In the back, stone-silent, leaning against the old brick wall. Dark black hair, full, tempting lips, strong and beautiful. Blue eyes on Rene, hands clapping when the president of the college called her name—her maiden name since she'd discarded his—standing up to give her an ovation for a job well done.

Seth. After all this time, all this agony, all this silence, *Seth!* He'd cared enough to find out about her graduation ceremony, cared enough to attend it! Cared enough to let his eyes meet hers, just once, while he gave her a hearty thumbs-up for a job well done.

Hope had suffused Rene, flapping at her insides like a wild rabbit abruptly thrust in a cage. When she'd called a mutual friend a few days later and learned that Seth had never married Fran—though he'd moved with her to Porter—a bizarre notion had taken root in Rene's heart.

Over time, her memory of the scene on the couch had faded. What remained was the collage of memories that surrounded those six other wonderful years of marriage. A kind of marriage she longed to celebrate again. Maybe, she told herself, she'd thrown the baby out with the bathwater. Cut off her nose to spite her face.

She loved him, she was lonely, and she decided to give him another chance.

But she couldn't just go to him. Her pride was too great and her wounds were too deep. She needed to plant herself near Seth, let him stumble across her path. Once they started talking again…a little here, a little there…well, anything could happen. And if it didn't happen on its own, she'd find a way to help things along.

Rene thrust from her mind the painfully domestic scene she'd studied at the farmhouse, reminding herself that if Seth had truly wanted Fran, he would have married her and started a family by now. It wasn't as though Rene were trying to steal another woman's husband! In Seth's heart, *surely,* Rene was still his wife.

It galled her no end that she could not take advantage of her local resources to find out more about him. But both

Johnnie Sue and Maxine seemed to be lying in wait for her to make a wrong move, so she didn't dare arouse their suspicions. Among the women she'd met, only Lotty treated her with honest warmth, but she was loathe to risk tipping her hand to such a garrulous soul. As to Larry, he seemed totally oblivious to her secrets, but Rene couldn't quite bring herself to deceive him further. It had something to do with the subtle respect he always offered her, something to do with his willingness to believe her trumped-up reason for coming to Porter, and something to do with the baby bird.

The bird arrived at Duncan's Drugs about the time Rene was beginning to wonder if she'd made a terrible mistake in coming to Porter. She'd certainly made several other errors in judgment since she'd arrived.

For instance, she had misread Larry Duncan considerably. She'd expected him to be overly friendly, unprofessional, and tolerant of a slipshod operation. Yet he'd consistently impressed her with his quiet, efficient management of his employees, his stock, and the doctors with whom he worked. He'd given her precise and cordial directions, but no shade of personal interest had colored his behavior at any time...except for her first day on the job, when he'd hovered over her so closely that she'd wondered what was on his mind. But he certainly didn't coddle her nowadays! He'd even rather pointedly checked his watch the one time she'd shown up late because she'd had trouble finding a spot to park in front of the store.

Of course, there *was* a back lot, but since her apartment was only three blocks away and the weather was clear, she was hardly driving to work in the interest of convenience. If Seth didn't learn she'd come to town by word of mouth, she was counting on the fact that sooner or later he'd drive by and spot her utterly unmistakable scarlet car. They'd picked it out together, and he'd always teased her about its unsubtle shade. When he saw it, he'd check it out, and when he learned that she'd come to Porter, he'd check *her* out. Seth was a thorough and curious man. He never sat still when something was amiss.

She'd told Larry that she was afraid to park in the back on the days when she closed up; it was too dark and isolated, after all. Her stomach had pitched in self-loathing as he'd nodded sympathetically, laid one firm hand on her arm and assured her, "You park wherever you want to Rene, but, believe me, you don't have to worry about that now."

He used the same tone a few days later when a frantic little urchin came barreling into his store around three in the afternoon, just minutes after Rene herself had come on duty. A noisy herd of children was passing by the front of the store on their way to Johnnie Sue's. This was not unusual; in fact, it happened every day right after summer school let out. Rene never paid much attention to the kids, though she had noticed that Larry usually seemed to be checking stock near the front of the store about the time they came by and stopped, eyeing them almost wistfully, as the sound of childish laughter drifted through the glass windows.

The child who rushed in the door—a very small, very dirty little boy—was wearing a loud orange T-shirt, bleach-spotted coveralls and a big smudge on his dripping nose. His cradled hands seemed to conceal something very small and fragile.

"Mr. Duncan! Ya gotta help me!" he burst out, oblivious to the fact that there were four women and two men crowded around the counter near Rene. "It fell outta the nest and it don't got no feathers or nothin'! I found it all bunged up on the sidewalk!"

Although Rene couldn't see the naked bird from her vantage point, she had no doubt that it was dying or already dead. The nest in that elm in front of the store was a good twelve feet off the ground, and no featherless chick could possibly have made the fall without sustaining grievous internal injuries. She would have told the child so—gently—and commended him for his thoughtfulness before disposing of the bird once he was out of sight. She was too busy to pay much attention to Larry's course of action, but she expected him to do the same.

He didn't. He abandoned his project—whatever it was—and hurried to greet the child as though the boy were a paramedic arriving at a hospital with a human heart attack victim. Larry took on the role of doctor.

"Let me see him, Artie!" he urged with a hushed, worried tone. "Open your fingers gently now, so he doesn't fall out."

The child gave a noisy sniff, which did nothing to restrain the oozing mucus now coursing over his upper lip, then opened his dirt-streaked hands. Larry knelt beside him, laying one brown finger tenderly against the child's wrist.

"Oh, he's a little one," he declared, nodding somberly. "It's a good thing you spotted him, Artie. I bet you got him just in time."

The little fellow's eyes misted. "You really think so, Mr. Duncan? You think we can save him?"

"If we put our heads together—" Larry pressed his forehead against the boy's with a wink and a tug on his mustache "—I think it'll come out just fine."

The little boy smiled, relieved and entertained, while Larry scavenged in the back for a box and some cotton, urging the boy to follow him into the semiprivate back area of the store. As he asked Artie for advice on every step,

he adjusted Maxine's desk lamp, explaining that they had
to keep the baby warm without burning it, then let Artie
cover the bird with torn wads of cotton before he sent him
off to get some raw hamburger from the Cornsilk. When
he was gone, Larry picked up the slack and filled a prescription or two, but the minute Artie returned, he left Rene
to juggle the customers while he showed the child how to
use a toothpick to feed the bird.

"Be very careful that it doesn't gobble too fast, or it'll
swallow that toothpick and strangle." His tone was warm,
paternal, sparking an indefinable sensation in Rene that she
decided must be envy. At Artie's age, she'd had no warm
father figure to teach her how to save a baby animal. In
fact, the one hamster she'd eagerly brought home had been
summarily squashed one night when it had somehow
slipped out of its cage. Her stepfather had called it a rat.

Larry spent a good half an hour with the boy and the
bird, ignoring the cluster of customers Rene and Maxine
had to field. Right about the time Rene feared that the child
might grow bored, Larry said, "Oh, Artie, we forgot to
call your mom! She'll be worried sick about you if you
don't get on home!" He promised to diligently care for
the bird until Artie came back to check on it tomorrow.

Satisfied, the boy thanked Larry and bounded off. Rene,
busy with customers, promptly forgot about the injured
chick. But when Larry got ready to go at the end of the
day, he told her briskly, "Rene, I'm going to take the baby
bird home with me. If Artie calls back, tell him I've decided to keep it as a pet until it grows all of its feathers."

Rene took a step toward the box and glanced at the
dying bird. It lay on its side, eyes closed, beak slack. Only
the trembling rise and fall of its tiny chest proved that it
was still breathing.

"Larry, it won't live until you drive home, especially if

you stop at the Cornsilk for dinner," she pointed out pragmatically. "It's probably internally bleeding to death."

Streaks of red slashed his normally genial face. "You think you're telling me something I don't know, Rene? You think I'm a stranger to hopelessness and death?"

It's odd how he puts those two things together, she thought. *He's so cheerful, I always assumed that he had hope enough for two.*

"Larry, I just—" suddenly she felt awkward and tongue-tied "—I didn't expect you to lie to a little boy, that's all."

"Even for his own good?"

"Lying never helps anybody but the liar. And even he, or she—" she gulped on the word "—pays for it in the end."

Larry's eyes narrowed. His lips thinned. "You're probably right, Rene. But it's hard enough for grownups to deal with death. Why break the heart of a little kid? Artie never comes to my house. If the bird's not here, he'll never see it again, and he'll never have to think of it as dead. If my son asked for help from a local grown-up, it's what I'd want that person to do for him."

Rene stared at him, dumbfounded. There was more than urgency in his tone, more than conviction that he was doing the right thing. There was pain in his voice, pain that seemed to splinter around the word "son."

"I...didn't know you had any children, Larry," she said, for some reason deeply shaken by his words. "I didn't even know you were married."

His curt response puzzled her even more.

"I *don't* have any children," he snapped. "I don't have a son. I don't have a daughter. And I sure as hell don't have a wife!" He glared at her and swallowed hard. "Not anymore."

Taken off guard by the rush of feeling, Rene whispered, "I'm sorry, Larry. I didn't know."

He shook his head, waving a hand as if to rid the room of the memory. "I find that hard to believe. Aunt Lotty's had time to give you my life story in chapter and verse by now, and if she hasn't, then somebody better call Doc Swanson because she's deathly ill."

Rene managed to smile. "Well, I'd have to admit that she has volunteered a tidbit or two about your childhood."

"But not my marriage and divorce?" he asked skeptically.

"Well, she's tried but—"

"But you weren't interested," he finished for her.

A slow, red stain darkened Rene's neck as she realized the implication of his words. There was fresh hurt in his tone, hurt that had less to do with his wife and kids than it had to do with her.

Rene felt sick. In her own way, she cared a lot for Larry; she wouldn't have hurt him for the world. Had she read him right the first time they'd met? Had he simply done an admirable job of keeping the lid on his feelings since she'd come to work at Duncan's Drugs?

"I didn't say that, exactly, Larry," she backpedaled kindly. "I just thought it was none of my business."

He shook his head again, as though he understood precisely what she'd tried so hard not to say. "And you were chewing *me* out for lying to protect somebody's feelings. You ought to practice what you preach, my girl."

Rene struggled to come up with a suitable reply, but everything she could think of only seemed to make things worse. In a desperate attempt to assuage his feelings, she blurted out, "Larry, it's not that I don't think you're…a very interesting man. It's just that, I work for you and…on top of that…I'm not really over my ex-husband."

It was more than she meant to tell him, but it was the most reassuring thing she could come up with. She hadn't expected him to be thrilled with her casual dismissal of his obvious affection for her, but the shock on his face took her totally by surprise.

"You're...*divorced?*" he asked, the word dropping like a rock into the stillness of a frozen winter's pond.

She nodded.

"You never mentioned that before."

She fought an odd sense of nausea. "I didn't think it mattered." She licked her lips. "To the job, I mean."

For a long moment Larry stared at her, then stared *through* her, as though she'd vanished into thin air. She watched a raft of feelings darken his gentle face, dissolving the kindly mask that had warmed to the heart of the child. Then he straightened, walked over to cradle the bird box, and tucked it under his arm.

"Of course it doesn't matter," he said briskly, but his husky tone gave away the lie.

HERSHELL HAD BEEN depressed since the day he'd heard that Larry was hiring Rene Hamilton, and his depression had grown deeper with each passing day. "He treats me like some rusty bent nail he can just pull out and replace," he told Aggie over breakfast one morning. At least, he directed his comment to the general direction of her chair at the kitchen table, one of the many places where he still carried on conversations with his late wife. "He thinks I'm some old horse too lame to pull the buckboard. Sometimes he forgets that I'm his dad."

Aggie didn't answer—she never did anymore—but he felt her healing presence just the same. After fifty-eight years of marriage, Aggie'd had no secrets from Hershell, and he'd known every one of her footprints before she'd even had time to don her shoes. It wasn't too hard for him to imagine what she'd be likely to say.

"He's just doing what he thinks is best for you, Hersh," she would have soothed him. "Don't you go getting your feelings hurt when he does things his own way."

"I just want a place where I belong, Aggie. Throwing me out of Duncan's is like throwing me out of my home. Can't the boy *see* that? I think he's got cataracts on his heart."

With apologies to Aggie, he poured himself a drink after breakfast and turned on the TV to some mindless game show. Or maybe two different shows, one after another; he wasn't watching closely enough to tell. After Aggie'd died, he'd blamed his indifference to daytime television on his cataracts, but now that his eye surgery was over, he had to face the fact that it was simply boring.

Nonetheless, he was still staring in the general direction of the television when he heard the car pull into the yard around 10. Thrilled at the thought of company, he steadied himself with both hands on the recliner chair, stood upright, and wobbled out to the porch.

Damn legs, he muttered to himself. *Getting shakier every day.*

Still, as he spotted Joel Carmichael coming up the walk, he didn't feel too lousy...until he saw the darkness on Joel's face.

"You goddamn, doddering idiot!" Joel shouted at him. "Why didn't you retire when Larry told you to?"

Hershell had sung in the choir with Joel for twenty-seven years, and he'd never heard Joel blaspheme, never heard him holler, and never heard him refer to anybody as a "doddering idiot," or even a fool. It was obvious that his old friend was terribly upset.

"Now Joel," he offered in his most calm and trustworthy tone, "why don't you come in and have a sandwich? You know I'll be more than happy to straighten out any little problem you might be—"

"Straighten *out?*" The other man's voice cracked hysterically. "How the hell can you straighten out the blunder you made this time? Goddamn it all to *hell,* Hershell! My Wanda is *dead!*"

Hershell was shocked. Wanda was a dear old girl who sang in the choir, too, except for the past month when she'd been recovering from surgery. But Johnnie Sue had mentioned only the other day that she was doing just fine and was out of the woods after that blood clot scare. Vaguely he realized that Joel had included him in some sweeping medical profession renunciation, but that was understandable when a man's wife was dead.

"Ah, Joel," he said almost tenderly. How clearly he remembered his own shock when Aggie had died. How closely the other man's pain surely mirrored his own! "I can't begin to tell you how sorry I am. Believe me, nobody knows how you feel any better then I do. Come on in and—"

Suddenly Joel's big brown hands were seizing his collar, shaking him as though he were a rat. Up close, Hershell could see the other man's eyes, rolling in furious despair, but there was nothing familiar about the pain-distorted features at all. Still, he could not feel angry with Joel; he knew how it was to lash out in grief. He felt utterly calm, utterly supportive, until Joel, incredibly, spat at him.

"Are you too far gone to get it, you old goat? It was your pills that did it!" His fury seemed to lace the very air. "You killed her, Hersh! You killed her just like you killed your own wife!"

There was probably more after that, but Hershell didn't

hear it. Right about the time Joel likened Wanda's death to Aggie's, he started to pass out.

WITH ONE HAND full of pills and the other holding a prescription label, Larry grabbed the phone and wedged it precariously between his neck and his shoulder. "Duncan's," he said briskly, trying not to let his voice reveal his gloom.

I've got no good reason to feel gloomy, he told himself. *I hired Rene to help me run the place, and as a pharmacist, she's been as good as gold.* It was a reasonable lecture—one he'd given himself several times today—but it didn't change the fact that ever since he'd found out that Rene was still pining for her ex-husband, he'd felt unaccountably morose.

Some other man would have assumed that in time she might get over it; he might even have volunteered to help her out. But Larry had already played that game, fallen for all the attendant lies, suffered the hidden heartaches of loving a woman inflicted with "still carrying a torch for my ex-husband" disease. He would sooner have fallen in love with a leper.

Since the day he'd hired Rene, he'd done his best to keep his feelings under wraps, especially after he'd come to grips with the fact that he was badly smitten. But even if Rene had never harbored suspicions that he was sweet on her before yesterday, he knew he'd given himself away. Which meant that he had to convince her instantaneously that his affection for her would not affect her job. He didn't want to look like an idiot, but—more important yet—he couldn't risk losing his part-time pharmacist.

"Larry, it's Joel Carmichael. I'm at your father's place and—"

"Hi, Joel. How's it going?" he asked genially, determined to turn his mind to somebody else's problems. "How's Wanda feeling?"

The dead silence that greeted the question should have told him everything, but it took Joel half a dozen sputtering sentences to get everything out. Once Larry got the whole picture, he knew that there was nothing he could do for Wanda, but a medical decision might still be crucial for his dad. "Have you called an ambulance? Can he breathe? Is he—"

"He's fine, Lare. Believe me. He's shaky and embarrassed, but that's all. He never really lost consciousness because I got him to lie down. It's my fault, Larry. I...went crazy. When I found Wanda this morning, I called Doc Swanson. He wasn't in yet, but I talked to his nurse, Sally Haywood, and she asked about which pills Wanda took last night. When I told her she only had warfarin and aspirin, she said you or Hersh should have told her never to mix the two! Sally said poor Wanda bled to death." He started to sob. "I knew you wouldn't make a mistake like that, Larry, but when I got to thinking about how you made Hersh quit working because he was so old I just..." He lost control completely then, and Larry did his best to comfort him.

Even as he spoke the right words of assurance, Larry's mind raced on to Super Mouth Sally's accusations...and the repercussions for his father if they were true. Could Hershell have forgotten to put a label on that warfarin bottle? And if he had, was there anything Larry could do about it now?

After he said goodbye to Joel, he made four quick calls—to Elwood Hazlett, Doc Swanson, Joel's daughter in Washburn and Pastor Ben. After that he told Maxine to hightail it over to his father's to "fill in for my mom."

But Maxine planted both hands on her hips and tongue-lashed him. "Do you mean to tell me, Larry Duncan, that your father is in terrible trouble and you won't even take half an hour to go to him?"

He considered telling her why he couldn't go, why the most important thing he could possibly do for his father at the moment was to stay right here in Duncan's and check Maxine's meticulous prescription records. He knew she'd understand the impact of a blow to his father like believing that he'd killed another dear friend; she might even be willing to alter evidence to protect him. But poor Maxine would wear sin-scars all of her life if she had to swallow her ethics and doctor the books, and Larry decided that it was a decision he'd have to make on his own.

JOHNNIE SUE DECIDED to call Gert Wilson at ten forty-five, exactly twenty-seven minutes after Elwood Hazlett first got the word that Wanda Carmichael was dead. She knew that Gert wouldn't be home, but she couldn't recall, right offhand, where she worked on Thursday morning, so she called little Julie first.

Julie, who still sounded as though she were only twelve, sounded sleepy when she answered the phone.

"It's Johnnie Sue. How're you doing?"

"Oh…okay, I guess."

That's what she always said, come rain or shine. To hear Gert talk, the girl was having the worst pregnancy in the history of womankind. According to Doc Swanson—who had told Johnnie Sue in the strictest confidence—Julie had morning sickness a lot worse than some, but her biggest problem was the oaf who shared her bed. Henry Clancy had bullied her into sleeping with him in the first place— an innocent young girl like that!—and now that she was seven months' along and looked like she'd swallowed a bowling ball, he still expected his voracious sexual hunger to be fully sated. If not by his wife, then by somebody else.

Johnnie Sue didn't like to talk to Julie, or even think about her much. This had nothing to do with the girl herself, who was colorless and wishy-washy but overall a nice-enough kid. The problem was that Julie was living out Johnnie Sue's personal nightmare, at least part of it, and Johnnie Sue knew that it was just a matter of time before the poor thing would have to face the fact that you can force a man to marry you, but you can never force him to be your *husband* in any way that counts.

The worst thing was that she'd seen it coming, way, way back, and hadn't done nearly enough to protect the girl. When Julie had started clerking afternoons and evenings for Larry, she'd ended up stopping at Johnnie Sue's for dinner or dropping by Clancy's Gas for candy bars. Johnnie Sue had been watching handsome Henry Clancy eye the girls ever since he was fourteen, and she knew that the fact that he was almost Larry's age and Julie was still in high school wouldn't get in his way. Once, she'd actually butted in and talked to Julie; she'd even talked to Gert. Half a dozen times she'd told Henry to keep his hands to himself or he'd find himself eating at the drive-in over in Washburn. Julie had blushed, denying everything; Gert had been incensed and unspeakably hurt. Henry had promised to keep his distance, and Julie had gotten pregnant within a few months. Nobody knew that Henry had agreed to marry her only after Johnnie Sue had tracked him down with her daddy's best bowie knife and threatened to cut off his testicles and his tab, in that order, if he didn't make things right.

Now she lied, "Your mom left her purse here and I want to make sure she doesn't worry about it. Where can I reach her this time of day?"

"She's at Toolie Hibbs's till noon. Do you want me to call her and tell her to drop by?"

"Oh, you don't have to worry about that, Julie. You go put your feet up, like Doc Swanson told you to. I can call Toolie. Now you give Henry my best."

She offered a few more crusty platitudes, then called Gert at the Hibbs's.

"When do you clean Wanda and Joel's place?" she asked without preamble. "Do you have a key?"

Gert gasped. "Why, Johnnie Sue, whatever do you mean?"

"I mean, I want you to get over there and check out the warfarin prescription bottle somebody at Duncan's filled in May. I want to know what it says on the label and what's inside. I also want you to check for some kind of warning about taking warfarin with aspirin."

This order was followed by a long, shaky silence, then a sputtered retort. "Why, Johnnie Sue, I never! To think of spying on that dear man with Wanda not more than a few hours' cold! How could you? Dear Wanda's dead and—"

"And Hershell might be next *if he thinks he killed her.*" Her words were blade-edge cold.

"But Joel said it was a mistake. At least that's what Vera Lawton said. And she lives just across the street, so when Elwood showed up, she—"

"I don't *care* what Vera said. I don't care what Elwood said! I want to know if there's any problem with that bottle of warfarin, and I want to know before anybody else does! You can walk right in the front door without a fuss, and if anybody asks what you're doing there, you just tell them you wanted to clean up the bed so poor Joel wouldn't have to face the sheets Wanda died in when he comes home from staying with his girl."

Johnnie Sue glanced behind her, making sure that her jackhammer voice didn't carry past the sounds of the kitchen fan. Not twelve feet away, Sam was grilling burgers, occasionally glancing in her direction. But he didn't look like he was paying much attention, and she made sure to look relaxed and happy when he looked her way.

"I can't do it, Johnnie Sue!" Gert whispered fervently. "It's wrong!"

"Wanda's dead," Johnnie Sue declared, each syllable a block of ice. "Tearing up what's left of Hershell's heart won't bring her back alive."

"I don't want Hershell hurt any more than you do," Gert whimpered. "But to sneak into Joel's home to…well, to *trick* him now that Wanda's gone…"

Johnnie didn't want to get dirty. She didn't want to threaten to tell Julie how she'd forced Henry to convert her status from unmarried mother into a respectable wife. But she was willing to do it if Gert didn't agree in another instant. There was no time to lose; it might already be too late.

"I'm not *asking* you, Gert," she growled. "I'm *telling* you it has to be done." When no further protest filled the gaping silence, she tacked on reassuringly, "Besides, I'm just asking you to check out the facts, not tamper with the evidence." She thought a moment, then added, "At least not yet."

LARRY STARTED to sweat as he tugged down the last box of original prescriptions, hoping it contained the one he wanted. He'd already checked the prescription register, and he'd found a warfarin prescription for Wanda filled a few days before Rene had come to town and plowed up his heart with her calm and capable indifference. It was hard to tell when his work had been more disconnected—before she came, when he'd been working thirteen-hour days and desperately searching for another pharmacist, or now, when it took every ounce of Larry's concentration to keep his professional facade from slipping.

Hershell had worked so few hours since Christmas that chances were excellent that he had not dispensed Wanda's medication…which meant that Larry had probably done it himself. Guilt reared its ugly head as he wondered if his blurry month of fatigue could have cost Wanda her life. Still, if somebody at Duncan's *had* made an error, he desperately hoped it was himself. Larry knew that if he was accused—or even convicted—of criminal negligence, he'd pay with his reputation, the family business and his career. But his father would never survive the knowledge that he had killed a dear friend through senile incompetence. One way or another Larry knew it would cost Hershell Duncan his life.

Fervently he prayed that he'd find his own initials scrawled at the bottom of Wanda's prescription. In that case there would be no moral questions to face, no agonizing decisions to be made. No humiliating explanations to make to ever-diligent Rene, who would surely, at some point down the road, ferret out any liberties he took with Duncan's pharmaceutical records. The truth—pure and simple—would be all he needed to get his dad back on his feet.

It only took Larry ten minutes to find the prescription, and on the top half, it held no surprises. One of Doc Swanson's gals had written it out for him—it looked like the prim printing of his longtime nurse, Sally Haywood—and Bob himself had scrawled his signature at the bottom on the appropriate line. The name of the drug, and the standard dosage—five milligrams twice a day—was perfectly correct and clear. It was obvious that since Wanda had left the doctor's office, nobody had added a thing.

Not even the letters "L.D."

CHAPTER FOUR

RENE NORMALLY WENT jogging just before going to work. She was just about to leave when a somewhat frantic Lotty wheeled up to her apartment with the news about Hersh and orders for Rene to drop everything and hustle down to Duncan's. She skipped the run, sacrificed breakfast and took off as soon as she could change her clothes.

She found Larry working on the books in the back—something he normally left to Maxine—and he jumped about a foot and a half when she softly said his name.

"Where the hell did you come from?" he greeted her coarsely. "Do you always sneak in like that?"

Hurt, Rene straightened, eyes watchful, as she replied with dignity, "Lotty said you needed me to come in early. If she misunderstood your message, I'd be happy to leave."

Larry slumped back on the small desk and sadly shook his head. "I'm sorry, Rene. I wasn't expecting you till noon. Lotty must have heard about Dad and acted on her own."

When Rene said nothing, he touched her arm and said softly, "Forgive me, huh? I really am sorry I barked at you. Nothing personal. I'm just having a terrible day."

Rene nodded, still confused by the unLarrylike display of emotion. Actually her own feelings had been in disarray ever since yesterday when Artie had arrived with the baby bird. To her amazement, she'd even had a dream last night that hadn't featured Seth. It wasn't an erotic dream, exactly, but when Larry had found seven-year-old Rene sobbing over her squashed hamster, he'd held her in his arms until she'd started to feel so good that she grew, in a matter of seconds, into a full-grown woman who wanted him to cuddle her in an entirely different way. Surprisingly aroused, she'd awakened just as their lips were about to meet in a decidedly unplatonic kiss.

Now, as Rene studied Larry's quietly sensual lips, she wondered what collection of motives had planted the dream in her mind. She'd never really given much thought to what Larry would be like as a lover. And yet—now that the notion had fluttered into her subconscious—she found that the idea of Larry's strong body close to hers was very appealing. But that surreal vision of happiness was peppered with guilt; every one of her deceptions now lived as a blot on her conscience. From the moment they'd met, Larry had been unfailingly kind and honest with her, while Rene had used him as a means to an end.

Good God, Rene, he's so much more to you than that, a voice within her cried out now. But as she battled with the strange new swirl of emotions triggered by the dream, she realized that she didn't know exactly how she felt about Larry. All she was sure of was that she felt warm and strong and cherished when he smiled at her…and sick inside when she thought of what would happen if he ever found out about her deception.

"Lotty says your dad is okay, Larry." She tried to soothe him, forcing herself to concentrate on the subject at hand. "But I don't mind postponing my run until tonight so you can go see him. Frankly I expected to find Maxine alone here. Lotty seemed to think that you'd gone out there right away."

He scowled at her, then tucked away a prescription in

the open file. "My father doesn't appreciate my attention very much, Rene. He wants to believe that he's just as brave and strong as ever. In his mind I'm still his baby boy. Number Two son."

Not quite sure how to handle his obvious depression, Rene said gently, "I've never met your father, Larry, but I've sure heard some nice things about him."

Larry chortled without mirth. "Why do you think you haven't met him yet, Rene? Did you think that was a co-incidence?"

Trying to ignore his sarcasm, Rene said, "I just assumed I hadn't run into him yet."

"That's because he's avoiding you like the plague. He refuses to believe that anybody can do his job, let alone a young female. Now that he's recovered from his eye surgery, he's going to start hammering at me to take back your job. He's already hinted once or twice."

Rene felt a sudden flip-flop of despair. Larry had warned her that the hours would be uncertain; he'd warned her that Pharmafix might ultimately make Duncan's Drugs go belly up. But he'd never mentioned the possibility that his father would replace her when she'd only been on the job for a few weeks.

"Are you trying to tell me something?" she asked tightly, hoping her fear didn't show. "Is my term here going to be a short run after all?"

Larry stared at her for a moment, looking befuddled. Then he blinked twice and said, "No, Rene! Good God, no. I was just trying to tell you how my dad looks at things. I never intended for him to risk filling prescriptions again, even before...well, before today."

Rene perched gingerly on Larry's stool, trying to catch her breath. She felt a bit dizzy. For just a moment there, she'd wondered if Larry had tricked her into uprooting herself to come to town for a job that would last only a couple of weeks after all. The very notion that Larry could so deliberately deceive her made her feel sick and insecure...and even more ashamed that she had, in essence, done the same thing to him. In fact, Rene was so disturbed by the notion of *Larry* laying her off for any reason that several moments passed before she realized that losing her job at Duncan's would mean she'd have to map out a whole new strategy to "accidentally" contact Seth and begin the long journey to win him back.

"He just hasn't been able to get a grip on himself since Mom died," Larry was saying, talking to himself as much as to Rene. "I think he even talks to her sometimes. Once I heard him rambling on in the kitchen just the way he used to recap his day for her while she was getting dinner." He stopped, pink shaming his neck, as he asked, "Are your parents old, Rene? Have you ever had to deal with anything like this?"

A tight band of muscle compressed Rene's heart as she struggled to think of a way to tell him the truth without giving any of her secrets away. But she basically had two choices—she could either tell him the truth or make up another lie, and she'd already told Larry all the lies she could ever muster. The closer she got to Larry, the more she ached to take them back.

"Larry," she confessed, "my parents are...pretty much nonexistent. I haven't the slightest idea who my father is, but I grew up with a mother that I'd just as soon forget. I moved out the instant I turned eighteen, and even though she knew where I was, she never made the slightest effort to contact me."

Larry's lips tightened in surprise. His gaze grew tender, almost sad. "Rene—"

"Never mind. It's not important," she cut him off. It

wasn't something she wanted to get into today. "What's important is your father's health. Do you need to go see him? Do you need me to stay? Or would you just as soon I get out of your way?"

He studied her quietly, differently from the way he'd studied her before. It made her feel strange…a bit tingly inside. She tried to think of something intelligent to say, but no words came out. Larry's quiet intensity left her shaken and curiously warm. In her haze of—was it sensual?—confusion, the only thing she was sure of was that she could not turn away.

"You're never in my way, Rene," Larry admitted quietly, his touching gaze caressing her face. "It's always a pleasure to have you around."

Rene pursed her lips, not quite sure of where he was headed…or even where she wanted him to go. "What I meant, Larry, was do you want me to—"

"Yes."

The word came suddenly, midsentence, and it was hard to tell whether he was answering Rene's question or answering one of his own. Yesterday's discussion about her indifference to Lotty's tales about his divorce seemed to fill the air between them, and Rene felt a strong urge to do something—step away or else press very close.

"Don't look so scared, Rene. I didn't mean…I didn't mean anything," he backpedaled quickly. "But the look on your face tells me that we need to get a few things straight. About yesterday, I mean."

She did not pretend to misunderstand him. "I thought we reached closure on that subject, Larry."

He shook his head. "No, we didn't. I made you uncomfortable and then I took off with that bird…which died late last night, by the way. I couldn't save it." His somber tone made it clear that he'd truly tried. "What I want to make clear is that I have no intention of...well, harassing one of my employees." His whole face turned pink, but he plunged on with his confession. "I'll admit to being attracted to you back when we first met, Rene. I'm only human. You're a beautiful woman, and you're about my age. I think you'd be more offended if you thought I hadn't noticed."

Rene was embarrassed but she managed to smile at him. Suspecting that Larry was drawn to her was one thing; having him tell her outright was another. And deciding the prudent course of action now was something else entirely. Especially when she felt so...well, downright off-kilter this morning.

But before she could get her bearings, Larry pulled the rug out from under her entirely. "But that has nothing to do with the job we have to do, or how I intend to treat you," he stated firmly. "You can hardly say I've been chasing you around the counter since you came to work here, can you?"

"Of course not, Larry. You've been quite professional at all times."

He nodded, looking a bit relieved. "And that's how I intend to remain. I don't plan to bring this subject up again unless you do." He raised his eyebrows until she nodded, accepting his decree. "Now, before we get to work, I want to say one other thing. You're new here. You hardly know a soul. I haven't wanted to be overly cordial because I didn't want you to misinterpret my...expectations. Personally or professionally. But if you ever feel the need for platonic company, or some avuncular advice, I'm here. I won't extend any specific invitations, because I don't want you to feel awkward about turning me down. At Duncan's, I'm the boss and you're the employee, but after hours if you need a friend, I'm perfectly willing to be...friendly."

He paused a moment, then tacked on, "And I do mean just that, Rene. 'Friendly' in the purest sense of the word."

For some reason, Rene felt more bereft than flattered by his straightforward speech. She knew he was trying to be generous, trying to make her feel at ease. And though she appreciated the gesture, she found herself disappointed, somehow, that he'd apparently given up the chase. Not that he'd ever hunted her, exactly, but until she'd told him about her divorce, she'd always felt his restrained interest and basked in its warmth. Now, abruptly, he was promising to be tepid. She should have felt relieved, but his change of heart left her sad and uneasy.

Still, she said crisply, "Thank you, Larry. You're really very good to me."

He grinned. Or maybe grimaced? "I try to keep my employees happy. And my customers, too." He glanced at the door as Gert Wilson trotted in, waving a prescription in the air. "Here comes one now. Would you do the honors? I'm not in the mood to listen to her gabble about my father."

Rene quickly greeted Gert—who'd come to get a prescription filled for old Toolie Hibbs—but her mind lingered with Larry. What was going on behind those sad, watchful eyes? Had he really told her the truth about his willingness to be her ever-so-platonic friend? And if so, why did that knowledge make her feel so disheartened?

After all, she hadn't come to Porter to find a new lover. She'd come to conquer Fran and win back Seth.

Hadn't she?

As HERSHELL SAT in what had become known as the Duncan booth at the Cornsilk waiting for Larry, he watched Johnnie Sue greet her customers with cheerful insults and salty wisecracks. When he'd arrived, she'd brought him

his coffee without a word, which would indicate to anybody watching that she understood what he'd been through
today. But the coffee, he realized in one slurp, wasn't de-
caf, and Johnnie Sue only brought him regular coffee when
she knew he was falling apart at the seams.

As he sipped the dark, rich blend, he thought about the
sturdiness of Johnnie Sue's friendship, the unflagging bul-
wark she provided for his scrambled life. Although everybody in town considered Johnnie Sue a friend, there were
"how's it goin' friends" and "even when the chips are
down friends," as Aggie used to say. And to the Duncans,
Johnnie Sue had always been the "when the chips are
down" kind.

As Larry slouched in a few minutes later, it occurred to
Hershell that Larry was a "when the chips are down" kid.
Paulie, who'd seemed to have ten times Larry's energy,
looks and brains, had always had somewhere to go and
something to do. Larry, on the other hand, had always been
willing to postpone his plans or cancel them altogether
when his mom needed somebody to drive her to Des
Moines or Hersh himself had wanted company pulling
weeds or mowing the lawn. When the boys got in trouble,
it was Paulie who'd come up with some high falutin'
story...Larry who'd always confess what they'd done
while he looked his folks straight in the eye. It was also
Paulie, from childhood, whom Hershell had groomed to
take over the drugstore. Larry had dreamed of working in
aeronautical design. If his brother was going to inherit the
drugstore, then Larry was free to follow his own dream.
But when Paulie hit a bad patch and dropped out of school,
Larry had switched his major. And when the army tried to
convince Hersh and Aggie that their firstborn wouldn't be
coming home, Larry, a pharmacist, by then had moved
back to Porter for good.

So where the hell was my boy today? Hershell asked himself. He was not angry; he was not hurt. Although he and Larry had been rubbing each other the wrong way a good deal of the time lately, he had no doubts about Larry's well-meaning, if misguided, intentions. His failure to come to the house today when Joel called had surely been for some reason that Larry believed to be in his doddering dad's best interests. The question was, what was going on in that boy's head?

The look on Larry's face tonight—so thoughtful it bordered on morose—did not encourage conversation. He sat down opposite his father, sipped from the frosty glass of Coke that Johnnie Sue had brought for him, and asked too tenderly, "Are you all right, Dad?"

"Of course I'm all right. I'm strong as an ox," he bluffed. "It's Joel who's losing it, son. Small wonder after what he's been through."

Larry glanced at him quickly, then focused on his Coke.

Ashamed of your old man, are you? Hershell wondered. *Ashamed because I nearly passed out, or ashamed because of what Joel said I might have done?*

Joel said somebody at Duncan's had forgotten to warn Wanda that she couldn't mix aspirin with warfarin. How could that be? Larry would never make a mistake like that, and Hershell would never have done it, either, unless his mind really *was* beginning to slip. He didn't remember the prescription, exactly—he'd filled dozens of them for Wanda in his life—but he'd never give any patient warfarin without putting on a bright blue warning label. He'd always been extra-cautious about things like that. Especially since Aggie and the others... Especially since then.

He glanced at Larry, wanting to ask if he'd checked to see who'd filled the prescription. Then he realized that *of course* Larry had checked it! Larry was a damn fine pharmacist, and Larry was his son.

At the moment, Larry was tapping on his Coke glass. Larry was playing with a spoon. Larry was…Larry was not looking at his father. Not looking at his father at all.

The small worm of worry that had been eating at Hershell's stomach all day now seemed to multiply in length and voracity. He stared at Larry, willed him to look back. But Larry's eyes were everywhere but on his dad this evening.

It was an ugly night—a summer squall was passing overhead—and all the regulars in the Cornsilk were chatting about the storm. Hershell was certain that by this time most of them knew what had happened, but none of them were brave enough to ask for details. He wasn't quite sure whether that was because they were also too kind to hurt him or because they knew that Johnnie Sue would drop them in their tracks if they did.

Despite his depression, Hershell almost smiled when Johnnie Sue marched back from the kitchen, slapped Larry on the back so hard he sputtered, and gave him her crusty, eye-wrinkling version of a grin. Without asking for their orders, she said, "I think you ought to have lasagna tonight, Hersh. And I've got corned beef hash for you, Lare."

Hershell didn't need to be told that neither meal was on the menu. Johnnie Sue had taken it upon herself to whip up each man's favorite dinner to help brighten this pathetically dismal day.

"Sounds great, Johnnie," Larry said without much vigor. "Maybe a salad first, okay?"

He didn't specify that he wanted the cobb salad, because Johnnie Sue knew that he liked lots of tomatoes when they were in season, no carrots, and plenty of her Cornsilk dressing on the side.

"You got it." She turned to Hersh. "You want anything special?"

I want my Aggie back. Oh, how I need to see Aggie today! The words cried in his heart and spoke from his eyes, and Johnnie Sue, who heard them, gave him one of those for-Duncans-only smiles. "Boston cream pie for dessert it is," she affirmed as though he'd requested it specifically.

Hersh managed to smile, but words were beyond him again.

Without writing down their order, Johnnie Sue turned to the kitchen, then stopped as the front door swung open on a gust of wind, admitting a stocky fellow, no taller than Johnnie Sue but about twice as wide. He wasn't fat—just bulky with muscles that testified to a lifetime of hauling freight. He stomped in the front door and stood there, dripping, as he gazed around inside.

"Well, you gonna sit down or just mop the floor with your boots?" Johnnie Sue called across the room in a cranky tone that a stranger might not have taken as a friendly greeting.

"Truck broke down on the highway," he replied as though she'd asked for the information. "Barely limped into that gas station down the block. Fellow there said this was the place to eat."

"Food's better here," she answered crisply.

"Better than where?"

"Than wherever else you were fixin' to eat tonight." Johnnie Sue stared at him a moment—he really was a mess—then ordered, "Sit yourself down." She grabbed a mug and slopped it full of coffee with such haste that a few drops leapt on to the spotless, worn Formica. As the new arrival followed her to the spot at the counter she'd chosen for him, Johnnie Sue barked, "Cream and sugar?"

"Two scoops, one drop of cream."

She opened the sugar packets and dumped them in, added a small spatter of cream, then handed him the spoon. Without another word she disappeared into the kitchen, returning moments later with two clean terry dish towels. "Go dry yourself," she ordered. "You like Italian?"

He nodded, then took the towels and headed off toward the men's room.

Hershell grinned. Hand it to Johnnie Sue to buck him up when he was feeling down. "Girl's got a real way with people, doesn't she?" he asked his son.

The tension in Larry's face began to ease. "I love her with all my heart, Dad, but I can sure see why she's stayed single all these years."

Hersh answered soberly, "She's stayed single because she never found anybody good enough for her in this backwater swamp." His eyes darkened for a moment, then he added, "Neither have you."

Larry didn't answer.

"Maxine says you're sweet on that new girl now," Hershell pressed. He knew it was not wise to aggravate Larry with unasked-for advice about such a touchy subject, but he felt so helpless, so put-out-to-pasture, that he clung to the notion that he could still counsel his young son. "She thinks she's all wrong for you."

Larry sighed dramatically, tossing both hands in the air. "Rene is an employee. A good one. That's all."

"That's not what Max says. Johnnie Sue's noticed the change in you, too."

Larry clenched both fists and gave the table a controlled but angry tap. "Look, Dad, I don't give a damn what either one of them thinks. Rene hasn't the slightest romantic interest in me, and even though she's a very…compelling woman, I'm not planning to pursue her.''

Hershell heard the words, heard the hesitation. He knew his boy. More gently he asked, ''What's wrong with her?''

Larry shook his head. ''She's divorced.''

It required no explanation, nor any further intervention on Hershell's part. She might as well have hoof-and-mouth disease. ''You didn't know when you hired her?'' he asked.

''She's an employee, Dad. What difference would that have made?''

They stared at each other for a moment, then Larry looked down again and said, ''She just mentioned it yesterday. I already knew that she…well, that she saw me only as a boss. It's no big deal. But when I found out that she was still carrying a torch for her ex-husband, it all felt so…well, so final.''

Hersh nodded. ''I'm sorry. But better now than some point down the road, I guess.''

''Sure,'' Larry agreed. ''I'm relieved, I guess. Now there's no question.''

A sudden thought occurred to Hershell, a thought that gave him both pain and hope. ''Are you going to keep her on? I mean, now that I've had my surgery and the eye doctor's given me the all clear?''

Larry stared at him, dead on. ''I said she was a good pharmacist. My personal feelings toward her have nothing to do with her employment.''

''But you said that after my eyes were fixed—''

''Your eyes are no longer the only issue, Dad!'' Larry burst out, his low tone not quite subdued enough to keep it from carrying to the next booth. But this early in the evening the Cornsilk was still half empty, and nobody but the sopping wet trucker was looking their way. He'd dried and combed his hair and taken off his soaked plaid shirt and was wearing only a white T-shirt with his jeans. Through the thin damp fabric his pecs and biceps bulged.

Catching Hershell's eye, he asked, "When she says 'Italian,' what does she mean? Pizza?"

"Finest lasagna this side of the Mississippi," answered Hersh. "And if you're crazy enough not to like it, you best keep it to yourself if you're interested in getting up with tomorrow's sun."

The trucker laughed, a deep hearty sound that shook off the gloom of the rainy evening. "I've got a lot of life in me yet," he commented brightly, then shrugged one shoulder toward the kitchen with a man-to-man wink. "And I reckon so does she."

Before Hershell could reply, Johnnie Sue sashayed out with a clean new apron—fuchsia—and a plate full of lasagna that electrified the whole room. It smelled so good that the trucker commented on it, earning a wry grin from Johnnie Sue as she plunked it down in front of him. Before Hersh could ask why he, who had arrived first, had not been served ahead of the trucker, she commanded, "Now you eat up. That'll get the chill out of your bones."

A moment later the front door bounced open to let in a Porter native and her outsider friend. Tall, voluptuous, crafty as a fox, Frannie Bixby was no stranger to the Duncans, or to anybody else in town. She was, after all, a hard woman to miss. But Hershell had more reason to notice her than the average man had. Her dad had left her his farm when he'd died after taking amethopterin for his psoriasis, and when Frannie moved back home, she'd started a class-action lawsuit against Duncan's Drugs. Fortunately the court had determined that the company who'd created the drug was at fault; Hershell and Larry had scrupulously listed all warnings and read them aloud to their patients. But the hard feelings lingered in Porter.

Hershell was in no mood to deal with Fran, but she spotted him at once and sauntered over with an infuriating grin. In her wake trailed a tall, dark man with thick wavy hair and deep blue eyes. Hersh couldn't recall his name, but he'd seen him once or twice before and knew that he was the lover Fran had brought back to Porter with her from Des Moines. A lot of the townsfolk—including Hershell—disapproved of the fact that they were living together out of marriage, but Hersh also wondered why they were still living together at all. Fran had started her career of man-stealing way back in high school—Johnnie Sue said she traded men the way other girls changed their underpants—and he found it hard to believe that she'd learned how to be faithful as she'd grown older. Even now—knowing that Larry hated her—she glided toward him with a saucy, inviting walk. Glancing at his son, Hersh watched Larry's lips tighten in disgust.

"Why, if it isn't my favorite defendant," Fran greeted Larry coyly. "I understand that you're about to have the pleasure of defending your shoddy little business again."

Larry glared at her but held his tongue. Calmly he said, "Good evening, Fran," then pointedly studied his Coke while he asked his dad, "So when is Orville Kensler going to start harvesting the corn out at our place? Will this late rain throw his schedule off?"

Hershell glanced at Larry, then at Fran. He swallowed hard, as though he were trying to speak, but no words came out of his mouth.

"You'll be happy to know that I talked to Joel Carmichael over in Washburn this afternoon," Fran trilled. "I shared with him everything I learned from our little lawsuit. I do believe he's almost ready to proceed on his own.''

Hershell suddenly felt light-headed. He'd thought it was over! Joel had said it was all a mistake! A strange, panicky feeling filled his throat, and he suddenly found it difficult to breathe, let alone focus on Frannie's words.

''In this case, of course, there's no question of trying to dump the blame on the pharmaceutical company. The blame for Wanda's death lies squarely with Duncan's Drugs.''

Hershell found himself gulping like a fish, fervently hoping that Larry would make Fran go away. But Larry was watching her with a deadly stare, immobile, almost paralyzed. While Hershell thrust his fingers inside his already unbuttoned collar, desperate to loosen the noose, help arrived from an unexpected quarter.

Fran's boyfriend laid a gentle hand on her shoulder. ''I'm hungry, honey,'' he said softly. ''Why don't we go sit down?''

''In a minute, Seth!'' She brushed him off and narrowed the distance between Hershell and herself. ''First I want to spell out the future to this blundering old bozo. He killed my father and he killed Wanda Carmichael. He even killed his own wife and—''

''That's enough!'' Larry burst out, rising to his feet with such force that the table pitched and his Coke tumbled to the floor in a spray of foam and broken glass. ''I respected your dad, Fran, and I'm sorry he's dead. Nobody in this town regrets what happened with amethopterin more than we do. But it's over and done and there's nothing any of us can do to change it! If Joel Carmichael has a problem with Duncan's Drugs, he can speak for himself.''

''Oh, he *will* speak for himself! He'll make sure that this old fossil is—''

"*I'm* the one who filled that damn prescription for Wanda!" Larry roared, grabbing Fran almost fiercely by the wrist. "So if you have any more ugly cracks to make, you can make them straight to me!"

Hershell began to gasp loudly. His head seemed to be circling freely above the rest of his body. He knew he should have intervened, protected his son, insisted that surely he, not Larry, had filled that prescription. He even had a vague recollection of doing so. But he'd filled so many prescriptions for Wanda over the years, so many prescriptions all jumbled up in his mind...

"Frannie, please," Seth begged, taking her hand as Larry released it. "I don't think this is the time or place—"

"But I do! I think—"

"*I think you better get out of here before I blow your head off!*" Johnnie Sue suddenly bellowed from the kitchen doorway. Legs apart, eyes black with rage, she was gripping her .30/30 with both hands and pointing it straight at Fran. "Hershell Duncan is the finest man ever to walk the face of the earth and I'll be *damned* if I'll let any fatmouth in this town stand in *my* place and talk to him that way!" Spittle spewed from her mouth on the last word. "So you turn your little tail around, Frannie Bixby, and hustle out that door because you are no longer welcome in the Cornsilk Cafe!"

Fran's eyes bulged, but she did not speak. For that matter, nobody in the restaurant so much as cleared his throat.

Larry, still standing, knifed Fran with his eyes. The trucker, clearly stymied by the sudden appearance of Johnnie Sue's rifle, couldn't keep his eyes off the scene, either.

It was Seth who finally spoke—not just to Larry or Hersh but also to Johnnie Sue. "We're sorry to have troubled you.'' With more vigor, he tugged on Fran's hand and led her away.

Her acquiescence surprised Hersh until he glanced at the kitchen doorway, and what he saw there knocked him flat. In all the years he'd known Johnnie Sue, he'd never seen such a vituperative look on her face. If he hadn't known that she loved him like blood kin, he would have been afraid of her, too.

Then he looked at Larry, but Larry looked away.

CHAPTER FIVE

JOHNNIE SUE WAS irritated when she first noticed that the trucker had gone before she'd written out his bill. Granted, she hadn't hustled with it, but he hadn't appeared to be in any particular hurry, what with his truck all broken down. And she'd figured that when he'd finished the lasagna, he might have wanted dessert. But shortly after the Duncans left, she'd found a ten-spot on the counter—more than enough to cover both the bill and the tip—but no well-muscled trucker grinning on the stool.

Truckers made up a good portion of her business—despite the fact that the freeway was six miles away—and she was always eager to encourage their trade. This fellow had a nice way about him—a friendly grin, a hearty laugh—and he would have fit in with her regulars. *Besides,* she decided as she busied herself with the evening crowd, *I'll need somebody to replace the Bixbys and the cowards once word of tonight's little set-to gets around town.*

Just thinking of Fran made her red-eyed with rage, especially because she still wasn't sure how much trouble that witch might raise. Poor Gert, bullied into sneaking back into Joel's house hadn't turned up quite enough to exonerate the Duncans. She'd found no trace of a warfarin bottle on Wanda's tiny bedside table, crowded with get-well cards, books and one bottle stuffed with five different-colored pills. Four of them matched the remnants of pill bottles in Wanda's bathroom cabinet, along with a dozen other odds and ends that dated back to 1962. But so far Johnnie Sue hadn't been able to identify the fifth—tiny round salmon-colored pills—that she suspected were warfarin.

She hadn't yet decided whether to take Maxine into her confidence or continue her research on the pills on her own. After all, Gert could probably find a sample of warfarin in somebody else's house. Already Johnnie Sue was trying to remember who'd had a blood clot in the past few years....

Gert, she knew, would be furious when she found out that Larry was the one who'd filled Wanda's prescription after all; her sleuthing had not been as vital as Johnnie Sue had first believed. Although she would cheerfully have taken on a Ninja warrior to protect either Duncan man, she knew that Larry could weather the ensuing storm if necessary. He was a young man of deep personal resources, and if he had to start life over in some new time and place, he'd find a way to do it. Just as she had.

Still, Johnnie Sue was determined to help him if she could, but she knew she'd have to go behind his back to develop her battle plan—starting with sending Gert back to search the Carmichaels' trash. Larry had always been such a straight-arrow—the kind who volunteered the information that he'd been going forty-seven in a forty-mile-an-hour zone when he was stopped by a state highway cop—and he'd rather face any storm head-on than take the risk of dirtying his own conscience. Unless—the idea nibbled at the back of her brain—he felt compelled to take action to protect somebody he loved as much as he loved his unhappy father.

Mentally she replayed the scene with Fran while she was cleaning up, hoping she'd injected the fear of God into the little harpy. She didn't really care if Fran ate at the Cornsilk or not, but she'd hoped to convince her that agitating grief-stricken Joel Carmichael just wasn't worth the trouble.

The problem still weighed on her mind when she heard a tap at the front door shortly after ten. Sometimes, especially on the weekends, she still had customers at this hour, but on Tuesday nights, even the theater was closed. Of course, Hershell often drifted in about this time during his evening meanderings, and since the rain had let up, she figured he'd be wandering back all het up about Fran. Or Larry might come by to sort out what had happened earlier. Even Gert might come whining in, in need of another pat on the head because she felt so guilty about her "break-in."

All in all, about the last person Johnnie Sue expected to see on the other side of the door was the trucker who'd come in sopping wet earlier. But he walked in the door—clad in a heavy denim jacket this time—looking like the cat that had swallowed the canary. Johnnie Sue felt a tiny jolt in her stomach that could have been pleasure or fear. In all the years she'd been running the Cornsilk, no man had ever tried to mess with her, but this one troubled her somehow. She was too alert around him, too prickly, too aware of his presence. And he looked…well, entirely too *happy* to be here.

"I'm closed," she growled. "Can't you read the sign?"

When he didn't even bother to glance at it, she was certain that he knew what it said. He also probably knew that she closed up pretty much when she felt like it, and she never closed the door on a friend.

But he wasn't a friend. He was a stranger. Worse yet, he was a stranger who made her itch.

Gotta be fear, she told herself. *I gave up itching for a man any other way a long time ago.*

"I came back for dessert," he said. "Can't get the engine part I'm missing till morning, so I've got all night to kill."

"This look like a hotel to you?" Johnnie Sue snarled, feeling the pearl-colored hair on the back of her neck stand straight up.

"I can sleep in the truck." His voice was calm, but there was no mistaking the sensual frosting in his tone. "I'm looking for more than a rented room."

She glared at him and tried to be insulting. "Then I reckon you'd be happy at Sara Mae's cathouse up the road. Take Main to the third stop sign and turn left on Elm. Second block on your right. Big pink place. Reasonable rates, the boys tell me."

To her surprise, he had no snappy comeback for that, nor did he turn to go. He just studied her quietly, like a fox getting ready to jump down a gopher hole.

"I've never felt the need to buy a lady friend," he claimed, his near-whisper somehow vibrating the whole room with the quiet aura of proud masculinity. "When I meet a special woman, I just tell her straight out that I'm in the mood for some company."

The words slithered cunningly over her heart and slid sensuously further down. Feeling strangely like a cornered wild beast, Johnnie Sue barked, "You think I'm running a lonely hearts club here?"

He studied her in the red-and-blue hues cast by the neon sign that blinked just outside the door...studied her until the masculine smell of him tugged at her senses...studied her until she had to look away.

"I think you've probably got a lonely heart," he dared to say.

"Bah!" She spat out the word, groping for anger to arm herself against his magnetic pull. "I don't even *have* a heart. It left my hometown with my husband thirty-four years ago.'' Johnnie Sue had no idea where the words had come from. Her story—short and sad—was hardly original, or clandestine, but it wasn't something that was common knowledge in town. Most of the locals just thought she'd come to town to visit Aggie Duncan, stayed on as a waitress, eventually taken over the Cornsilk, and grown as tough as any man. Surely, nobody would have expected a passing trucker to express interest in her as a *woman*.

Even now, as Johnnie Sue flinched under the sensual stare of this muscular stranger, she wondered what he saw in her. Rag-mop hair stuffed on top of her head, mustard-yellow T-shirt and jeans, ten extra pounds on her hips and thighs. *This man must be out of his mind,* she decided. Yet a whispery ghost of female pride danced in her head.

"You're strong as an ox, Johnnie Sue, and you fight for your own. I like that in a woman," he said with a virile, inviting grin. "But you're not sleeping with that old man. You've got another kind of love for him."

Johnnie Sue gave him her fiercest glare, the one that had felled all lesser men. "None of this has anything to do with you."

He took a step toward her. "I just want to spend some time with you."

"I told you Sara Mae runs—"

She stopped, stunned, when he reached out to touch her cheek. No man had touched her there since the last time her husband had hurriedly kissed her goodbye on his way to work, without bothering to mention that he would not be coming home again. She'd waited for hours, for weeks, for years, it seemed at times....

"Get your hands off of me," she commanded. At least, she tried to command it, but her order came out as a squeak.

He didn't move. "You wanted me the minute I came in the door, Johnnie Sue. And I wanted you. But that don't mean I gotta rush you. You just wanna talk tonight?"

Johnnie Sue felt dizzy. His callused fingers were slipping now, grazing her jawline, gliding across the lower part of her face.

"I want you to go," she croaked.

"Or you'll shoot me?" He gave her a grin that was half pleasure, half triumph. "You can't run a business here if you kill *everybody* off."

Johnnie Sue swallowed hard. She felt drunk. Crazy. Like somebody had slipped her an overdose of Hershell's sleeping pills.

"Why do you keep your hair so long?" he asked, his voice now a low hum. "That's a fine woman's head of hair. I bet it flows clear down to here." His fingers crawled down her neck, her shoulder, her bare arm. The heel of his hand warmed the side of her breast. "How long is it, Johnnie Sue?" His free hand reached around her waist, then slid down to lightly cup her hip. "When I pull out the pins, will it reach clear down to—"

Johnnie Sue reached up on the wall beside her and grabbed the nearest knife. She could tell by the feel of it that it was the one with the Roy Rogers handle—a lot more decorative than strong—but nonetheless she jabbed the point against his chest.

Startled, he jumped back, his eyes smoldering. "What the hell?"

"I told you to get out!" she repeated furiously. She was shaking with rage, but the rage, she knew, was directed at herself. This damn trucker had read her right from the moment their eyes had first met! She felt stupid, helpless, ashamed. Not since her divorce had she felt so vulnerable. If anyone in Porter ever found out what had happened in the past two minutes she'd be the laughingstock of the whole damn town! She peered toward the darkness but found nobody outside the door.

"You've seen me with a rifle, pal, so don't press me with a knife. If I—"

To her shock and unbearable chagrin, the big man closed his hand over hers, crushing her tough fingers, until she had to release the knife and let it clatter to the floor. Humiliation now mingled with rage and—though she'd damn well fight it—a tiny blip of fear.

"Don't be stupid, Johnnie Sue," he snapped, his sensual mouth only inches from her own. "If I were the kind of man you seem to think I am, that stunt could have gotten me good and riled, and you'd be lying naked on the floor."

He released her then, stooped and picked up the knife, while Johnnie Sue, trembling, stood perfectly still. By the tone in his voice she knew he wouldn't use it on her, but she had the feeling that he wasn't about to give it back.

For a long, tense moment he studied her face while Johnnie Sue prayed he wouldn't touch her again. She was still angry, but also—ludicrously—aroused. She had been certain that Bulldogger Johnnie could handle this man, but she seemed to have misplaced that Johnnie Sue. The woman who had let this stranger caress her breast was remembering that the only bed in the refurbished Cornsilk storeroom she called home was a twin that she'd never shared with anyone.

Slowly the trucker straightened and tucked the knife inside his wide leather belt. He stared at her—eyes grave and angry in the poor light—then shook his head.

"It could have been a real nice night for both of us," he whispered, his voice a low, dry hiss. "You're a damn fool, Johnnie Sue."

LARRY WAS SACKED out on the couch with a good book at ten o'clock when he heard the volley of shots. Normally a rifle shot meant nothing in Porter. Half the men in town owned rifles, and some of the women did, too. Most people kept one in the gun rack on the back of the family truck. They used them to show bravado, to go hunting or shoot skeet—none of which generally set their womenfolk to screaming.

The scream was high-pitched and terrified. And it continued even after the gunfire ceased.

Larry realized in an instant that the sound was coming from somewhere near Duncan's and the Cornsilk. He couldn't imagine Johnnie Sue screaming if her life depended on it, but a twist in his gut told him that the woman could have been Rene. She could still be closing up, or—now that the rain had stopped—she could be out jogging in that vicinity.

Alone at night because he'd given her late hours.

He was on his feet and running before the second scream, even more high-pitched and terror-laden than the first. He noticed instantly that he wasn't the only one to hear the blood-shrinking sound. He was running down the street with half a dozen other people.

By the time he'd sprinted the four blocks to Porter's "downtown," a siren was warbling and a black-and-white swerved ahead of him on the way to the scene. Cars and trucks were starting to spring up everywhere, making it hard to dart through the streets. A big rig, red with white stripes and some fancy name on the side, paused to let him pass. Two bikes jetted by, and he spotted Lotty's wheelchair rolling rapidly down the street.

The panic that had seized him when he'd first heard the rifle fire did not abate. Absolutely desperate to find Rene, he bolted after the police car, catching up just as Clayboy jumped out and tried to clear a path through the crowd that was gathering at Clancy's Gas.

"Who is it, Lotty?" Larry called over the hubbub. "Have you seen Rene?"

She shook her head, looking frustrated and confused as she wheeled toward him at top speed. "I counted four shots. One right after the other. I don't think the girl got hit because she never stopped screamin'."

It was a good point, one which Larry had not thought of in his panic. Whoever the woman was, she was probably only frightened, not hurt. She was still screaming, though the sound had lapsed into mild hysteria now.

As he spotted Orville Kensler's truck pulling over—with Maxine at the wheel—he crossed one more beloved female off of his list and plunged through the crowd. He felt as though he were in some sort of a terrible dream. *Nobody,* but *nobody* got shot on a Tuesday night in Porter! Least of all a woman!

He had nearly clawed his way through the crowd when he heard a voice cry out, "It's Frannie! Fran, are you all right?"

Larry froze where he was—sandwiched between a shaggy teenager on his left and a buffalo-sized farmer on his right—and took great gulps of air. It was Fran. Just Fran. Making a mountain out of a molehill, as usual.

By this time, Clayboy Billings was taking control. He carved his way through the crowd as fast as he could, looking for all the world as though he actually *cared* what happened to horrible Fran. "Get back, everybody!" he ordered the milling group. "Henry, call Elwood, will you? Frannie, are you all right?"

By this time, Fran's loud sobs could be heard a good twenty yards away, and Larry, who heartily disliked the girl, almost felt a moment's pity. If any woman in Porter deserved to get a good scare, it was Frannie Bixby, no doubt about it. What had she been doing alone in the field in back of Clancy's at this time of night, anyway? Up to her usual tricks, no doubt. Living with one man, carrying on with another—he wouldn't put it past her. Still, Fran did belong to Porter, and what happened to her could have happened to anyone.

It was a notion that gave him little comfort as he realized, after that first great moment of relief, that whoever had fired the shots might still be wandering around the vicinity and Rene was still nowhere in sight. He'd been dead serious when he'd promised her that afternoon that he would be her friend. And as that friend, he was determined to find out exactly where she was tonight.

It occurred to him that there was no reason why Lotty would have checked her apartment on her way over here; she might be safe and sound inside. He decided to walk back in that direction to put his mind at rest.

That's when he saw her, hovering next to the wheelchair, looking absolutely shell-shocked. She was wearing a pink sweatsuit and breathing hard; obviously she *had* been out running. Her dark hair was loose, flowing haphazardly over her shoulders. Her green eyes glistened, perhaps with tears. She was pale and visibly trembling.

It was the first time Larry had ever seen Rene look vulnerable and out-of-control. It touched something deep within him. She was so alone in this town. She pressed against Lotty's wheelchair as though the old woman were her only friend. But Lotty was eagerly chewing over the details of the attack with Maxine and Johnnie Sue, who'd just joined the others. Not one of them was paying any attention to Rene.

As he hurried toward her, he wondered why she looked so much more frightened than the other women. Was it because she'd been out jogging alone? Or was it because she'd come to Porter for safety after her friend Finch had been so brutally beaten?

By now she looked pearl-gray, almost faint, even though her gaze was no longer fixed on Lotty. She was staring blankly at the street, at a space between two trucks, where a green Volkswagen Rabbit now screeched to a stop and double-parked. A tall and very handsome young man leaped out and scrambled toward the crowd, calling, "Frannie! Franieeeee!" as though his heart would break.

It was the fellow who'd trailed Fran into the restaurant— Stu, Seth, Steve, something like that—and Larry guessed that somebody had had the sense to call him. He looked terrified, yet almost homicidal with fury, as he pawed apart the mob of bystanders and seized Fran by the shoulders. She was still sobbing, but her terror seemed to fade as she clutched him.

In a strange and ghostly counterpoint, it was right about then that Larry reached Rene and gently put his arms around her. By this time she was crying, too, and she melted against his chest as naturally as breathing. Even though he knew that she gripped him only as a shield against her fear, her instinctive trust touched him deeply. Fiercely he vowed to protect her from whatever danger lurked in the Porter night.

"It's okay, sweetheart," he crooned before he could stop himself. His lips brushed Rene's lush hair.

Rene raised her head, as though to draw comfort from his loving eyes, but she did not look directly at him. Her gaze was focused just beyond his shoulder, where Fran was flinging herself melodramatically into her boyfriend's arms.

"I won't let anybody hurt you," Larry vowed in an intimate whisper.

Rene shuddered, as though the reality of danger still lingered. Then she pressed her face against his chest and began to sob.

in Rene exploded. As though she'd repeat the offer, Janice withdrew. "With the press of her fingers on his chest and pushing to stop..."

CHAPTER SIX

IT WAS NOT UNTIL that familiar green car chugged off, leaving the crowd still gawking, that Rene realized she was cradled in Larry's arms.

It came to her as a shock that anyone was near her, because she'd felt so utterly alone. But quite suddenly she was aware of a warm male body pressed against hers, soothing hands stroking her head and shoulders, quiet words promising comfort, offering to take her home.

Rene's embarrassment staggered her. How long had she stood here blubbering incoherently in her employer's arms? What had she said to him? What had she done?

"I'm sorry," she murmured against his chest. "I'm not...please don't think I'm usually like this."

When Larry patted her head, she realized that the gesture was familiar because he'd done it so many times since she'd first heard the shots. Even the feel of his arms around her, strong and remarkably comforting, felt almost...right.

"Sometimes things just catch up with you when you aren't looking," Larry said gently, as though he knew that her fear of the gunshots had triggered a far deeper hurt. "I live just a few blocks from here, Rene. Why don't we go over there and talk for a while?"

She knew that he was offering to listen to her heartaches and hold her while she cried. She wanted to tell him that it wasn't necessary, that she was fine, but she still felt wobbly. Besides, she couldn't think of anything she'd rather do than spend a few quiet moments with Larry. Never in her life had she so badly needed the kindness of a friend.

Larry slung a brotherly arm around Rene's shoulders as he steered her toward the street, calling good-night to Maxine and Lotty. Then he focused on Rene as they walked, chatting about the trees and houses and neighbors that they passed. Vaguely she recognized what he was doing—giving her the same sort of comfort he'd given that little boy with the bird—but she wanted his support too much to deny her need of it right now.

As they strolled through the well-kept older neighborhood, he told her all about Fran Bixby, who used to steal boyfriends, tease her friends and cleverly get her classmates in trouble. His voice was a steady hum, and the details all ran together. Rene knew they didn't matter; Fran didn't matter anymore.

Suddenly, neither did Seth.

Fran had won. Rene had lost her husband to her rival, and she was never, ever going to get him back. She would probably never see him again. She had known it in her head for at least two years, but until tonight, she had not *really* known it in her heart. She'd thought of Fran as a toy to Seth, a sexual playmate he would eventually tire of. She had not ever realized that he truly loved her as a woman. Seth's world had once revolved around Rene. Now Fran was the center of his life.

Rene grappled with a host of conflicting feelings as she walked silently through the cheerful neighborhood, her body close to Larry's. It wasn't until they reached the small blue house on the next block that she realized it wasn't just shock that made her dizzy. It was, incredibly, *relief.*

It's over, she realized deep in her heart. *I never could have brazened this out, never could have stood up to a hussy like that to reclaim my husband. And even if I had, what good would it have done? Could I ever really have forgiven him? Taken him back? Pretended that he hadn't done what he'd done?*

The sense of relief grew greater, sweeping over her like a hot prairie wind, as she stole a glance at Larry's dear face. The deceit that had choked her for weeks now lifted like a veil, and the anguished years of futile hope—of asking why, why, *why?* over and over again—suddenly vanished.

As Larry steered her toward his white-picket fence, she dimly realized that he was leading her into the house, settling her against his chest on the couch. He probably thought she was going to cry some more, but she had no more tears for Seth. Still, it felt good to snuggle into his embrace as she talked out the last of the old hurts, clearing out the mess she'd been storing for years in her heart. She told him about her childhood, her long years in school, her wonderful first years with Seth; they'd done everything together—gone to the grocery, walked the dog, cut each other's hair. She told him how she'd found Seth with Fran and walked out at once but had never quite given him up. She told him everything except for her husband's name and the name of the woman he'd left her for. And she did not mention that it was because of her husband that she'd ended up in Porter.

Tonight she desperately needed Larry's comfort, and she was not about to tell him the one thing that would surely push him away. Besides, now that it was over—now that she was no longer going to waste her life waiting for Seth—she didn't have to leave Porter, didn't have to leave Duncan's Drugs. She could stay forever if she wanted to. The only question now was—did she still want to stay?

It was not until Rene heard the cuckoo clock bang away

eleven times that she grew quiet, spent, as she realized that she lay sprawled across Larry in a thoroughly unprofessional pose. She wasn't in Larry's house as his employee, and she seriously doubted that he'd give quite the same brand of comfort to any other female friend. Nor would she have responded the same to one of her platonic male friends. Greg Finch had been a good friend ever since she'd started graduate school, and though he often hugged her hello or goodbye, she would not have spent an hour curled up in his arms.

As Rene realized that the last dregs of her life with Seth had finally been exorcised from her system, a comfortable kind of silence stole over the house, as did a change in the nature of her peaceful feelings. While Larry's warm hands continued to caress her temple, Rene's contentment grew, took root, blossomed into something more compelling than peace. It took her awhile to put a name to the feeling, but once she recognized it for what it was, there was no turning back.

Somewhere within her, Larry Duncan had planted tiny seedlings of desire.

At first she thought she was imagining her physical need for him; after all, she'd been alone so long! But then as the warmth spread throughout her body—as her nipples began to tighten and her thighs began to tense—Rene realized that she'd been fighting these very feelings almost since the day she and Larry had first met. Always Seth had blocked the process, dampened her quietly growing admiration for Larry and her building romantic interest. But her affection for Larry had bloomed in spite of Seth, pressing at the edges of her consciousness, tugging at the fringes of her desire. And now—now that Seth had been zapped from her heart in a strike of lightning—she could see Larry clearly. In fact, as she opened her eyes and slowly sat up to study the man who had so gently touched her heart, she could see nothing in the world but Larry's loving face.

As their eyes met, Larry stopped stroking her temple. Wariness darkened his gentle expression. Rene struggled for words to tell him—tell him what?—as she marveled at the multitude of new feelings crashing through her.

Ever so slowly, Larry stiffened. He did not release her, but he did pull back.

He knows, she realized with a jolt. *He knows that suddenly everything has changed.*

Rene wanted to tug him back beside her, wanted to snuggle back on his lap and touch his bristly mustache. But she didn't know where that step might lead her... didn't know just where Larry might want to go.

Before words came to her, Rene heard a car drive up out front, heard a sharp rap on the door. Larry touched her face once more, as if to apologize for the interruption, then rose and disappeared through the front hall.

"'Evenin', Lare," she heard a man's firm voice declare a moment later. "Sorry to get you up so late. Can I come in for a sec?"

There was a pause before Larry answered, "Uh, actually I have company, Elwood. Is it something quick or can it wait?"

Another pause. "How long've you had company tonight, Larry? Since you left the Cornsilk or just a little while?"

"What difference does it make?" Larry asked.

It seemed like a reasonable question to Rene. But the first question, asked by Elwood—the Porter sheriff, if memory served—didn't make sense at all. It sounded like something Perry Mason might hurl at a recalcitrant suspect.

"Larry, I've got to ask everybody who's crossed swords

with Fran Bixby lately. Somebody tried to shoot her tonight.''

''I know that. I just got back from Clancy's. I heard somebody say they heard rifle shots, but that doesn't mean much; there's a rifle on the gun rack of half the trucks in this town. But if you—'' Then Larry stopped, disbelief sucking the warmth out of his heretofore genial tone. ''Elwood? Are you serious? Are you…hell, are you *questioning* me?''

''Lare, I've got to do my job. I know you'd never hurt a fly, but—''

''Good God, Elwood! I don't believe this!''

''Larry, please! I'm the sheriff! I'm paid to uphold the law! Now, if it was Max or Lotty or Johnnie Sue who'd almost gotten shot tonight, wouldn't you want me to be questioning likely suspects right now?'' After a moment's pause, he added, ''After the ruckus at the Cornsilk tonight, I—''

''God damn it, Elwood! You know Johnnie Sue is always threatening folks! It doesn't mean a thing,'' Larry insisted. ''Besides, she's a deadeye shot. If she'd taken it in her head to shoot Fran Bixby, Frannie would be dead.''

''Unless she just meant to scare her, which I figure would be enough for Johnnie Sue.''

''Elwood, for God's sake! Have you lost your mind?''

''Larry, can I come in, please? Can we sit down and talk this over rationally? I need to talk to your… company…also.''

Again Larry paused. Rene sat up and tried to run her fingers through her hair. Suddenly she felt embarrassed, as though Elwood had caught them…doing what? What, in fact did Rene even *want* to do? Had she imagined that strange new pulse of desire she'd felt for Larry as she'd lain on his lap? Had she imagined that suddenly their roles had reversed, that now *she* was the one reaching out for him and *he* was the one turning away?

"Is that really necessary, Elwood?" Larry asked.

"I'm afraid it is. But you can count on me to be... discreet Larry. It's my job."

"Oh, hell, Elwood, it's nothing like that! It's just that Rene is pretty shook up about what happened tonight, and she's in no condition to be grilled by a storm trooper."

Elwood didn't answer, but a moment later he appeared before Rene in the living room. He took off his cap, nodded in her direction, mercifully made no comment about her disheveled appearance even though his eyes told her that he'd quickly assessed the situation and drawn his own conclusions.

"Sorry to trouble you, Miss..."

"Hamilton. Rene Hamilton," she said quietly, certain that he already knew who she was.

He nodded again. "Glad to meet you, Miss Hamilton." He sat down opposite Rene even though Larry had not invited him to do so. Larry stood by the door, his eyes on Rene.

"We had a shooting in town tonight, Miss Hamilton. The intended victim was Miss Fran Bixby. I don't imagine you know her, but she's about your age and I'm sure you realize that what happened to her could have happened to anyone. So it's really for your own protection that I determine who perpetrated this crime so he or she can be stopped."

"Elwood, you don't have to scare Rene! She'll tell you the truth! Besides, what happened to Fran couldn't have happened to Rene or any other decent woman in this town! Fran's the only one that everybody hates."

Elwood silenced Larry with a terribly official glance. Then he turned back to Rene.

"Miss Hamilton, how long have you been with Larry this evening?"

Which Larry? she longed to ask. *Larry my boss or Larry my friend? Or this new Larry-lover I'm suddenly reaching toward?*

But clearly the sheriff didn't care about her befuddled feelings. He was trying to solve a crime. Instinctively Rene glanced at Larry, wondering for the first time if he needed some sort of alibi. And then, when he said, "Just tell Elwood the truth," Rene suddenly realized that maybe *she* needed an alibi, too.

It was a shock to Rene, a shock that made it difficult for her to focus on Elwood's surface questions or his underlying ones. Neither Larry nor the sheriff knew that she'd ever met Fran Bixby, let alone that she had a first-class motive for wanting to see her rival dead or injured. Rene had come to town to get Fran out of the way—not to kill her certainly, though hadn't she mumbled something like that to more than one friend or co-worker in Des Moines after she'd first found Seth with Fran? If the sheriff delved into Rene's background, or even into Seth's, might he find out enough to put two and two together and come up with what seemed like a suspicious four? *Thank God Fran wasn't murdered,* Rene breathed to herself. *If I get into any trouble, at least it can't be too bad.*

Doing her best to look serene and mildly irritated instead of shaken, she announced, "I've been here since about half an hour after the shooting, Sheriff. Larry thought I was too upset to go home alone. I was just about to leave when you got here."

"Thank you, Miss Hamilton," he said, looking a bit surprised that she hadn't lied and said she'd been with Larry for hours. Then he turned to Larry and asked, "Can you recall where you were between the time you left the Cornsilk and the time you ran into Miss Hamilton?''

"I was here, *Sheriff* Hazlett," he responded sarcastically. "I was reading a terrific book by Tony Hillerman—" he gestured toward the open, facedown copy of *Coyote Waits* on the coffee table "—when I heard gunshots and a woman's screams. I took off at once."

"How did you know where to go?"

"I followed the crowd. Good God, Elwood, there must have been thirty people following the sound of those gunshots. And Frannie kept screaming to wake the dead. I could even hear her over the sound of that semi."

"Semi?" repeated Elwood.

"Yes, there was a semi pulling out of Clancy's just before Fran's boyfriend showed up." He glanced at Rene. "Did you notice it?"

Rene wanted to back him up, but he'd told her to tell the truth. Besides, she was already in a vulnerable position. "Maybe, Larry," she conceded. "I think I heard a big truck or two, but my memory is pretty fuzzy. To tell you the truth, about the time you got there, I just sort of fell apart."

And that's okay, Larry's eyes tried to warm her, neutralizing the sting of Elwood's questions. *I'm glad I was there for you.*

He's always there for me, Rene suddenly realized. Of course, this afternoon he'd promised to be her friend in the "purest sense of the word," and tonight the comfort he'd offered had surely been platonic. But wasn't that because he'd thought that Rene had only wanted platonic friendship from him?

What do I want from Larry? she asked herself now. *An hour ago I wanted Seth, but now I can't remember why. All I can remember is the way I felt with Larry's arms around me, his fingers rubbing my temple, his lips brushing my hair....*

Vaguely she realized that Elwood was interrogating her again. "Frightening as this experience appears to have been to you, Miss Hamilton, why did you join the crowd at Clancy's?" he queried snidely. "Or were you...already in the vicinity?"

"Elwood, are you accusing *her* now? My God, if this is how you drum up suspects, I—"

"Larry, that's *enough!*"

It was an order, a gun-and-badge order, and his old pal's command clearly rocked Larry back on his heels. Still, he looked hurt more than frightened. And Rene knew Larry well enough to know that by this time, if he'd harbored even a shade of guilt, he would have been sweating with self-recrimination. Rene, who had done nothing to Fran but wish her ill, was nearly soaked.

"Please answer my question, Miss Hamilton."

Again Rene looked at Larry, who nodded encouragingly from his post by the door. His silent support filled Rene with hope, underlined her deepest faith in Larry's true affection for her. It also reminded her that Larry would unquestionably vouch for her veracity and believe anything she said. In front of Elwood, she didn't dare reveal her connection to Fran Bixby, but sooner or later, she would have to find a way to confess her subterfuge to Larry.

"I was out jogging," she said simply. "I normally go in the morning, but I had to go to work early today so I didn't get the chance till I closed up at nine. I was over on Elm, in front of that garish pink house—" Elwood nodded "—when I heard the gunshots. I stopped because I was frightened. Then I heard a woman scream, and I sort of...well, drew back against that big tree."

She was embarrassed to admit her cowardice, but neither

Larry nor Elwood said a word. Suddenly she wished that Larry would come sit beside her and hold her in his arms again. His comfort had been so natural, so sweet, so unassuming. Like Larry himself. Larry who might well be in trouble, but whose first thought this evening had been Rene's peace of mind, Rene's protection, Rene's welfare.

Oh, Larry, you are such a sweet man, her heart's voice whispered. *How ruthlessly I've trampled your feelings! How brutally I've pummeled you with my ludicrous love for Seth.*

Now she looked at him, really looked at him, while his gentle gaze sought only to build her up. For a moment she just let his affection seep into her pores, clearing out the last dregs of Seth's poison. And as it happened, she felt her evening's grief metamorphose into something new and fresh and beautiful.

Quite suddenly, Rene couldn't get enough of Larry's eyes, his tenderness, his strength. She knew that his name had been echoing in the dark corners of her soul ever since they'd first met, and her long night of deafness had finally passed.

Surprise streaked Larry's face as Rene's eyes revealed her imminent surrender. Her looked confused and a little frightened...not altogether pleased. But he could not turn away from her, could not shake his head to tell her no.

Suddenly it was more than a quiet, warm moment. More than a tentative question or probe. It was a straightforward confession in Rene's soul that vibrated her new and irrevocable truth to Larry: *I am ready to give you my heart.*

She watched him reel from the impact, watched his jaw go slack. She watched him wrestle with his own set of feelings as he tried to tell her no. Then she saw him jam his hands in his pockets, as though he needed cuffs to keep them from caressing her face.

And then there was nothing between them but Elwood. They could not kiss, could not embrace, because the sheriff still crowded the living room. But the sensual ache that sprang from deep within Rene was mirrored on Larry's virile face, and the newborn hunger wrestled between them as potently as if she'd wrapped her arms around his neck and he'd claimed her mouth. She rocked with a crazy, exhilarating need of him, one she would have flatly denied an hour ago. And though she could see that Larry was stunned by the force of his own feelings, his tense dark eyes could not conceal the simple truth: he adored her, and as soon as Elwood left, she knew he would tell her so.

Their eyes talked for so long that Elwood finally prompted, "And then?"

Reluctantly Rene turned back to the sheriff, tried to make some space for him in her mind. It was not an easy task.

Still tingling with her new discovery, she continued, "And then people started running by. And driving. When I saw Larry, I knew I'd be safe. I took after him as fast as I could."

Fresh surprise colored Larry's cheeks, but he made no comment as Elwood said, "So you actually joined him before he reached the scene of the crime?"

She shook her head. "No, I couldn't catch up. He was going too fast. I called after him, but there was so much noise that he didn't hear me. He disappeared in the crowd and didn't see me for about…oh, I don't know…maybe five more minutes? By then I'd found Lotty Barrington— my landlady—and I was sticking close to her."

Elwood couldn't stifle a smirk. "You thought Lotty could protect you from a gun-toting marksman?"

"I wasn't looking for protection by that time. Your deputy was already there. I just wanted—" she swallowed hard at her already-fading memory of Seth coddling Fran "—to be with a friend."

And you got your wish, Larry's warm brown eyes reminded her. Then they seemed to draw her close, weaving the strands of her life into his, and Elwood's presence didn't seem to matter anymore.

Larry didn't even glance at the sheriff when Elwood asked, "And why were you in such a hurry to reach Clancy's, Larry? Did you have some…premonition of doom?"

"I was in a hurry because I suspected that Rene might be out jogging after dark tonight," he admitted quietly, making no effort to hide the depth of his concern for her.

There was a possessive "she's my woman" tone in his voice that Rene had never heard before. It filled up her heart with summer air and dawn's first light. It kindled her quietly mounting desire for him and suffused her with fresh longing for his touch.

"When I first heard a woman scream," Larry openly confessed, his gaze still locked with hers, "all I could think of was Rene."

Then, without fanfare, he crossed the braided rag rug and joined Rene on the couch. She could no longer see his face, no longer speak silently to his beautiful, loving eyes. But she didn't feel a moment's lapse in his support because the moment she felt Larry's knee brush hers, he slipped one protective arm around her shoulder and drew her close.

He felt warm and loving and so virile that even his most guarded public touch set Rene on fire. She couldn't tell him how she felt with words, but not even Elwood's dark presence could keep her from gripping Larry's hand.

CHAPTER SEVEN

HERSHELL WAS STARING at the TV—some nameless criminal had just shot some nameless victim in some nameless town for some nameless reason—when he heard the knock on the front door. It was rare that anybody dropped by anymore, especially at this time of night. Larry, most likely, he figured.

"Come in!" he called, not bothering to get up.

The unlocked door swung open, off to his left where he could see it if he craned his neck. But he didn't bother to do so until he heard an unexpected voice announce, "Hersh, it's Clay Billings. Can I come in?"

He craned his neck. "Clayboy? What the hell are you doing out here at this time of night?" Suddenly he bolted upright, trembling. "Is it Paulie? Have you heard something about Paul?"

He regretted the words as soon as they left his mouth, because the chunky deputy's response was an embarrassed, sympathetic smile. The last thing Hersh wanted from Clayboy or any other young whippersnapper was *pity*. It was the last thing he wanted from his sole surviving son.

Clay shook his head. "No, Hershell, I'm sorry," he answered gently. "I'm here about Fran."

"Fran?" He stifled a savage expletive. "I've spent the whole night trying to get my mind off that horrid girl and I *don't* want to talk about her!" He sat down emphatically, then remembered his manners. Aggie, he knew, would not have approved of such a greeting. "But pull up a chair, Clayboy. Take a load off. You want something to drink?"

Clay shook his head, but he did sit down, albeit gingerly, on the piano bench across from the recliner chair where Hershell spent most of his lonely hours at home. Strangely he asked Hershell where he'd spent the evening in a tone that gave Hersh the impression that he already knew.

Before he could answer, they were interrupted by a call from Johnnie Sue.

"Don't say a word if Clayboy's there," she ordered brusquely. "He just left here, and he said Elwood was over at Larry's. Somebody tried to kill Fran tonight, and they're collecting alibis for the shooting. You've got to have one, Hershell, so don't argue with me. I told Clayboy you were here all evening."

He stood there, phone to his ear, trying to make sense of Johnnie Sue's words. Except for the first moment he'd told her that Aggie was dead, he'd never heard her sound so grave. She wasn't joshing him. The details of the attempt on Fran's life made it seem all too real.

Johnnie Sue's explicit orders involved an alibi that placed them together from the time Fran left the Cornsilk until long after her screaming started.

"But Johnnie Sue," he protested. "You know that I—"

"Hersh, I already told Clayboy you were here. If you say anything different, you'll make it sound like I lied."

Well, damn it, Johnnie Sue, you did lie! he wanted to protest. But he was not in the habit of questioning Johnnie Sue's judgment, and besides, he was starting to get the picture now. Fran had hollered unspeakable things at him in front of a dozen witnesses; Larry had stood up to her; Johnnie Sue had threatened to kill her; and a few hours later somebody had taken a few shots. All three of them could be in trouble up to their eyeballs if they'd lived in some town where they hadn't known the head cop since he'd drawn his first breath.

By the strange, stern look on Clayboy's face, Hersh had a hunch that they all might be in Dutch anyway.

LARRY STARTED the next morning jumpy as a long-tailed cat in a room full of rocking chairs. In the past few years he'd learned to cope with his mother's death and Sandra's defection; he'd recovered from the loss of her kids. He'd managed to face the families of the friends who'd died from amethopterin when he saw them on the street, and he'd conquered his desire for a woman who had not expressed the slightest shred of romantic interest in him. But yesterday, everything had changed.

Fate, it seemed, had conspired against Larry Duncan. To honor his father, he'd had to break his obligation to the truth. To give comfort to a friend in trouble, he'd had to break down the wall he'd built to protect himself from caring too much for Rene. And when the story of Fran's near-shooting was linked to last night's Cornsilk fiasco, all the heinous doubts about the integrity of Duncan's Drugs raised during the first lawsuit would surface again.

Larry didn't have an alibi for Fran's shooting, nor did he have a clue as to who else might have been involved. The thought had occurred to him that the guy driving that big rig might have had something to do with it; according to Elwood, Henry Clancy had suggested the same thing. The trucker, said Henry, was a mean son-of-a-bitch who'd gotten hot under the collar when he'd learned that Henry couldn't get the truck running right away. In fact, the reason Henry had come back to his station so late was because he wanted to get the guy rolling before business opened the next morning. But if Henry couldn't fix the semi, why had it taken off, anyway? And even if Henry had had a good reason to be working so late, what had Fran Bixby been doing in the field next to his station?

Larry had no answers to his questions about the shooting, let alone for the host of others that plagued him. Questions like, *Would Rene still want him this morning? Was he really foolish enough to get involved with a recent divorcée? Could he ever forget that she'd reached out to him just twenty-four hours after confessing that her ex-husband still had his talons in her heart?*

Rene arrived about noon. Her long black hair—caught at the nape in a richly ribboned barrette—brushed ever so gently across her back, making Larry long to do the same. She greeted Maxine with a rapturous smile; Maxine grumped and glared. In fact, it was the coldest greeting Maxine had delivered since Larry had told her to shape up with Rene, and her blatant chilliness surprised him.

So did his own cowardice. He greeted Rene quickly, without meeting her eyes, and ducked out the back door for his lunch break the instant a customer asked her a question.

But he'd barely taken a deep breath of relief when Rene, pushing open the store's back door behind him, called out, "Larry? Got a minute?"

He stopped, turned around, tried not to face her head on. "Can it wait till I eat?"

She didn't answer him at once. In the back lot, there were people coming and going, all at a distance, all minding their own business and oblivious to Rene. No helping hand there. But Larry needed time to think, time to steel himself to those pleading green eyes…time to summon the courage to tell her it had been a mistake for either of them to pretend they could find happiness together. "I'm hungry, Rene," he stalled.

For several moments she stared at him in total silence,

but he could hear her pain as fully as if she'd sobbed out loud. Finally she said, "If you're just rushed and hungry, it can wait all afternoon. But if there's some other reason why you haven't looked me in the eye since I came in today, then I don't think it'll wait another minute."

That's all she said, but she'd said it all. Larry glanced down at his hands, found his fists clenched, untangled his fingers and took a few steps closer to Rene. Slowly, painfully, he managed to look at her. "I thought you might be a little embarrassed at the way you fell apart last night, Rene. I just thought it'd be easier for you if I didn't make a big thing about it."

Rene licked her lips. Then she did something he'd never seen her do before. She tugged a lock of long black hair between two nervous fingers and started to weave it into a knot. "Are you going to tell me that's all that happened last night? I fell apart and you tried to comfort me while I cried?"

He glanced away. He couldn't face her squarely while he remembered those unspoken moments of eye-to-eye surrender when Elwood might just as well have not been there. It didn't matter that Elwood had volunteered to take Rene home in his cruiser and see her safely inside; it didn't matter that Larry, knowing he was falling into a deep and bottomless pit, had welcomed the night's reprieve to try to get a grip on his common sense before he headed blindfolded into disaster. It didn't matter that neither of them had said anything or done anything last night to change their lives.

Without a word of spoken promise or so much as a sizzling kiss, they had *joined*. They had bonded. They had crossed the friend-to-lover line.

Still, he tried to roll back the clock. "Rene, that's all that should have happened. That's all I had in mind. I can't take it any further." He did face her then, as honestly as he knew how. "I wish I could, but I can't. I'm sorry that I let you believe it could be otherwise."

Her fingers stopped twisting her hair. Her eyes pinioned him. "Why?" she asked bluntly. "How did it all change overnight?"

Larry shook his head, bleakly took a step closer. He knew he owed her the truth. "Two years ago Sandra stumbled into town with a bleeding lip, a busted jaw and a broken heart...all courtesy of her ex-husband," he told her simply. "I nursed her back to health. I married her." And then, because he knew there was no other way to make Rene understand, he confessed, "I gave her my soul."

Rene studied him intently, but she did not speak.

"A year later she went back to him. She took my kids. They were his by blood and hers by law, but they were *mine*, Rene, after the year we spent together. They thought so, too."

He saw his own pain reflected in her eyes, and he realized, in a strange and distant fashion, that despite her own pain, she was hurting because *he* had been hurt. Sandra, he knew, had never felt his pain at all.

"I don't know if I can ever risk falling in love again, Rene," he confessed in a low, hoarse tone, wishing she weren't standing so beguilingly close. "Frankly, I'm just not ready yet. And even if I were—" he shook his head as he took hold of the unchanging reality "—I'd never be able to trust a woman who'd already given her heart to somebody else. I'd never know for sure when he might come back to claim it again."

She got it then. He could see it in her eyes, in the tight set of her ever-so-kissable mouth. He watched her fingers tighten and tug on her hair, watched the color drain from her face.

"He...won't...come...back," she promised him. Her eyes met his as she waited for her solemn vow to sink in. "There's no doubt in my mind."

He fought the temptation to believe her. He'd learned from his mistakes, and this time he would not be taken in. "Sandra said the same thing," he crisply told Rene.

She ignored the comparison and plowed right ahead. "Yesterday, if he'd come for me, I might have gone," she confessed. "But not today. And *not* just because of you. Something happened last night, happened inside of me. I don't belong to him anymore. That's the reason I'm free to belong to *you.*"

Larry felt dizzy as he listened, and he tried to blame it on the sun, which was rising fiercely overhead. He started to sweat. "Rene, you don't know how much I wish I could believe you. But I've heard this speech before. *Believed* this speech before. Planned a life full of dreams and hopes and *lies* around this speech and—"

"What's my name?" Rene suddenly barked at him, abandoning both her knotted hair and her death grip on the half-open door. "Look at me and tell me who you see!"

"That's not the point, Rene. It's—"

"What is my name?" she demanded in a mighty voice. Larry couldn't answer. He couldn't speak. He stood there, feeling the weight of her anguish, feeling the weight of his own.

"They're gone now, Larry. Both of them," she reminded him tersely. "Now there's only you and me."

He longed to touch her, to caress her pain-lined face. But he knew it could only get worse after this. After all, how far had it gone? He'd never even kissed her. Surely they could get past this, ignore it, continue to work side by side! Jamming his hands in his pockets in self-defense he said softly, "No, Rene, that's where you're wrong. There's four of us. There always will be."

Fiercely she shook her head, the long black ponytail flying in its own rage. "No! I've beaten higher odds, Larry Duncan. I escaped a hellish childhood home. I dragged myself through nine years of school! I kept from going belly-up when my husband betrayed me, and I can damn well kill off a couple of shadow-ghosts if they get between you and me!"

Larry closed his eyes and turned away, praying that she would not start to cry. He ached to touch her, to tell her what she wanted to hear. But he knew he'd never be able to forget the way she'd wept for the other man last night, and she'd never understand that he'd resented every tear.

He faced her then and stood up straight. He met her eye to eye.

"Rene, I've been as straight with you as I can be. I desperately wish that we could be together, but it's just not going to happen. There will never be anything but friendship between you and me."

She stared back at him, eyes dry and angry, for a full thirty seconds until he blinked. Then she said softly, "Larry—" his name sounded so intimate on her loving tongue "—what do you really want?"

He *wanted* to touch her face, to kiss her, to take her in his arms. He *wanted* to tell her to forget what Sandra had done to *him* and what her husband had done to *her*. He *wanted* to blindly promise that together they could forget the past, heal their wounds, ride off into the sunset together. But he knew that to do those things would be foolish, if not absurd, and he also knew that if he did any one of them, the rest would surely follow.

"Rene," he said, trembling, "I honestly don't think—"

And then he stopped as her eyes suddenly brimmed with tears.

Briskly she dropped her glance and turned away, plunging toward the safety of the drugstore.

Don't cry, Rene, his heart begged her. *I can't bear it when you weep.*

Before she'd reached the doorknob, he'd taken three quick steps and laid a hand on her bare arm. Her woman's tender flesh trembled at his touch, but she did not turn around until he tugged her ever so slowly in his direction, aching to take her in his arms.

Rene's tears were flowing freely now, and Larry could not dry them until he touched her face.

IT WAS JUST about nine when Johnnie Sue spotted that outsider, the one who was living with Frannie Bixby, in the corner booth by the door. He wasn't bad-looking, as city boys go—nice hair, nice eyes, nice clothes. But Johnnie Sue had made a career of reading men's intentions—it was no accident she kept her rifle in the back—and she knew how to read trouble when it bit her on the kneecap.

For one thing, he was nervous. He ordered coffee, but he only gave it one perfunctory sip, then used the mug as a base on which to drum his fingers. For another, he looked as though he were waiting for someone. *But nobody who lives with a woman meets her at a restaurant this late at night*, Johnnie Sue concluded, *especially a woman I've threatened to shoot on sight.*

Johnnie Sue served a family from nearby Washburn, plopped down four scoops of vanilla on four pieces of apple pie for some kids on their way home from the show, then thrust a menu at a trucker who'd just stumbled in off the highway, eyes puffy with fatigue.

He looked nothing at all like the other one, the one

who'd stolen her knife and her pride. This one was tall and skinny instead of short and strong. No smile lurked beneath lips that were much thinner than those others; no hint of mischief lurked in these tired eyes.

He didn't take the menu. Instead he asked, "Are you Johnnie Sue?"

She nodded, wondering which of her regular drive-by customers had been kind enough to recommend the Cornsilk to a pal. Forcing herself to be more friendly—not an easy task, considering her mood—she said, "Sure am. Who sent you?"

"Fella named Big Shorty," he reported blandly, pulling a knife from his belt. It was her Roy Rogers knife, the one she'd used to defend herself from the other man. The trucker laid it on the table before her, handle first, as though the gesture said it all. "Said he forgot to return this and you might have need of it."

Johnnie Sue stared at the knife and swallowed hard. She fought a wash of desire low in her groin as she remembered the bizarre moments she'd spent with her would-be lover last night. Her sudden fear and temporary surrender made even less sense to her now than then.

She hadn't breathed a word of the exchange to Clay or Elwood, though she'd thought about it long and hard. The trucker—Big Shorty—had angrily stomped out of the Cornsilk just a few minutes before somebody had shot at Fran. His rig had been parked right there by Clancy's for most of the evening, but when Johnnie Sue had heard the screams and hustled over there, she'd spotted it barreling off toward the highway. Shorty had been the only outsider in town last night. An obvious suspect. He'd even seen Fran in action during that set-to with Larry and Hersh.

Fran could have taken a shine to him, tracked him down and bitten off more than she could chew. It was a story that anybody who knew the tart might have believed. But Johnnie Sue did not believe it, and she wouldn't help anybody else string Big Shorty's noose.

No man crazy enough to want a tough old bird like me would take an interest in a flibbertigibbet like Fran, she rationalized. *And even if he did—and things went wrong— he wouldn't shoot her with a rifle.* Johnnie Sue had given Big Shorty plenty of reason to turn on her, but he'd simply taken the knife from her hand and told her she was a fool. Surely he would have done the same to Fran.

Besides, if she told Elwood about Big Shorty, she couldn't provide an alibi for Hersh. And under the circumstances, that seemed considerably more vital than protecting Fran from any possible harm. It would serve the damn shrew right if somebody knocked her off.

Gert had found the warfarin bottle in Wanda Carmichael's trash, and Johnnie Sue had already squared things between the Duncans and Joel. But that didn't change the fact that Fran had sorely wounded Hershell…and may have gotten Larry to falsify a prescription record as well.

She licked her lips and looked at the tired trucker. "You want something to eat? You look about done in."

He tried to smile but failed. "I've got a long way to go tonight. Some coffee would be nice. Maybe a ham and cheese to take along for later."

Johnnie Sue nodded. "Sure thing. On the house tonight. I 'preciate you coming all this way off the road."

This time his weary smile managed to reach his eyes.

Johnnie Sue found herself asking, "Big Shorty…he a friend of yours?"

He shrugged. "We show up at the same place sometimes. He just asked who was heading this way, and I was."

Johnnie Sue splattered some coffee in his mug. "Did he...say anything else? Except to bring the knife?"

This time he chuckled, but it was a warming chuckle, not a mean one. "He said you'd kill me if I asked for anything off the menu." He studied her closely, as though he wondered why any man would even consider it. Then he finished soberly, "And he said that if you didn't, *he* would."

For a full five seconds Johnnie Sue stared at him, wondering if she'd heard the man right. *Big Shorty, Big Shorty,* she wondered as the name began to throb in her heart, *was I wrong to toss you out? Is it possible that just once in my life, giving in to a man could have turned out right?*

Briskly she hollered the trucker's order to the cook, then picked up her coffee pot and made the rounds.

When she reached Frannie's fellow's table a moment later, she found it empty, with not so much as a penny's tip. She had no doubt at all that he'd snuck off to meet some other woman, and she felt a moment's glee that Fran Bixby was finally getting what she deserved. *What goes around comes around,* she cheered. *You deserve to love a cheating man, you little tramp.*

She glanced across the street, where his gaze had focused, and realized that it was dark now at Duncan's Drugs and the shades were pulled down. Larry had asked her to keep a special eye on Rene at closing time tonight, especially if anybody suspicious was lurking around. Until Elwood found out who had tried to shoot Frannie, all the men were keeping a special eye on their womenfolk, so his request had not surprised her. Nor had the almost-bashful way he'd begged her not to let his concern get around town. She'd promised to keep his secret, though she knew that any fool could tell by that pie-eyed look on Larry's face whenever he mentioned Rene that even if she didn't give a fig for her employer, poor Larry loved her with all his heart. Despite her suspicions, Johnnie Sue had never been able to turn up any dirt on Rene, and now that Larry had fallen for her, she'd resolved to do her best to find some good in the girl.

It was a resolution that dissolved in a fizz of motherly rage a moment later when she spied Fran's unfaithful lover across the street, clearly visible beneath the streetlight in front of Duncan's Drugs. He was furtively approaching Rene's little red car.

Damn you, Rene Hamilton! Johnnie Sue swore to herself. *It'd serve you right if you got the bullet meant for Fran.*

She tried to think of a way to get the fellow off the street before anybody could see him; she tried to think of a way to protect Larry from the humiliating truth…at least until she found a secret way to run Rene out of town.

But a moment later she realized that Fran's lover had no intention of waiting for Rene in front of God and everybody. As he reached the Datsun, he turned the handle as though to sneak inside, stopping for just a second when he realized that the car was locked. And then, without a moment's hesitation or a single finger's fumble, he pulled out his keychain, grabbed the right key and neatly slipped it into the lock on the passenger's side of the car.

As though he'd done it a thousand times before.

IT WAS TOTALLY DARK when Rene closed up the pharmacy and strolled outside. It was terribly humid, but she really didn't mind. Something wonderful had happened today. Something even more wonderful was likely to happen tonight.

Larry hadn't come right out and said that everything was going to be okay between them, but she'd felt his surrender as clearly as if he'd hollered the words right out loud. In the parking lot, with no one around to see them, he'd taken her in his arms and begged her not to cry. He'd kissed her temple tenderly, and though she hadn't dared to lift her lips to his, she knew it made no difference. He could not hold her divorce against her forever. Seth was gone from her heart. She realized now that the only reason he'd lingered there so long was that she'd had nobody new to replace him.

But now there was only room for Larry.

She slipped her key in the lock, pulled open the car door, and let out a strangled scream when she spotted a denim-clad leg in the passenger seat.

"Shh, Rene! It's only me," a man's voice said gently.

Her heart was pounding so fiercely that it took a moment to register the voice. It was one she knew as well as the sound of her own name, and it belonged to a man who she knew would do her no harm. But she'd been expecting Larry to show up any time now—all evening, in fact—and it wasn't until she climbed in and stared Seth full in the face that she realized that he wasn't the man she wanted to see.

Dear God, how I waited for this moment. How I counted the minutes, laid the grand plans! And now that he's here, all I can think is, what if somebody sees me with Seth and tells Larry before I can explain?

"Close the door, Rene," Seth ordered furtively. "We need to talk, but I'd rather not do it in the middle of Main Street. I suspect that nosy old bird at the Cornsilk keeps track of everything that goes on out here."

"Did she see you?" Rene asked. "Did she see you get into my car?" She might have added, "More important, did she rush to the phone to call Larry?" but Seth wouldn't have known what she was talking about. She'd been hoisted by her own petard.

Seth looked perplexed. "I was expecting a little more personal greeting, Rene. I presume you tracked me to ground in Porter for more than a casual hello."

Rene flushed. She could not face him. Even if Larry had not been involved, she realized in embarrassed hindsight, her ludicrous plan would never have worked. She would have been sitting here, face-to-face with Seth, while he told her in person what she'd always known. When she'd walked out, he hadn't tried to stop her because he'd wanted her to go. And the last thing he wanted was to be with her now.

"Seth," she said evenly, "my being in Porter has nothing to do with you."

"Right." Sarcasm radiated throughout the car. "There are dozens and dozens of puny little farm towns in Iowa, and you just happened to get a job in the one where I live."

Her humiliation was complete. How could she ever have imagined that this bizarre plan might work? And why had she ever tried to get him back in the first place? Looking at him now, she didn't see the man she'd sobbed over for so many hard months. Now she saw a very ordinary fellow, a memory of time gone by. The most important thing about him was that he might cripple her new life with Larry.

"All right, damn it, I came here because of you," she blurted, just to get it over with. "But that was weeks ago. Things have changed since then."

He studied her thoughtfully. Across the street a loud guffaw bellowed out from Johnnie Sue's place. The rest of the town was silent.

"Would you turn on the engine? Let's go somewhere quiet to talk. I need to get back before Fran gets home."

He said it straightforwardly, as though Rene, an old

friend, should understand that Fran was the center of his life.

It didn't hurt the way it once had. Now it was an old wound, a wound less of love lost than of betrayal. She wanted to reply, "I've got to get home before Larry shows up," but she didn't. It would have sounded catty, and besides, she wasn't sure she wanted to share Larry with anybody yet. She wasn't even positive that she had anything to share.

She agreed with Seth on one thing: they needed to go somewhere private to sort out how they were going to handle the awkwardness of living in the same small town. The gossips would have a heyday with the information when it came out. It was a problem Rene had not considered when she'd first arrived in Porter, because she'd expected to leave—with Seth or without him—about the time Fran figured out what she was up to. Now she realized that both of them were going to stay. Both Fran and Larry had deep roots in Porter.

"Drive over to the back of Henry Clancy's place," Seth suggested. "Nobody can see us there."

Rene shivered, despite the heat. "That's where somebody shot at Fran last night, Seth. I'm not sure it's a very safe place."

His whole face tightened. "Fran was alone. Nobody's going to take a potshot at the two of us."

"Seth, I'm not sure—"

"Oh, for Pete's sake, Rene, be reasonable. This isn't Des Moines; it's a little bitty town. That wasn't some random shooting. Fran ticked somebody off. Whoever shot at her didn't mean to kill her or she'd be dead. He just wanted to scare her half to death. He's not going to shoot at anybody else."

He seemed so certain that Rene couldn't argue. Hadn't

Lotty said pretty much the same thing last night? And it did make sense. Even back in the old days before Rene had had good reason to hate Fran, she'd always realized that the other woman had a knack for ruffling feathers.

She turned in where Seth indicated and turned off the engine. It was suddenly quite dark, quite still. It should have felt perfectly natural to be sitting in silence with a man she'd lived with for so many years. And yet...it didn't feel natural at all.

"Rene," he said softly, "I'm sorry. I really am."

She didn't answer. There was nothing to say.

"I knew it was over—at least ending—for us. But I should have had the courage to tell you outright. Please believe me, I never meant for you to find out about Fran like that."

There was a time when she would have hurled accusations at him, asked how he could have taken another woman to her home. But it didn't matter anymore. All that mattered was that she found a way to explain Seth's presence in Porter to Larry before he found out about her past.

Now she asked softly, "What happened, Seth? I mean, what really happened? Did you just get tired of me? Did you want a woman with more splash?"

He gazed at her softly, almost tenderly. His expression gave her an odd sense of déjà vu. It was as though she'd been plopped down in the past. "I'm surprised you still haven't figured that out yet, Rene. I didn't leave you for Fran. I was already...quite alone when I got involved with her."

Rene's eyes widened. "I loved you, Seth!" she protested. "I never even looked at another man while we were married. Even afterward, I—" She stopped herself in time; he didn't deserve to hear how long she'd cut herself off from men following his betrayal.

"Rene, it didn't have anything to do with another man. You left me for...well, for this." He gestured disparagingly toward her smock. "Night and day, school and work. You kept collecting kudos while I kept collecting bills. It was all right when we were in the same boat. But gradually I started to see that even though we were both working our socks off, you succeeded at everything you tackled, while I kept going one step forward, two steps back." His tone was bitter, sad, ashamed. "You left me in the dust, Rene. I couldn't keep up with you."

She couldn't argue with him. It was true. She could have told him that, given the choice back then, she would have carried him on her back sooner than lose him. And she could have told him that now—with the twenty-twenty vision of hindsight—she was glad that their marriage had dissolved. She deserved a man who was her equal—morally, intellectually and professionally. Larry was all three.

For a long time there was nothing to say. Then Seth said calmly, "Tell me what you're doing here."

She licked her lips. He'd been honest with her; he deserved the truth. "When I saw you at graduation, I had this crazy idea that...well, that there was still some hope. You hadn't married Fran and—"

"Oh, Rene." He sounded genuinely regretful. "I couldn't let you go through graduation alone after all you'd been through. I knew I was the only family you had."

To her surprise, tears filled Rene's eyes. She hadn't imagined the love she'd once shared with this man. He *did* still care about her, in his way. She blinked once or twice, then hurriedly glanced away.

"Seth, the bottom line is, I came here hoping to get you back. But after I settled in, I met somebody else, and now, as far as I'm concerned, you're welcome to Fran."

He studied her closely. "Really?"

"Really." She met his eyes without reserve. "My only concern is that he'll find out why I came here before I get a chance to explain about us. He's really touchy about ex-spouses."

For a moment Seth was silent. Then he said, "It's Larry Duncan."

She didn't deny it; she didn't even ask how he knew. From what Lotty had said, everybody in town knew Larry's story. There was no reason why Seth shouldn't know it, too.

"Please don't tell anybody you know me, Seth. You owe me one."

He nodded, his face a mask of chagrin. "You don't need to rub it in, Rene. I've got no reason to cause you any trouble. And quite frankly, I'd just as soon not have Frannie know you're here, either, because she won't like it one little bit." His eyes darkened as he suddenly tacked on, "Rene, if I spotted your car, it's just a matter of time before Fran does, too. She doesn't shop at Duncan's because of what happened to her dad, but unless you junk this heap..."

In that instant, Rene knew she'd have to tell Larry everything before he found out in the worst possible way. But surely she could buy some time! If she told him now, when things were still so unsettled between them, he'd never give her a second chance.

"I can hide the car, Seth, or sell it. I started out leaving it out front so you'd find it, and then I forgot about it after that."

He shook his head. "I didn't see it, Rene. Not until tonight, and I came into town to catch you after work, anyway." His eyes were troubled. "I spotted you last night in all the hubbub. If Fran hadn't been so hysterical, I'm sure she would have spotted you, too. And it's a damn good thing she didn't, and not just because of Duncan.''

''What do you mean?'' asked Rene, suddenly feeling queasy.

Looking profoundly troubled, Seth took her hand. ''Rene, look at your situation here. The avenging wife who's come to Porter to reclaim her husband. Hell hath no fury and all of that. The cops are looking for the person who shot at Fran! If they ever figure out why you came to Porter, the finger of suspicion is going to point right to your door.''

CHAPTER EIGHT

"IT'S NOT RIGHT, Johnnie Sue," Hershell whispered as his old friend served him rhubarb pie at noon the next day. He'd given all of his arguments over his chicken-fried steak, but Johnnie Sue hadn't paid much attention to him then and he didn't think she was paying much attention to him now. Earlier she'd been too busy explaining why they both needed an alibi. Now she had her eyes on that trucker, the one who'd shown up so wet a few nights before.

He was dry now, of course, but otherwise he looked about the same as he had the first time. Hershell noticed that though he was not a tall man, he gave the illusion of wielding great power. His muscles seemed to bulge in ostentatious places, and his grin was just short of cocky.

Johnnie Sue had served him coffee the minute he walked in, right after she'd changed aprons. Hershell had noticed that she'd put in the cream and sugar, too—something she often did for her favored regulars, but rarely for a stranger. He couldn't imagine why she'd bothered to remember the man's preference in the first place.

"Sheriff's lookin' for you," said Johnnie Sue, as though she were announcing the latest weather forecast. "We had a shooting the last time you were in town."

The big man shrugged. "Don't see what that has to do with me. I don't know a soul in Porter, and besides, when I travel armed, I carry a knife."

Johnnie Sue's eyes flashed up at his, and she bit her lip.

Big Shorty held her gaze. A look of tension passed between the two.

"It was the girl who was in here causin' such a fuss. I chased her out with my .30/30." She started wiping down the countertops that she'd finished scrubbing about ten minutes before. "You remember her?"

His lips twisted in a wry grin. "I remember the fireworks. Takes a woman of more substance than that young filly to hold my attention."

Johnnie Sue's eyes flashed up at him again, and Hershell wondered why she looked almost…afraid.

She can't be afraid. Johnnie Sue hasn't felt a moment's fear in over twenty years! Hershell reminded himself. Then he remembered how adamant she'd been about alibis for both of them, and he wondered if she knew something else she wasn't telling. He also wondered why she was warning the trucker to get out of town when she ought to be calling Elwood. After all, Hershell had pointed out once or twice before that the trucker might be a suspect they should mention to the sheriff, but Johnnie Sue had insisted that he was just a passing stranger who meant no harm. But Clancy had mentioned the big rig parked at his place before he'd gone home for the night, and Larry had seen it pull away right after the shooting. It probably didn't mean anything, but with a stranger, you couldn't be too sure.

"The shooting took place out by Clancy's. Didn't you say you were waiting for him to fix some part on your truck?"

That's better, Johnnie Sue, Hershell silently snorted. *Get him off guard, then grill him for Elwood. Now you're doing your job.*

Big Shorty nodded. "Yep. But I got tired of waiting. Went on down the road and found somebody who could take care of it that night. I was hell and gone from Iowa by morning.''

''Best explain that to Elwood or move on before he finds out you're here.''

Now, don't start warning him again, Johnnie Sue. One would almost think you were taking his side instead of Elwood's. Of course, that was unbelievable—unless Johnnie Sue actually knew that he'd shot at Fran and figured he'd done them all a favor. After all, the girl had been scared witless, but the shot hadn't ruffled a hair on her head.

''What time did the shooting take place?'' the trucker asked, his tone slightly less nonchalant.

''Right around ten, while I was closing.''

The big man's eyes met Johnnie Sue's. ''I've got an alibi for ten o'clock.''

A tense, unreadable look passed between them before she answered, ''I guess you'd found somebody to fix your truck by then.''

There was a moment's silence. When the trucker spoke again, Hershell didn't hear him, because Maxine was calling out a cheery greeting as she rolled in for her afternoon break. Hershell knew the girls liked to gossip without him—girl talk—but sometimes he was so lonely that he hung around anyway, just to listen to their voices. They always sat in the same configuration—Gert and Maxine on the left side, Lotty facing the table in her wheelchair, Johnnie Sue slipping into the edge of the right-hand part of the booth, leaving the space near the wall empty in memory of Aggie.

Today Hershell sat in Aggie's place. He'd asked her about it a dozen times, and he knew she wouldn't mind.

''Hershell, your poor boy has just gone off the deep

end!'' Maxine muttered as she slid into her regular seat. She didn't sound as though she were kidding.

"What do you mean, 'off the deep end'?" he asked, a little concerned.

She shook her head. "It's that new girl. He's falling for her hook, line and sinker. He's walked around all morning like some addlepated schoolboy. And that was *before* she came in!''

Hershell stifled a sigh of relief. He didn't want his boy hurt again, but that was a fairly minor concern at the moment. He was afraid Max was going to tell him something he didn't want to hear—like the possibility that Larry had done something really foolish, like trying to scare off Fran or doctoring the books. Neither seemed possible for the boy he knew. But on the other hand, Larry had refused to look him in the eye last night, and that wasn't like him, either.

As Hershell studied Maxine—who spent the next ten minutes complaining about the favoritism Larry was showing the new girl—he pondered on Larry's odd behavior. There was something his son wasn't telling him, something he ought to know. He might be old, but he was still alive.

He was still the founder of Duncan's Drugs, and still part-owner of the store.

When Maxine started to run down, he asked, "What do you know about Wanda's prescription?"

For just a moment, her eyes grew huge. He was afraid she was going to look away, just as his boy had done. Then she blinked a couple of times and started looking normal, just like good old Max. "Larry checked it out while I ran over to your place the other day, Hersh. Says it had his initials on it. Didn't he tell you that?"

He nodded. "That's what he said." Then he waited. Maxine was loyal to the bone. If Larry had changed that damn prescription—or if Max had done it herself—she'd tell him. "Max, I need to know."

Her glance flitted off, toward the trucker who was leaving Johnnie Sue one helluva tip, if the clunky sound of the change on the counter was anything to go by. As he sauntered toward the front door without a backward glance, Johnnie Sue scooped up the coins in a flash and dumped them in her pocket, where they jangled as she walked.

"Max," he tried again, but suddenly Johnnie Sue was heading in their direction, almost rushing to ask Max what she wanted to eat. Before he could ask about Larry again, Gert showed up and the three women started talking about the spell that new girl had woven over his son.

He was secretly glad that the moment was lost.

BY THE TIME Maxine had returned to work and Hershell had followed Lotty home, Johnnie Sue was so itchy she thought she'd scream. The hotel key Shorty had left with his pile of change seemed to be burning a hole in her pocket. But Gert lingered over a second cup of coffee, babbling about the different drugs she'd inadvertently located in the various houses she cleaned while searching for a warfarin sample.

At the moment, Johnnie Sue was not interested in Myrt Hazelwood's asthma and Horace Cutler's eczema. Nor was she intrigued by Gert's lamentations about her son-in-law's poor treatment of her precious girl. She knew Henry was a bum and she knew that Julie was a sweetie. She also knew that Gert grossly over-protected the poor girl. If she'd ever given Julie a chance to grow up and get her feet on the ground, she might have been better able to cope with her situation. A girl with some savvy could have seen what Henry wanted a mile off.

And a woman my age would have to be blind not to see what Big Shorty wants.

She didn't know why he bothered to come back. *Some men just like a challenge,* she told herself. But he *had* come back, and he *had* left his key, and she had to run off Gert so she could get rid of the damn thing before anybody found out. She'd be the laughingstock of three counties if anybody knew that a man had actually propositioned her.

And if anybody ever found out that she half wished she could join him at the Washburn Hotel, she'd be the laughingstock of the world.

By the time she shooed off Gert, things were quiet in the Cornsilk, and Johnnie Sue knew she could disappear until supper without anybody asking questions. Mary Lynn could cover the few drop-ins she might have until five-thirty.

She took off her apron and glanced down at her jeans. She'd spilled a few drops of coffee on them earlier, but nothing seemed to show. Her shirt was one of her favorites—a flaming red—and she'd taken a bath just the night before.

I'm only going to the goddamn mail box, she reminded herself tersely. *Sure as hell don't have anywhere else to go.*

But then it struck her, as a vision of Big Shorty's dark, steamy eyes filled her mind once more, that somebody might see her toss the damn key in the mailbox and ask her questions. It would be smarter to return it to the hotel in Washburn. It was a good ten miles from Porter, and nobody was likely to see her there. Nobody ever went to the Washburn Hotel unless they had something to hide.

I've got nothing to hide, she told herself fiercely. *And I'm not going to have anything to hide. I learned my lesson thirty-four years ago.*

She was suddenly struck by a vision of her husband—not as he'd left her but the way he'd looked in the early days, when they'd bed-wrestled every night. In a flash, the feeling was replaced by the memory of Big Shorty's giant hand on her face, in her hair, on her hip. She'd felt his power, restrained by a streak of gentleness. But she didn't know the man, not really.

Not yet.

Johnnie Sue's old truck lumbered out of town without raising much of a ruckus. She passed Julie Clancy driving in from Henry's farm and waved absentmindedly, braking twice for loose cattle on the road. It took her fifteen minutes to reach the hotel. It took her twenty more to open the truck cab door.

I can't be seen in the office, she told herself stoutly. *I'll just give this thing to Shorty himself and tell him where he can shove it.*

Johnnie Sue checked the room number, as though she had not memorized it hours ago, then drove the truck to the back parking lot where it couldn't be seen from the road. She marched toward the room with more confidence than she felt, determined to summon up her normal chutzpah before she faced the big-handed man again.

She knocked on the door belligerently, then waited for an endless moment until it briskly swung open.

He was dripping, the way he'd been dripping on the night they'd met. Only this time his jeans were dry. Beads of water pooled on the short-cropped hair on his head and the dense curly fur on his naked chest. His just-shaved face was slick with shower steam.

He grinned. "You're late, Johnnie Sue. I'd just about given you up."

She flushed. His cockiness was more than she could bear. Had he really been so damn sure that she'd come to him? Another voice answered, *Did I really believe I could stay away?*

"You left your room key at the Cornsilk by mistake," she said gruffly. "I just dropped by to return it."

His smile vanished. His whole huge body grew still. Eyes full of need swept over her body, setting tiny campfires in parts of her she'd thought had ceased to exist. She realized, with keen regret, that something was missing from the look she remembered in those eyes.

Before this moment, he'd always looked at her with respect.

"Never figured you for a coward, Johnnie Sue." It was a half-whispered growl.

Instinctively she raised one hand to slap his face. "Damn you, Shorty, if you—"

He caught her hand in his meaty fist, completely immobilizing her without bringing her a moment's physical pain. The pain was all the other kind.

"Excuses are for little girls, Johnnie Sue, and I drove a good fifty miles out of my way this afternoon in hopes of spending some time with a first-class woman." He dropped her hand, then rested his fingers at her waist. He didn't try to slip under her shirt, but she could feel his warmth through the fabric, anyway.

Above and below that masculine hand, female parts of her sizzled.

"If you can't own up to the fact that you came here to be with me, then I made a mistake coming back, Johnnie Sue. You crawl on back to your Cornsilk Cave and lock yourself in like a good little girl. I need a woman hard as nails and stuffed with courage. Looks like I was wrong thinking it was you."

Fury and shame did battle within her; common sense wrestled desire. It was pride, as much as anything, that finally propelled her through the door, shoving him aside with her roomy purse. She slammed the door and locked it, then tossed the purse beside the bed.

She turned to face him, still angry, still afraid. She wanted to tell him that no man called her chicken and lived to tell about it; she wanted to tell him that she didn't give a damn about sharing his bed.

No words came to her.

Shorty leaned against the door, arms crossed over that muscular, hirsute chest as he studied her with tentative approbation. She couldn't read his eyes. They were dark, distant, waiting.

At last he said calmly, "Ball's still in your court, Johnnie Sue."

She knew then what he wanted; she knew what he expected her to do. She had to prove that she was as brave in the bedroom as she was in the Cornsilk. Suddenly she knew it would not be an easy thing to do.

She faced him squarely, eyes meeting his, as she pulled off her clothes. She did not strip in a sensual way, but neither did she act like a terrified virgin. She just took everything off in her own straightforward manner. At first it was hard, but when she saw a flicker in those stern eyes as she took off her tired old bra, fresh courage raised her full breasts.

She didn't bother to suck in her stomach as she stood by the bed, naked, and began to unpin her hair. She was who she was, and either he wanted her or he didn't. Either way, she realized with astonishment, she desperately wanted him.

Nobody—not even the Duncans—had seen her hair loose for years and years. She was gratified to hear a tiny gasp as the locks came flooding down over her back and shoulders, licking her hips. One slender strand fell in front of her ear and covered part of her right breast. It was the strand that she expected Shorty to touch first when he crossed the room and stood before her by the bed.

To her surprise, he slipped his big fingers through the thinning hair at her right temple, gentling her scalp for a moment or two before his fingertips slid slowly down the slope of hair and ultimately came to rest on her nipple. She closed her eyes as his thumb brushed across the taut surface once, twice, three times. Desire ricocheted through her when he cupped her hip with his free hand.

She gripped his waist, as much to steady herself as to enjoy the feel of his damp skin. She pressed her lips into the hollow of his throat. She heard him groan—a low, feral sound—and she knew that in a moment, he would pull her close.

She was already lost. She knew that it was way too late for talking. But she had something she had to say to Big Shorty, this man who touched her as she had not been touched in years. There was one thing he had to promise her.

"There's something you got to do for me, Shorty," she barked more loudly than she'd intended. "Something you gotta promise."

His fingers froze, but he did not release her. "You oughtta know by now that I'm not a promising sort of man." Disappointment rippled through his low tone.

Johnnie Sue slapped his chest in frustration, but he didn't budge an inch. "Don't be stupid, Shorty. I'm not asking for moonlight and roses. This is different."

"I travel prepared," he said quietly.

"I figured as much, or I wouldn't be here," she barked, "but that's not it, either."

His hand left her nipple and traveled down the length of her torso, circling around to inflame her back. His fingers splayed out, dipped lower, pressed her toward him. When her body met his jeans, it was hard to concentrate, but somehow she persevered.

"You go when you want. You come back when you want. Or you don't come back at all." She glared at him until he nodded. He was starting to look confused.

"But the last time—whether it's tonight or ten years from now—you let me know it's over. Tell me to my face. Send a homing pigeon, write a postcard or give me a call."

Shorty took a deep breath; she could feel it throughout the whole powerhouse of his body. His abdominal muscles clenched against her own.

"How long did you wait for him?" he asked softly.

Johnnie Sue closed her eyes and looked away. Her silence said it all.

Slowly the big hands slid upward, warming her naked back. Before, his touch had been gentle, but sensual. Now she had the oddest feeling that he was cuddling her as though she were a dear friend.

She felt his breath heat her forehead, fan her hair. Caring fingertips stroked away the hurt of those old memories, healed the lingering scars. Then he took her face with both hands, tipped her chin up until they met each other eye-to-eye.

"I promise, Johnnie Sue," he whispered, his gruff voice almost gentle. "When the time comes, I won't forget to say goodbye."

To her astonishment, her fingers swept up his chest as she boldly claimed his mouth.

Moments later, she tugged him down beside her on the bed.

RENE NEARLY LEAPT out of her skin when the back door to Duncan's opened at five to nine; she was certain she'd already locked it. After her encounter with Seth the night before—not to mention fencing with Larry all afternoon—she was uncommonly jumpy. Elwood still hadn't turned up a clue as to who'd shot at Fran, and that knowledge troubled Rene for a number of reasons. Aside from the fact that it *might* have been a random shooting by some wacko who still lived in town, Seth had brought home the fact that Rene was a prime suspect.

"It's just me, Rene," Larry's familiar voice called out from the shadows.

"Thank God," she muttered with two-fold relief. She was thrilled that he wasn't an intruder...and thrilled that he'd come back to see her tonight. All day he'd been sending out quiet signals, but Maxine's disapproving glances had skewered their communication. "I'm just wrapping things up here, Larry," she answered, not quite certain whether she should be reporting to him as a boss or greeting him as a date. "It's almost nine."

He moved toward her then, his gently warming smile only half visible in the unlit shadows. He looked hesitant. She wasn't sure if that meant trouble or could be taken as a good sign.

"I'm glad you're here," she blurted, unable to restrain the confession. She hovered near him, not quite ready to move closer without an invitation, not willing to move back.

"Rene—" his voice seemed to crack "—if you don't need to rush right home, I thought maybe we could talk."

"I'd like that, Larry." It sounded silly, but it was true. Besides, what else could she say? *I've waited all day to see a sign of surrender from you. Every day this week you've changed...one day you're my friend, then you want to be my lover, then you tell me there's no hope for us at all.* But yesterday, he'd melted, despite his words of denial, and tonight…well, tonight maybe he could say it all.

"Let's go," he said brusquely.

Rene didn't remind him that it wasn't quite nine. Nobody was going to show up in two minutes, and besides, it was Larry's store. He could shut it down for a month if he felt like it.

She quickly marched to the front door and locked it, then joined him at the back. She'd walked to work, not wanting Fran to recognize her car. A quick glance at the parking lot told her that Larry had come on foot tonight, as well.

Rene wanted to invite him to her apartment, but she wasn't quite sure how he'd take it. She'd been desperately forward the last time they'd stood together in this parking lot; she'd been painfully clear about her feelings. The ball was in Larry's court. She'd have to wait until he served it.

"Rene, could we just…sit down and talk?" He glanced toward the bus stop bench beneath the streetlight. It wasn't the most romantic spot he could have chosen, but with the tiny city park behind it, it was green, at least, and tiny clusters of sweet alyssum flanked both sides.

Rene nodded and headed toward the bench. Larry touched the small of her back for just a moment, as though he were ushering her into a room, but almost at once he drew back.

By this time, fear and hope were battling inside her in equal measure. Obviously he'd decided to set the record straight, but if he'd just decided to say, "To hell with your divorce, Rene, I want you," he surely would have said it by now. At least with his eyes.

Rene perched on the edge of the bench. Larry slid back and rested an arm along behind her. His fingers did not touch her back. A sudden ache for his touch assailed her.

"Rene, you've got me between a rock and a hard place," he said softly, not looking at her. "I'm going to be dead honest with you. I really don't know what to do."

She turned toward him, eyes wide, as she wondered just what he meant. Had he already found out about Seth? Had Elwood been to see him? Or was he just talking about his own chaotic feelings for her?

"I told you yesterday how it was with Sandra."

She felt the need to say something, anything, to show she was still paying attention. "You gave me the rough outline, Larry."

He shook his head. "You want all the sorry details?" At last he looked at her.

"If you think it would help. I'll even tell you all the sorry details of *my* divorce if you think that would help. If you knew what my husband did to me, it might be easier for you to understand why I'd never go back to him even if I could."

"Rene, you were still hurting for your ex when I met you. I'm not sure you're over him yet."

"Larry—" she turned to face him squarely "—*I'm* sure I'm over him. I'd stay single forever sooner than take him back. The only doubt I have in my mind about us is whether or not *you're* really over Sandra."

The notion seemed to surprise him. Taking advantage of the moment, she pressed on. "Didn't it ever occur to you that *you* might be the one who ended up hurting *me?*"

It was obvious, from the ensuing silence, that it hadn't occurred to him. He studied her in utter silence. The nearby cricket chorus seemed to grow louder. Somebody shouted a punch line across the way at the Cornsilk, and two or three people laughed out loud.

"Rene, I found them together in my bed."

"I found them together on my couch."

He took a deep breath. "It was Christmas. I came home early to give her her present. A brand-new car."

Rene couldn't top that; she didn't even try. "She was somebody I worked with," she said evenly. "Not a close friend, but someone I knew quite well."

He didn't seem to hear her. He was telling his story now. "I met her the night she left him. She pulled into Aunt Lotty's place around two in the morning, face all battered, bleeding like hell. There was a room-to-let sign out front, and the Washburn Hotel was full, so she pulled into Lotty's parking lot and tried to sleep. Lotty woke up when she heard a child crying, which struck her as odd because no kids were living in her apartment house. She checked it out and found Sandra trying to comfort her little girl, Ellie—" he seemed to choke on the name "—even though Sandra was crying as hard as she was. Lotty got the truth out of her in a jiffy."

Rene waited to hear the truth, waited for Larry to clean this wound and turn to her with his heart whole and fresh. He was staring blankly in the general direction of the Cornsilk, still talking in that low, numb tone. She almost had the feeling he'd forgotten her.

"Her husband was a mean drunk. 'The salt of the earth' most of the time, she maintained, but every now and then he'd get ugly and slap her around. On this night, her boy, Timmy, had heard them fighting and come into their room to see what was going on. He saw his dad hit his mom and tried to stop him. Then the bastard hit Timmy, too."

Even now, she could see that the story hurt him. It wasn't just Sandra this man had lost, she realized all over again. Larry loved those children! Their loss was a second brand of suffering, a kind Rene had been spared.

"For the first time, Sandra was more frightened for her son than she was frightened for herself. Instead of cowering, she tried to fight back. That's when he went berserk and hit her with his fist. He cracked her jaw, but she didn't realize it then.''

Rene felt his pain, his disbelief that any man could so mistreat a woman, especially a woman he claimed to love. She wanted to touch him, to ease his hurt, but there didn't seem to be any way for her to do it. Both of his hands were spread out far away, and it seemed too personal to stroke his knee or the front of his shirt.

''Lotty called me to open the pharmacy, just to get some painkillers and more antiseptic than she had on hand. She took care of the kids while I took care of Sandra. Once I got a good look at the swelling, I realized that she needed medical care. I called Doc Swanson, and he came on over, even though it was almost 4:00 a.m. by then.''

For a long moment he was silent. His gaze had dropped to the ground.

Rene longed to hug him, to squeeze his hand, to do *something* to ease that pain in his low voice! He'd told her the end of the story before, and she didn't want him to have to admit it again.

''It took him awhile, but he found her. At first he tried to bully her into coming back to him. She held firm; I backed her up. When she filed for divorce, he got desperate. He grew humble. He pleaded. He begged. Then he went on a bender and threatened to kill her. He threatened to kill *me*. And we weren't even dating then.'' He grimaced. ''I was just good ol' Larry, trying to be nice to a lady in distress. Johnnie Sue says I'm a sap. Everybody comes to me looking for a handout.''

Rene wanted to tell him that his open-handed kindness was one of the things about him she loved best. It made him a modern-day hero, not a sap. But it was still time for her to be silent. Time just to listen.

"It didn't happen all at once. I just sort of grew into her life, and she grew into mine. The kids were a big part of it, I guess. But the bottom line is that once I fell, I fell hard. One hundred percent." Slowly he turned to face Rene, as though to underline his next words. "I don't know how to love a woman any other way."

Rene bit her lip. Against her will, she edged closer. She was just about to touch his chest when he said softly, "Looking back on it, I don't think she ever really loved me. Not the way she loved him. I was handy, I was kind, and I was good for her children. She decided to love me in her head, but in her heart, it was still him." Suddenly he shifted both arms, letting his hands fall on his knees in a way that seemed to shut out Rene. "I think you care for me, Rene, but I think if you're honest with yourself, you'll realize that you feel the same way."

It was time to tell him; it was the only way she could explain that it was her love for Larry that had ultimately conquered her need for Seth. But she couldn't say it without revealing why she'd come to town, and if she told him now, she knew he'd slam the door on their future.

"I didn't plan to fall for you when I came here, Larry," she hedged. "But somewhere along the line it just happened. It's because of you that I finally let my ex-husband go."

He shook his head. "It's because good ol' Larry gave you comfort when you were frightened. Good ol' Larry patted you on the head and took you in."

"That's only part of it," she insisted.

"Oh?" he taunted her. "What's the rest?"

She didn't want to tell him, not when he was baiting her like this. But she knew this was her only chance, if one could even call this a chance at all. She had to lay her cards out on the table.

"It's the way I feel when I see you coddling a baby bird or comforting a small child. It's the way I feel all shaky when I hear the back-door bells jangle and I know you're in the store. It's the way I feel when you touch me in passing and I desperately wish you'd do more."

She had planned to continue, but suddenly Larry stiffened. His fingers plucked the knees of his jeans. "What kind of 'more' do you have in mind?" he asked tensely.

She leaned toward him. "Kiss me and find out." She waited in agony while he pondered her invitation, and suddenly she couldn't take it anymore. "Oh, hell, Larry!" she burst out. "Let me make it crystal clear."

Rene slipped both hands around his neck and pulled him toward her; her lips pressed hungrily against his. She had wanted him to kiss her for weeks, and as scared as she was of blowing everything, she was more afraid that she might never get a chance to kiss him again. Instinctively she pressed her body close to his as her tongue slipped between his lips.

She held nothing back. She surrendered her heart to him.

For a long moment, he fought her. He didn't pull away, but he didn't kiss her back, didn't touch her, didn't melt or let her rev his motor. She felt his stiffness, his fierce internal struggle, and suddenly she knew she could never win him over by sheer force of will or even sexual surrender.

Abruptly Rene pulled back, her eyes on her hands. She felt ashamed and silly. Red branded both cheeks. It was the first time she could remember blushing since she'd been a kid.

"That wasn't what you wanted?" he asked, his voice half sorry, half mad.

Her eyes flashed up at his. She was surprised to see the

sheen of perspiration on his forehead. Had he responded more than she realized to her aborted kiss?

Slowly, with all the dignity she could muster, Rene stood up. Feeling foolish, hurt and angry—a deadly combination if ever there was one—she forced out, "I'm sorry, Larry, if that was out of line. I thought...I thought you wanted it as much as I did, but I guess I was wrong."

He studied her carefully, but he did not move from the bench. "Do I really arouse you, Rene? I mean, not just male-female proximity, but...in some way special?"

Rene closed her eyes and covered her face with her hands. Suddenly she knew that the make-believe world she'd created in Porter was about to crumble. Even if Larry never found out about Seth, she knew she couldn't go on working for him. Not after tonight.

She felt irrational, angry, aroused. Keenly aware of how close his right knee—and the ever-so masculine hand that rested on top of it—was to the pulsing center of her ever-so-feminine body.

Suddenly he grasped her hand. "Answer me, Rene. Do you *really* want me?"

"Yes." She almost choked on the word, confused and embarrassed by his change in tactics, not to mention her own sudden surge of desire for him. Knowing that she would never know Larry's love only made it worse.

And then he was standing, his body unbearably near. His grip on her fingers grew tighter, hotter. His thumb stroked the outside of her thigh where their joined hands rested.

"Did you want me like that before the night of the shooting? Did you want me then the way you want me now?"

If anybody but Larry had been asking her these questions, she would have thought he was teasing her cruelly,

or else indulging in verbal foreplay. But she knew that
Larry was testing the depth of her feelings. She desperately
wanted to believe he might yet give her a chance.

"What do you want from me, Larry?" she whispered,
her voice almost drowned by the backfire of a passing car.
"You want me to beg? I don't think I can do that. You
want me to admit that I want you terribly? I already have.
You want me to promise I'll love you forever? There's no
guarantee in this life, Larry, but right now, that possibility
doesn't seem too remote to me."

His eyes deepened in the shadows. His free hand cupped
her face. His voice was low, truly husky now, as he asked
her point-blank. "Are you absolutely certain that he's completely gone from your heart?"

It was the one question she could answer without equiv-
ocation, especially after last night. "One hundred and fifty
percent certain." She let her eyes meet his again—half
hopeful, half afraid—as she finished fiercely, "There's no
room left in there for anybody but you."

That's when he kissed her—kissed her the way she'd
longed for him to respond when she'd dared to kiss him.
It was a kiss of desire mixed with anguish and surrender.
It was not as gentle a kiss as she'd expected from Larry,
but his frustration and self-reproach could not mask his
tenderness for her.

He released her hand to hug her with both arms as his
kiss deepened. His tongue teased the corner of her mouth.
She squirmed as she clung to the sides of his shirt, instinctively pressing herself against him. She didn't know what
had happened to change his mind; she wasn't even sure if
he'd decided to give her a second chance. But she knew
that she longed for his touch too much to hold him off
while she asked searching questions.

She loved him too much to say no.

His thumbs flanked her jawline as he cradled her head, kissing her temples, her cheeks, then her yearning lips again. She opened her mouth to admit his seeking tongue, desperately wishing they were somewhere private so she could admit him into her body as well as her soul. He tried to pull her closer, but Rene was already as close as she could get. It wasn't nearly close enough, she decided a moment later, when she realized that he was quivering.

"*Rene,*" he whispered, the single word a surrender of his entire heart. He kissed her again, more tenderly this time. He'd stopped trying to hide his true feelings from her. She could feel the change in his grip as he yielded to his inevitable surrender.

"Don't make me sorry," he begged her as his fingertips evoked wildly urgent sensations along her nape and spine. "Please don't betray me, Rene. Don't make me sorry for this."

She ached to tell him about Seth, to get it off her chest. But she couldn't possibly interrupt this moment, spoil it with the mention of her ex-husband's name. Besides, she wasn't even sure she was still capable of speech. The only words she wanted to utter were, "It's only three blocks to my place." She was almost tempted to suggest that they duck back into the store.

"I love you, Larry," she whispered against the sweaty valley of his throat. "Please, let's get out of here. My place is closer than yours."

They were safe enough for the moment—it was dark and there wasn't a soul in sight—but any minute she was going to start tearing his clothes off, and this wasn't the place for that. Besides, they needed privacy for other reasons, too. Sex aside, this conversation didn't lend itself to interruptions for casual "howdies" and "how are yous."

Larry pulled back slightly and took a deep breath. His

hands were gentler on her spine, but that only made his touch more arousing. "I've wanted you right from the beginning," he confessed. "I would have hired you anyway—I had no choice. I never expected you to fall in love with me, but I hated being treated like your big brother."

Her eyes were wide with desire, but she tried to respond to his comments. "Larry, you were my boss. I didn't dare think of you as a potential date."

"I'm still your boss," he pointed out. And then, joyfully, he smiled. "Are you going to sue me for sexual harassment?"

Rene grinned back. She pulled him closer. "I haven't given it a thought."

His nose nuzzled hers. "I'm glad to hear that, Miss Hamilton, because I intend to harass you quite a lot."

They kissed again, and this time the kiss was mutual. For the first time since that nonverbal bonding the night Elwood had interrogated them at Larry's house, Rene was certain that Larry returned her feelings and was willing to take a chance on her. Everything was going to be okay.

She melted into his searing kiss without thinking of anything but the feel of his full lips and the warmth of his strong body.

An instant later the night exploded with the sound of gunfire. Simultaneously Larry knocked Rene to the ground.

She'd never heard a gun fired at such close range before, but she still recognized the sound. She'd never been knocked flat by a man who was making love to her before, either, and she could hardly believe the speed with which she went from a state of profound arousal to one of half-conscious agony. Her head hit the pavement so hard she thought she'd pass out—and almost wished she had because of the pain.

Larry was lying on top of her, fiercely shielding her body with his own. "Don't move," he ordered.

And she didn't. For at least sixty seconds she was absolutely paralyzed by shock and fear.

But the instant she felt the blood gushing between her chest and Larry's, Rene lost all power of rational thought.

By then all of Porter could have heard her screaming.

CHAPTER NINE

LARRY WAS COLD. It seemed to him that all the summer heat in Iowa had vanished in the wake of some inexplicable off-season arctic temperature drop. His shirt was soaking wet, which didn't help any. He was shivering convulsively.

Below him was concrete, wet and chilled. Something softer was under his head, something that seemed to smell like Rene. He couldn't see her, but he knew she was touching his head. Those gently stroking fingers had to be hers.

He heard shouts and the sounds of boots on blacktop, running. He heard a police car's siren, followed by Clayboy Billing's high squeaky voice. Once he glanced up and saw Lotty's wheelchair. The next time he looked he saw Johnnie Sue.

It was Johnnie Sue's face that frightened him the most. It was pasty white, a color he'd only seen it once before, on the night his mother died. She was not crying—Johnnie Sue had surely forgotten how—but her terror hurt him worse than the pulsing pain in his side. And that pulsing pain was unbearable.

He'd been shot. Of that he was certain. Why, who, how—he couldn't even contemplate. But he understood clearly that there had been only one shot, and it had hit him from behind. He had managed to protect Rene from the impact. Although he was growing dizzy and uncertain about almost everything else, he was sure she was okay, and it greatly relieved his mind. It was Aunt Lotty who seemed to be shaking violently, weeping and calling his name.

Johnnie Sue was tearing off her apron, rolling it up and using it to staunch his bleeding. Clayboy and one of the Cornsilk men—he thought he recognized Orville Kensler's voice—picked him up, gently but painfully, and slid him into the back seat of the police car. In the front seat, he heard a scuffle. Then Maxine's voice called out, sharp and shrill, "He needs family with him now! I've got to stay with him while Johnnie Sue comforts Lotty and my husband goes to get Hershell!"

Maxine must have won the tussle, because when the siren started up again and Clayboy roared off toward Washburn, Maxine was in the front seat, chanting a litany of assurances.

"You're going to be all right, Lare. We'll get you there in time. He will be all right, won't he, Clayboy?" And then back to Larry. "You're going to be just fine."

It was just before he passed out altogether that he realized who Maxine had pushed away, whose face he'd seen whey-faced outside the window of the black-and-white, tears streaming from her anguished green eyes.

His last thought was, *I would have told Rene I loved her if I'd known I was going to die.*

THE HOURS PASSED with all the speed of aeons as Rene waited for the news. She considered driving over to the hospital on her own, but she knew she didn't have the courage to face Maxine's possessive stare. Larry was surrounded by people who loved him; he didn't need her. In fact, at the moment, the confusion she offered his life was probably the last thing he needed to think about. When he recovered—she couldn't bear to think of it as "if"—there would surely be time to sort everything out, if they needed to go back to the drawing board again.

There had been a moment there—a long, erotic moment there—when Rene had believed that the waiting was over. But she'd believed that with Larry once or twice before, and she knew by now that he wasn't a man who was helplessly ruled by emotions. Getting shot was bound to make him reconsider everything about his life...or even deny that he'd all but confessed that he loved her.

But he didn't confess it, she remembered with pain. And even as he'd yielded to his desperate need to believe he could trust her, his half-whispered pleas had made it clear that he did not.

Shortly after the police car left, people began to ramble back into the Cornsilk. Johnnie Sue, who looked like she'd been run over by a truck, didn't follow the crowd. Instead she marched stiffly alongside of Lotty as she wheeled back toward her apartment. At the rate she was moving, Rene could have crawled and kept up. It made her wonder how on earth Lotty had reached the scene so quickly. Maybe she'd been at the Cornsilk or visiting somewhere else.

In a matter of minutes, Rene found herself alone on the bus stop bench, still sweating and shaking, desperately wishing that she had a single friend in the whole town. Normally Lotty was kind to her, but at the moment Lotty was so near hysterics that she didn't even realize that Rene had been with Larry when he'd been shot...let alone that Rene's head and back had been badly bruised. Both Maxine and Johnnie Sue seemed to dislike her because she'd edged out Hershell, and nobody else had strong feelings about her one way or another.

She didn't want to go home to that empty apartment, calling the hospital every half an hour for news. But she didn't feel welcome at the Cornsilk, or even at Lotty's at the moment, and sure as hell wasn't going to sit out here alone with a gunman on the loose.

In their panic to get Larry to the hospital, nobody had asked about the shooting. Nobody had even considered the possibility that Rene, too, might have been injured, let alone that she might have been the target.

At least nobody considered it until Elwood Hazlett showed up at her apartment less than an hour after Clay Billings had driven Larry away.

Rene rushed to the door and whipped it open before the second ring. Panic all but crippled her tongue as she faced the sheriff.

"Is he...is he?" she stammered.

Elwood looked surprised. "Larry? He's hanging in there, Miss Hamilton. He's gonna hurt like hell for a few days, but from what I hear, he's gonna be all right."

Rene snapped. She collapsed as though some spring had broken inside her. Oblivious to the sheriff's close scrutiny, she sank into the armchair by the door and let the tears gush.

Thank you, God, she wept silently. She grabbed a throw pillow and buried her face in it. For a while she felt nothing but the great rush of relief, the release of the bright knots of pain from the way her body had been clenched. Only vaguely did she realize that somebody was gently patting her bruised back, and even then it wasn't until after she'd begun to calm down.

She was embarrassed when she remembered the sheriff sitting there, but grateful that he, at least, had cared enough to let her know that Larry was going to be all right.

"Maxine almost pushed me out of your deputy's car," she admitted, still trying to dry off her wet, red cheeks. "I've been calling the hospital every fifteen minutes, but nobody would tell me anything. I wanted to go and wait there so much, but I thought I could help Larry more if I just stayed out of the way.''

Elwood nodded. He moved his hand off her back.

''Thank you so much for coming over,'' she told him earnestly. ''It's been so horrible, waiting here all alone.'' Suddenly her bruised face crumpled up again, and some leftover tears spilled over. ''I was so afraid he was going to die!''

She cried for a few more minutes while Elwood sat silently beside her, shifting uneasily once or twice. When she got herself together once more, she said politely, ''Would you like some coffee or soda before you go? I must have something in the—''

Slowly he shook his head. ''I can't stay long, Miss Hamilton. I'm in the middle of an investigation.''

She straightened then, sensing the change in his voice. ''The shooting, you mean?''

He nodded.

''Did anybody see anything? Do you know who did it?''

He licked his lips uneasily. ''I was, uh, hoping that you could tell me.''

He studied her face with a look she'd seen before, the night he'd questioned her at Larry's. Suddenly she realized that he hadn't dropped by to tell her Larry was going to be all right, after all. It was just fortuitous that he already knew his status.

Rene tried to get herself together to act businesslike, but the effort was overwhelming. ''I can tell you what happened, Sheriff, but quite frankly, I don't think it'll help you much.''

She knew what he was going to say just before he said it: ''Let me be the judge of that, Miss Hamilton.''

Rene shivered. Something about his tone told her that he wasn't just asking for information from her as a witness.

His eyes told her that he suspected she knew far more than she was willing to share.

"Larry met me just before nine as I was closing up," she started slowly, choosing her words with care. "We left about a minute later, out the back. We walked over to the bus stop bench and sat down and talked for maybe ten minutes or so. We could hear people laughing over at the Cornsilk, but other than that we didn't see a soul."

"You were sitting there talking when Larry was shot?"

She shook her head. "No. We were standing up, getting ready to go."

"Go where?" he asked.

Rene wanted to point out that it was none of his business, but she wanted desperately to find out who'd done this terrible thing to Larry. Embarrassed or not, she wasn't about to get in the sheriff's way.

"I asked him to come over here with me."

"And he agreed?"

"Well—" she tried to remember exactly what he'd said "—not explicitly. But I'm pretty sure that he was heading in that direction."

Elwood studied her for a moment, then asked bluntly, "Why?"

"Why what?"

"Why did you ask Larry to come to your apartment?"

Rene flared, "Why do you think? We were kissing on a public park bench. We wanted to be alone!"

He nodded, unembarrassed. Rene was certain that he'd known what they were doing all along; for some reason he just wanted to hear her say it.

"When the shots were fired, were you holding still, walking, what?"

She tried to think; she tried to be patient. She tried unsuccessfully to thrust her embarrassment aside. "I was more or less facing the street. Larry was facing me."

"You were facing the street when he got shot and you didn't see anything?" he asked disbelievingly. "Not even some motion in the shadows?"

Angrily Rene stood up. "Sheriff, my eyes were closed," she snapped. "I was excited. I was thinking about Larry. I'd forgotten anybody else existed!"

He pulled out a small notebook and scribbled a few lines. Then he said, "He fell when he got shot, right where Clayboy found him? You didn't move him?"

She shook her head. This part she remembered quite clearly. "He didn't fall. He threw me down, threw himself on top of me, the instant after I heard the shot. He was hurt, but he was trying to protect me. I didn't know he'd been hit until I felt the blood all over my chest." She shivered at the memory. "I kind of went crazy, I think. I know I started screaming. I remember wriggling out from under him and rolling up my smock under his head because I didn't want him lying there on the concrete bleeding to death. I didn't want to leave him to go for help, but I didn't have to because I could hear people pouring out of the Cornsilk. The first person who saw us hollered back that somebody ought to call you or Clayboy."

"Who was that person?" he asked. His tone was all business now.

Rene shook her head. "I don't know. I don't know the voices of very many people in town, and I wasn't, well, thinking very clearly. I can tell you the people I know that I remembered seeing, but I really don't know in what order they showed up."

He made another note. "Who do you recall?"

"Lotty Barrington, in her wheelchair. I remember being

amazed at how quickly she got there. Of course, I'm always amazed at how fast she wheels that thing around.''

He did not reply.

"Johnnie Sue Rawlings charged over with a bunch of the men who always hang out over there. I don't know their names, but I'd recognize their faces.'' She frowned. "Actually I couldn't tell you which ones were there. They just all looked familiar. I remember feeling safer when they got there.''

"Safer?''

"I guess I figured that whoever shot Larry was a stranger, and I knew everybody who gathered around us. At least, I know them by sight. I know they belong here in Porter.''

Slowly Elwood stood up, and he seemed to tower over her. "We don't get many strangers here, Miss Hamilton.''

"I know that.''

"In fact, right now, you're the only one.''

He let his words sink in. Rene felt an odd glitch in her heartbeat as he said slowly, "We sometimes go two, three years without gunfire in this town except for huntin' and skeet on Saturday afternoons. We've had two shootings since you moved here, both with a rifle.''

Rene stiffened. "There's a rifle in nearly every house in this town, Sheriff.''

"That's a fact.''

"And the other shooting was of a floozy that half a dozen people probably wanted to kill. I can't see that it's got anything to do with me.''

"Maybe, maybe not. But it might have something to do with Larry.''

Rene was starting to feel queasy. "What do you mean?''

"I mean, jealous lovers and jilted wives aren't the only

folks in this town with a score to settle with Fran. The Duncans have a pretty score of their own to make right.''

Rene stood up and firmly faced him. ''Have you forgotten that *Larry* was the one who was shot tonight? And the night somebody shot at Fran, I saw Larry running toward Clancy's from the direction of his house. Even if you're crazy enough to think Larry would harm a woman—which means you know nothing about him at all—you can't deny that evidence.''

Elwood's earlier comforting demeanor had completely vanished. ''Miss Hamilton, I've known Larry Duncan all of my life. And I know damn well he wouldn't shoot a woman, but he might be willing to scare the daylights out of one as bloody awful as Fran.'' He gave her a moment to ponder that before he added, ''I also know that you'd throw yourself in front of a truck to save Larry's reputation, so I'm not too impressed with having you as his alibi.''

''You know I love him, but you have no reason to believe I'd perjure myself for any man,'' she maintained stoutly. ''Besides, Larry doesn't need me or anybody else to vouch for him. His reputation stands on its own.''

''So it does.'' The sheriff scribbled one last note, then snapped his notebook shut. ''But you haven't been here long enough to establish your own reputation one way or another. You could be…almost anybody. With almost any reason for being here.''

Rene tried desperately to hold his threatening glare, but she couldn't do it. Helplessly she glanced down.

''I came here to work, Sheriff. If you check out my credentials, you'll find that I'm qualified for my job.''

''I *have* checked out your credentials, Miss Hamilton, and I'd say you're overqualified for this job. In fact, I can't imagine why a woman with your background would choose to leave a good job in Des Moines to work part-time at odd hours in an out-of-the-way little burg like this unless you were hiding from something or somebody.''

Her eyes flashed up to his. ''Nobody's looking for me, Sheriff.''

He grinned without humor. ''That doesn't mean you don't have something to hide.''

Rene's resentment battled with her fear. She wasn't terribly frightened that she'd get charged for anything relating to Fran's shooting; even if the sheriff came up with some connection, Fran would have to press charges, and she was almost certain that Seth could stop her from doing that. But if Elwood kept nosing around, he might discover that she'd been married to Fran's current lover before Rene had time to break it just right to Larry. Nothing frightened her more than that.

She marched to the door and briskly threw it open. ''I'm very tired, Sheriff. It's been quite a night.''

''Gonna be a busy week, Miss Hamilton. I reckon you'll be working long hours the next few days.''

She gave his odd comment a moment's thought. ''I guess...I'll need to take over while Larry's laid up.'' She didn't mind at all. In fact, she was thrilled that there was something she could do for him.

''I'm glad you feel that way, Miss Hamilton. Some of the part-time help he's had in the past would say 'to heck with it' and just take off.'' He took one more step in her direction and said slowly, ''I'm sure Larry's counting on you to stay put till we get this whole thing sorted out.''

He was halfway to his car before Rene realized that the Porter sheriff had just ordered her not to leave town.

AT NINE O'CLOCK the next morning, Larry had not regained consciousness. Hershell had not moved from his boy's bedside since Orville Kensler had wakened him up and rushed him over here. Every bone in his body ached, and he'd talked to Aggie all night to no avail. The doctors said they'd patched him up, that he'd be all right, but Hershell was not convinced.

"Come on, son," he whispered, as though his gruff and desperate voice might wake the boy he'd cradled as a child. "You can't die on me yet. We've got things to talk about. You gotta tell me if you changed Wanda's last prescription to save your old man. I gotta make you see that I can't carry on if you won't let me work."

He choked back a sob. Larry didn't answer him, but he carried on.

"Just because I love Paulie doesn't mean I don't love you, son. Paulie was always different. He was the butterfly; you were the workhorse. When you came back, I knew you'd given up your own dreams for me. I was too ashamed of Paulie to let you know it. I didn't want to need you, Lare, not so bad, like some old man who can't stand on his own."

He wiped a fresh tear from his right eye, covered his forehead, crushed back the fear. "We lost Paulie so long ago. Then Aggie passed on. It's just the two of us, Larry. The two of us and Johnnie Sue." He swallowed hard. "Don't you ever tell Maxine that I said that, now, because she'd be jealous as all get out. She's as good a friend as they come, you know, but she's not family. Not like Johnnie Sue."

He stood up and walked toward the window, stared dismally at the brilliant summer sunshine pouring in. It had been a beautiful day just like this when Johnnie Sue— Aggie's girlhood friend from summer camp—had first arrived at the Porter bus stop, so young, so frightened, so broken in spirit and heart.

"It was Aggie said it. 'We're all she's got, Hershell, so we're her family now.'" He shrugged. "I didn't know Johnnie Sue from Adam's off ox, but I did just like Aggie told me. I took her in." He turned back to his sleeping son. Larry's face was gray, and blood seeped through the bandage on his chest. "And I thought *I* was doing *her* a favor! And now look who's picking up the pieces, keeping me alive. I'd move heaven and earth for that girl, Larry." Then, more gently, he added, "I'd move heaven and earth for you."

He considered pointing out that Johnnie Sue had been acting kind of squirrely lately. Jumpy as all get out at lunch and happy as a clam by suppertime. He sure hoped she wasn't coming down with something. He'd never seen her act so strangely.

He'd called her once at 3:00 a.m., to tell her there'd been no change. She was still at Lotty's, holding down the fort, but she'd promised to come over in the morning. He'd been surprised that she'd let Maxine take her place last night. It made sense for one of them to stay with Lotty if she was that upset, but he would have expected Johnnie Sue to insist on going with Larry.

When the door swung open, he expected Johnnie Sue, but it was Elwood Hazlett, looking grim. "Any word?" he asked.

Hershell shook his head. "They say he's gonna be okay, but he won't wake up."

"Did they give him something to knock him out?"

Hershell nodded. "Yeah, but I still don't like it. I won't feel right till he opens up his eyes and tells me he's not dead."

Elwood clapped him on the shoulder, then gingerly sat down on a vinyl chair beside the bed. "He's going to be just fine, Hersh. And while he's getting well, the best way you can help him is to help me figure out who shot him."

Hershell turned basset-hound eyes on his young friend. "Promise me, El. Promise me you'll find the trash who did this to my son."

Elwood took his hand, gripped it hard. "You've got my word."

Hershell blinked a few times before he asked, "How can I help?"

Elwood leaned closer, kept his voice low. "I need to know about anything different in the past few weeks. Any changes in Larry, any changes at Duncan's, any changes with you."

He shrugged. "Nothing's happened that you don't already know about, Elwood."

"You're talking about that Cornsilk scene with Fran?"

The shrug was more elaborate this time. "Ah, that was nothing. I mean, it was awful, but it wasn't *new*. Just more of the same old thing. That's just Frannie being Frannie. It's got nothing to do with my son."

Elwood pulled out a notebook. "Nobody new in his life?" he tossed out nonchalantly.

Hershell pulled a face. "Only that girl. The one he hired to take my place." He couldn't hide his bitterness. "Fran's been a pain in the neck for twenty-five years but nobody ever tried to shoot her until Rene Hamilton came to town. And Rene was with my boy last night when he got shot, too." The expression on his aging, sleepless face grew hard and determined. "You're looking for changes at Duncan's? Start looking at her. If Larry's shooting wasn't just some random thing or freak accident, then somehow, some way, Rene Hamilton's in the middle of it." His grieving eyes met Elwood's. "You mark my words."

CHAPTER TEN

"AND THERE WAS poor Larry just lyin' there, covered with blood, and Clayboy's siren's running like crazy. We all bolted outta here like a bat outta hell and..."

Johnnie Sue sloshed coffee in Henry Clancy's cup and wished she could pour it down the front of his jeans to make him shut up. One of her regulars had been out of town, visiting his in-laws in Tulsa, during the shooting, and Henry was bringing him up-to-date. In the past forty-eight hours she had listened to a half dozen different versions of that night's god-awful events. Elwood had questioned everybody and asked her to keep one ear open for any clue that might come her way. He was certain that sooner or later, somebody would say something in the Cornsilk to give the shooter away.

Johnnie Sue sincerely hoped not. In fact, the only thing she hoped more desperately was that Big Shorty would manage to meet her at the Washburn Hotel on his way back from California. Despite her anguish over Larry, she'd found herself counting the minutes until his return.

He was due back this afternoon.

"You want me to stop back when I'm headed this way?" he'd asked her nonchalantly after they'd spent two glorious hours in his room.

"If it's no trouble."

He'd given her a sleepy-eyed grin that reminded her what it meant to be a woman. A feeling she'd all but forgotten before the night he'd strolled into the Cornsilk. "It's hell and gone from the beaten path, but I'd say you're worth the fuss."

She grinned like a school girl and felt like a sap. But he'd kissed her goodbye in a way that left her with no doubt that he'd be coming back.

She'd driven back into town almost too happy to be scared of how rotten she'd feel if he didn't show, a possibility she knew she had to get prepared for. Still, she'd made it back in plenty of time to serve dinner to her regulars without anybody figuring out where she'd gone. And when Rene had closed up shop at nine o'clock, she'd been waiting for her.

From the Cornsilk, Johnnie Sue could see the front of Duncan's, not the back, but it took no genius to notice that her little red car was not parked out front. Though she'd never seen it parked in the back, she circled around once to make sure. No red car. She could draw only one of two conclusions: either Rene planned to walk home or she planned to meet somebody with a car.

She'd never known Rene to walk to work, but she *had* known her to meet a man afterward. The night before, in fact. Johnnie Sue had slipped back into the Cornsilk, mingled with her folks, and nonchalantly disappeared out the back right at nine. In the dark, at such a distance, she couldn't overhear her conversation with the man on the bench, but she sure as hell could see the way that hussy kissed him. She'd slipped back in to get her shotgun in a flash, planning to scare the bejesus out of that little tart. She'd have to wing Frannie's lover instead of Rene because that was one thing Larry would never forgive her for. She was a dead-eye shot; she knew she could graze him somewhere harmless.

And then, in his passion, the man's body had twisted in

some terribly familiar manner. With instinct more than conscious thought, she'd realized, just as she'd squeezed the trigger, that she was shooting Larry! Desperately she'd tried to stop, but her frenzied effort only wrecked her aim.

There was no agony—prison sentence, execution or fine—that could possibly be any worse than knowing she'd nearly killed Aggie's son, and it wasn't fear of the law that kept her so desperately silent. It wasn't even the look in Larry's eyes if he ever found out what she'd done, or even the look in his eyes if he ever found out why she'd done it. The reason she couldn't fess up was Hershell.

He couldn't take another blow. Not from life, not from a stranger, absolutely not from Johnnie Sue. Larry loved him terribly, but Johnnie Sue knew that she was the glue that held his dad together. He wouldn't blame her for trying to get rid of Rene—for his sake as well as Larry's—but he could never forgive her for nearly killing his son.

What worried her the most was that poor Elwood was stumbling around in the wrong direction, looking for a suspect involved in both shootings. She hadn't a thing to do with Fran's attempted shooting—though the thought of Fran lying dead didn't bother her any—but if Elwood ever found out she was guilty of one shooting, he'd figure she was guilty of the other one, too. But she wasn't. And even though anybody in town who wanted to kill Fran had her blessing, the fact remained that a genuine murderer might get around to killing somebody *else*.

She hadn't uncovered a clue as to Frannie's shooter. Privately Big Shorty had admitted that he'd heard the gunshots on the way out of town, but there were so many people milling around that he didn't think the girl needed help...and he was afraid he might be fingered for the crime if he stuck around, especially in view of what had just transpired at the Cornsilk.

Johnnie Sue believed him. Well, she believed him more than she didn't. But she knew that if Elwood got hold of the same facts, he'd add up two and two and come up with a very unsavory four.

Especially if he ever figured out that the night Larry had been shot, Big Shorty had come through Porter, too.

LARRY WOKE SLOWLY, fading in and out, until he became aware of the presence of a new person in the room. Since he'd been in the hospital, his father had almost lived there, and the nameless nurses—kind, helpful but interchangeable in the fog of his pain and grogginess—had come in and out so often that he never even stirred unless they asked him to.

This presence was different. It wasn't Maxine, who'd wept all over him yesterday. It wasn't Johnnie Sue, who'd given him some crusty orders and then tearfully turned away. And it certainly wasn't Elwood, who wanted to know anything and everything that might assist his investigation.

It was Rene.

She was sitting in the vinyl chair beside the bed, her eyes on his face, her lovely mouth tense and drawn. She looked exhausted, uncertain. An ugly bruise ran the length of her jawline and dotted her temple.

He didn't try to speak to her at once. His tongue was a bit stiff from the painkillers and sleeping pills, and considering what he'd been doing with Rene when he'd seen her last, this conversation was bound to be a bit awkward, anyway.

"You don't have to talk if you're not up to it," she said softly. "I just had to see for myself that you were okay."

Under those simple words he felt the pressure of a dam

breaking. He could still remember the sound of her screams in his ears. She'd been terrified.

And she was still afraid.

"I'm going to be fine, Rene. I'm better already. The doctors just want me to take it easy for a while."

She nodded, sucking briefly on her lower lip. "I didn't see who it was, Larry. Elwood asked me—" She broke off, as though she didn't want to discuss Elwood. "By the time I realized what was going on, I was flat on my back."

Carefully he asked her, "Were you hurt much, Rene?" He gestured toward the bruise that marred her lovely face. "I knocked you down awfully hard."

"Thanks for asking. Nobody else ever did." She smiled weakly. "I'm pretty stiff and my head's still throbbing, but my biggest problem is that I'm worried about you."

He considered reaching for her hand, but it seemed too far away. Everything in the real world seemed too far for him to reach, and Rene had always seemed beyond his grasp, anyway.

Had he really been kissing her when he'd been shot? Not just *kissing* her, like hello and goodbye, but kissing her like *Good God, how I want you?* And had she really been kissing him back the same way?

"I figured you'd want me to keep the store open."

He nodded.

"The place has been packed with people who just want to get the latest gossip on you, but most of them picked something up to justify their nosiness, so we've been making a powerhouse profit the last two days. Poor Julie just sobbed her little heart out when she heard what happened to you. Maxine had to take her in the back and calm her down before we sent her on her way."

He tried to grin, and was surprised to find that the effort didn't hurt much. If Rene leaned over and kissed him, he could probably move his lips without causing himself any pain.

But she didn't bend over, and he realized, in his haze, that he wasn't at all sure he wanted her to. Just before the shooting, he'd convinced himself that he could take the risk of loving her, come what may. But in his mind, "come what may" had not involved nearly dying. And it made him wonder what other surprises might be coming his way.

"Can you think of anybody who might want to kill you, Rene?" he asked. Vaguely he remembered telling Elwood to keep an eye on Rene. In his memory, there had been something intense about Elwood's answer that had troubled him. Was she the one in danger? Had the bullet hit him by mistake?

Rene shook her head and gulped in surprise.

Eager to soothe her, he suggested, "I suppose it could have been Fran."

Her face whitened.

So much for trying to help, he berated himself. "Well, it had to be somebody, Rene. And I can't imagine anybody else angry enough to try to shoot me."

"You really think he was shooting at you and not me?" she asked. "I don't know whether that's good news or bad."

He met her eyes and tried to understand the mixture of fear and loyalty that battled there. But it was hard to think clearly when his chest was throbbing and his mind was numb. The only thing he was sure of was that he was glad he'd been the one to get the bullet, no matter who it was meant for. The thought of Rene lying injured was more than he could bear.

"Rene," he said softly, as his consciousness started to waver, "promise me you'll be careful. Start driving your car to work again and park out front where everybody can see you.''

She blanched again, and he wondered what she wasn't telling him.

His eyes closed against his will, but he forced them to flutter back open.

''Larry?'' she whispered, her voice suddenly close to his ear. She was leaning over him now. He could feel one soft hand against his face. It felt delicious. Natural. Incredibly right.

''Larry, when you're better, I need to talk to you about some things.''

Groggily he murmured, ''Trouble at the store?''

''No.'' Her hand lovingly stroked his cheek, brushed the edge of his mustache. ''The night you were shot, you told me everything about your marriage. If you want to listen, I'd like to tell you everything about mine. Then we can put the past behind us and never think of it again.''

He didn't want to think of the past, now or ever; he didn't want to think about the man who'd been too stupid to value Rene as a wife. He wanted to tell her that she was precious to him, that he was profoundly touched by her visit, that he desperately longed to get well so they could be together again.

He longed to tell her that he knew it would be a mistake to love her—a mistake he'd regret down the road.

Then he struggled to open his eyes once more, saw her angelic vision, remembered the way he'd surrendered to her kiss. He wanted to kiss her again, with tenderness now and with passion some time later, but he couldn't seem to find his voice at all.

He wasn't sure whether he was still awake or already dozing again when he heard her whisper, ''I love you so much, Larry. I only hope that when I tell you the truth, you'll still be able to love me, too.''

His sleep was troubled all afternoon. He had nightmare after nightmare about the shooting. Everybody he knew faded in and out of the picture as shooter or victim—his dad turned into Henry; Maxine ended up in Lotty's wheelchair; Gert's red hair was in a bun like Johnnie Sue's. Once, Fran drew a bead on Rene and shot her through the heart.

Larry woke up with a start, profoundly relieved to find the room empty.

But he could still hear Rene screaming.

FOR THE NEXT few days, Rene worked from nine in the morning till nine at night, with only an hour off for lunch and dinner. During most of that time, Maxine was by her side.

Maxine knew what Rene and Larry had been doing when he'd been shot. Rene didn't ask how she knew, but it was obvious by her increasing bad temper and constant potshots that she not only knew but disapproved.

"These girls nowadays," Maxine grumped when one of the high school girls who clerked in the evening showed up in a miniskirt that came within an inch or two of her knees. "No respect. No decency. In my day a woman didn't show off her body or throw herself at her boss. She didn't drive around at night and meet men in strange places."

And so it went; if there was any way at all Maxine could tie Rene's behavior to somebody else's, she did. She also seemed to blame Rene for the shooting itself, though she never said so in so many words. "Strangers coming into town, bringing all kinds of riffraff with 'em."

But Rene's problems with Maxine seemed to pale in the

face of the potential disaster that threatened Duncan's on the day that she got a run-of-the-mill call from Sally Haywood, Doc Swanson's gossipy nurse.

"Got another one for you folks, Rene," chirped Sally, who'd grown rather friendly after a month of daily phone calls. "From Larry's favorite customer." She giggled. "Frannie Bixby, can you believe it?"

Rene couldn't believe it. She couldn't believe that Fran would voluntarily choose to have a prescription filled at Duncan's. She couldn't believe that Fran was going to find out she was there.

Somehow, she had to tell Larry about Seth before that happened. But how could she press the issue when he was lying so still and pale? She had known she loved him long before he'd gotten shot, but seeing him in the hospital had profoundly crystallized the situation for her. As he'd slipped off to sleep, she'd realized how she'd feel if he ever died. The notion had shaken her so thoroughly that she'd had trouble driving home.

He didn't need to die for her to lose him, though. The truth hung over her head like a waiting guillotine. For Larry's sake, as well as her own, she desperately wished she could make this prescription vanish, but that was impossible. The next best thing she could do was make sure that Fran would have nothing to complain about.

And hope and pray that she was out of sight when Fran came back to pick it up.

Rene wrote down the prescription carefully—cimetidine, generally prescribed for ulcers—and repeated it back to Sally. This was standard procedure, but, just to be on the safe side, she did it twice.

Sally wanted to know all about Larry, and Rene told her what she knew. When she got the garrulous woman off the phone, she gave careful thought to Fran's prescription. If anything went wrong—if Fran could uncover even the slightest little bit of trouble—she'd come down on Duncan's like a ton of bricks.

And if she found Rene behind the counter, she'd make a scene that rivaled Mount Saint Helens's spewing lava. Larry would hear about it in the worst possible manner— from half the damn town—before Rene had a chance to tell him her own version of the story.

Before that happened, she had to tell him the truth herself.

"YOU COULD HAVE called," said Johnnie Sue, staring angrily at the big man who'd just let her into his room. After their second time together, Shorty had promised to come back in three days. It had been over a week.

He shrugged. "I told you I'd swing up this way if I could. I couldn't. And I went out of my way this time because I thought I'd find a warm welcome here. If I was wrong, I'll check in my key and be on my way."

Johnnie Sue wasn't sure what to tell him. She was so relieved that he'd come back, so afraid he'd go away. She hated the way he made her feel. So tearful, so afraid. *So alive, so much a woman!* And she hated wondering where he'd been during the first shooting. Hated the fact that she'd never mentioned his name to Elwood...hated the fact that a tiny voice kept warning her that she should.

"I thought you weren't coming back," she finally told him. "I thought you'd changed your mind."

He eyed her quietly. "As I recall, I made you a promise, Johnnie Sue. If I'm not coming back ever, I'll send you a message. Otherwise you can expect me whenever I happen to be coming through."

She felt a great ghost of relief surround her; it was going to be all right.

But suddenly Shorty said, "It seems to me that I'm the one getting the short end of this stick, anyway."

His tone made her palms feel clammy. She sassed him, anyway. "What the hell does that mean? You want something you're not gettin'?"

He glared at her. "Yeah, as a matter of fact, but it's not what you think. I've got no complaints about the time we spend in this bed."

She swallowed hard. She was so damn rusty at making love that she was surprised she still remembered how. Of course, Shorty provided all the inspiration any halfway normal female could ask for. Still, it was a relief.

"So what's your beef?" She tossed out the question casually.

He sat down on the edge of the bed and started pulling off his shirt. "I don't like feeling like I'm something you want to sweep under the carpet, Johnnie Sue. At first I could see why you didn't want everybody in town to know your business, but I'd like to think things are different now."

"Different how?"

She knew she sounded belligerent, but she couldn't help herself. Any minute he was going to ask if he could just sashay into the Cornsilk any time he pleased and kiss her hello. Gert would twitter, Lotty would grin and Maxine would scold. Clancy and Elwood would tease her to tears and Clayboy would turn red. Larry wouldn't believe it, and Hershell wouldn't understand at all. In a funny kind of way, it would be like losing Aggie again.

"Johnnie Sue, we're cut out of the same piece of cloth. I'm not looking for a woman to put dinner on my table every night and you don't want to hustle around with some man's slippers and pipe."

"Got that right," she growled.

"But you're not in the habit of meeting passing truckers at the Washburn just for sex. This—" he motioned from himself to her and back again "—has always been more than that to both of us. I'm proud that you're...well, that you keep coming here to meet me. I'd be happy to show you off to my friends." For one incredible moment, a flicker of pain slithered across his face. "I just wish you felt the same."

It troubled her to know she'd hurt him, but she couldn't say so outright. The best she could do was explain it all over again. "They think I'm hard as nails, Shorty. It's how I keep the lid on the place. If they know I'm sleeping with you they'll think I'm wide open to anybody. As it is they think my only recreation is shooting skeet."

And shooting my best friend's boy by mistake. She longed to share that pain with Shorty, but it would have been too hard to explain. In bits and pieces she'd told him about Hershell and Aggie, but Larry's past was his private business, and Shorty wouldn't understand why she'd shot him if he didn't know about Sandra as well as Rene. She hadn't even told him about her ongoing efforts to unearth dirt about the girl.

Apparently Maxine had been doing research of her own. She'd come bursting into the Cornsilk one day with the news that she'd spotted Rene's little red car at Clancy's one night when she was driving home from choir. Rene had looked surprised when Maxine had asked if her car had been repaired; she'd denied taking it into the shop. After talking her hunches over with Orville, Maxine had astutely recognized the similarity between Fran getting shot at Clancy's when she had no right to be there and Rene being there late at night without a good reason, either, and had come up with the logical conclusion that Frannie wasn't the only one in town who found that big open field behind Clancy's a good place for a secret rendezvous.

But Maxine didn't know who Rene was meeting, and Johnnie Sue wasn't sure that she wanted to tell her just yet. She had recently learned that Seth Rafferty had once been married to Rene, but she wasn't about to tell Larry in his current condition, and she wasn't sure Max could hold her tongue. Worse yet, Johnnie Sue couldn't even start a plan in motion to run the girl out of town until Larry got well, because Duncan's couldn't carry on without at least one pharmacist.

"You don't need to hide behind all that false bravado to keep the Cornsilk going," Big Shorty continued almost gently. "I saw through you the first time we met. You think those regulars who've been watching you take care of the whole damn place for twenty or thirty years haven't figured out you've got a heart of gold?"

She knew it was a compliment, but it left her shaky. He was getting too close.

"Shorty, I've got three hours till supper," she told him straightforwardly, hoping to deflect his concentration as she sat down beside him on the bed. "After that I'm free all night."

It must have been the right thing to say because after that he gave her a steamy smile that made her rush with her clothes. "I've got to be on the road by four-thirty, but I figure that's long enough to say hello."

It was long enough to say hello and long enough to give each other all kinds of welcoming pleasures, and that's what they did for the next two hours. At the time, it seemed damned near perfect. It wasn't until later that Johnnie Sue felt as though he'd rushed her.

And it wasn't until Clayboy popped in to ask some more questions about the big rig seen in the vicinity on the night of Larry's shooting as well as Fran's that she realized what would happen if anybody ever figured out that the rig belonged to Big Shorty.

Somebody might figure out *why* he kept coming back to town...and *who* he kept coming back to see.

Desperately she hoped that if there had to be a third shooting in Porter, it wouldn't happen tonight.

"I'M OKAY, DAD. Really. I don't need a nursemaid."

Hershell's long face grew grim. "That doesn't mean you couldn't do with a father. I don't like the idea of your staying alone when you've just come out of the hospital. What if you get worse?"

"I'm not going to get worse, Dad. In fact, the doctor said I could have been released the day before yesterday, but he was out of town and the message didn't get relayed."

"And nobody here noticed that you were well enough to go home, either," Hershell maintained stoutly. He'd seen how gray his boy's face was during those first few scary hours. It was going to take a long time for him to feel comfortable about Larry's health. Besides, Elwood hadn't turned up hide nor hair of a potential murderer. He'd gone to interview Fran and that boyfriend of hers, but they'd claimed to be off at a movie in Washburn together that night. Fran insisted that the same person who'd shot Larry had also shot at her.

Hershell wasn't sure about that. Fran was nasty, but she was sharp. He wouldn't put it past her to stage a fake "attack" on herself to cover her tracks when she shot Larry. He'd suggested as much to Elwood, but he'd said that the evidence indicated that the shots had been fired several yards from Fran's car. She couldn't have fired them herself.

But the boyfriend could have, and he'd told Elwood so.

Elwood had said it was a possibility, but it was obvious that he thought it was pretty farfetched.

"Dad, they kept me so doped up that I didn't know what was going on. Now that I'm on straight acetaminophen, I won't be so groggy. I'm going to check in with Rene and see what's going on at the store."

Hershell's lips tightened. Larry had told him more than once that he needed his father at the hospital more than at the store, and Hershell had pretended to agree. But the sore truth was that even now, with his eye surgery behind him, Larry still didn't trust him to dispense medication. Until Wanda had died, he'd believed that he would still be able to return to Duncan's. Since then, Larry had refused to even consider it. It was so damned unfair! Nobody at Duncan's had done anything the least bit negligent, and Hershell hadn't even been the one to fill the prescription, anyway. At least that's what Larry still maintained.

There's no room for error, Dad, not even the breath of a suspicion, his boy had told him. *Unfounded or not, if we have another lawsuit for any reason whatsoever, Duncan's could be finished.*

He knew his boy was right, and it gave him no comfort to believe that a stranger—a mere slip of a girl—was running things in Larry's absence. Thank God for Maxine! He hadn't had a chance to confer with her much the last few days, but he was planning to join her for lunch tomorrow now that Larry was home, and then he'd get the lowdown.

"If you won't come home, could I at least come back and spend the night? Just in case? I don't want you here alone."

It was then, for the first time, that he noticed the change in Larry's face. It wasn't impatience or irritation so much as embarrassment that darkened his eyes.

"Dad," he said clumsily, "I'm...expecting company this evening."

He got it then. It had taken awhile, too long, perhaps. Or maybe there were just too many things going on for an old man to sort out what was what when he was so frightened for his boy.

He didn't ask who she was. He knew his boy. This would be no casual fling. This would be it. This would be forever.

Unless the damned female changed her mind and left Larry flat.

"You told me she was divorced," he pointed out, fighting a protective urge not unlike the way he'd felt when a teenage bully had beat Paulie up when he was only ten. "You told me she only liked you as a friend."

Larry looked down. He blinked once or twice, but he couldn't quite meet his father's eyes.

"Things have changed. She says she loves me now."

"Some things don't change. She's still divorced."

"She says she's over him."

"Sandra said she was over Ralph."

This time his eyes shot up. "And I'm finally over Sandra."

The assertion surprised Hersh. Gladdened him. "Are you really?"

Larry nodded slowly. "When I look at Rene—" he swallowed hard "—there's only Rene."

There wasn't much Hersh could say to that, at least not out loud. But in his head a voice kept asking, *Does that damn Hamilton girl feel the same?*

He still had never met Rene, not face-to-face. But everything he'd heard about her from Max and Johnnie Sue told him that his boy was being led down the garden path.

Even if the girl had nothing to do with whoever was prowling Porter with a rifle.

But he had a hunch that she did.

SHORTY SHOWED UP hours after he usually did. In fact, the suppertime crowd was already clearing before she got the call.

Johnnie Sue's relief was instant, sweeping, joyful. Almost as great as it had been when she'd seen Larry at noon. He looked so healthy, so happy. She'd almost told him that she'd shot him, just to get the great weight off her chest. But the words were too terrible; they just wouldn't come. Instead she'd promised to bake him a strawberry pie for supper. Now she'd have to send it to his house with Maxine.

And now that Larry was out of the hospital, she'd have to decide what to do about Rene. But that would have to wait until after she saw Shorty.

Johnnie Sue hated feeling helpless. She hated waiting for Shorty to call. Most of all she hated knowing that she'd done the one thing she'd always vowed never to do again: given a man the power to break her heart.

She didn't want to relinquish any more of herself to this man who had such control over her. When he greeted her at the hotel with a chuckle and heart-melting smile, she decided to test her own power by wiping the smile off his face.

He stopped laughing when she boldly thrust her hand down the front of his jeans. His eyes widened as she took him in her hands, then closed as she worked her tough magic. She was proud that she made him groan. He braced himself against her shoulders as she tugged his belt loose and let his jeans fall. Boldly she took him in her mouth.

As she brought him to a quick climax with her nipping teeth, he collapsed dizzily on the bed.

He took a minute to recover, but he was still breathing hard when he pulled her down on his lap.

"That's not bad for a howdy, Johnnie Sue. Beats the hell out of having to wrestle a knife away from you."

She managed to chuckle as he started to undo her hair. He liked to wrap the long strands around his wrists to pull her close. It was a personal embrace that always thrilled her through and through.

His jeans pooled around his ankles, but his solid legs were naked now. Even through her jeans, Johnnie Sue could sense his fresh arousal. It incited her own.

"That first night when you asked me to play games, I thought you just wanted to use me, Shorty. I never figured it could be like this."

He laced her hair through his big fingers and laid them on the front of her shirt. His pinkies nudged her nipples. "Dammit, Johnnie Sue, you make me wish I had a lot more time."

"I've been thinking 'bout what you said before, 'bout wanting more time together," she said bravely, not yet yielding to the fire. Now that she felt back in charge, it wouldn't hurt to give him a little bit of what he wanted as long as she was the one who made the suggestion. "I haven't had a real vacation in five or ten years, Shorty. If we planned ahead, maybe we could go off for a few days. Anywhere, I don't care. But—" Suddenly she realized that he was shaking his head, looking downright disgruntled.

"I wasn't talking about that kind of time, Johnnie Sue. It's a great idea, but we'll have to discuss it next time I'm heading this way. Right now I'm afraid I've got to rush. I'm carrying a load that's got to get to Denver by the crack of dawn. I got a real late start out of Pittsburgh—some turkey at the plant screwed up the order. I shouldn't have stopped at all, but I just couldn't pass this by.'' He grinned and patted her bottom. "I'll drive a lot better now that I got what I came for.''

Johnnie Sue stared at him, suddenly incensed. She'd tried to respond to his plaintive plea for some time together outside this room, and now he couldn't even spare the time to listen to her suggestion! He'd gotten what he'd come for, had he? She hadn't even gotten a kiss!

"How long were you planning on staying, Shorty?'' she snapped. "Five minutes? Ten? Are you planning to leave your money on the nightstand before you go?''

"Oh, for Pete's sake, Johnnie Sue!'' Mechanically he rubbed her breasts. "I didn't mean I didn't have enough time to spare a little sugar for you.''

Angrily she pushed him away. She wasn't sure what she'd wanted this afternoon. Sex, yes, but more than that. Much more. She'd wanted to feel special, really special, to this man who'd become so special to her. She'd wanted him to reassure her, in some unique wordless way, that he'd had nothing to do with shooting Fran. And she wanted to tell him that she'd shot Larry...and that she desperately hoped Larry would forgive her.

"Johnnie Sue, I can stay only another twenty minutes or so,'' he persisted. "Let's not waste what time we've got left.''

He tried to kiss her, but Johnnie Sue pulled away. She jumped to her feet, suddenly too angry to be aroused, too desperate for his reassurance to tolerate his obligatory touch.

"What am I to you, anyway? Just a one-choice cathouse, a quick stop on the road? Isn't it bad enough that you only meet me here in secret for a few hours every time you happen to be driving through? Do you have to insult me by counting the minutes and coming before you even kiss me hello?''

Abruptly he dumped her off his lap and roughly pulled his jeans back on. "You're the one who couldn't wait to get her hands on me, lady, so don't go throwing the blame. And as for these 'secret' meetings, they're your idea, too. You're the one who doesn't want anybody to know you're seeing me. I've made it damn clear that I don't take that as a compliment."

"I explained it to you clear enough. I don't want them laughing at me when it's over. I don't want them feeling sorry for me when you go."

He tucked his shirt back into his jeans and glared at her. "You know, Johnnie Sue, if you'd spent more time enjoying the present and less time worrying about the future this might have worked out."

Sudden panic clutched her heart. She'd just been letting off steam! But Shorty was stuffing his wallet into his pocket. He was picking up his keys.

"What do you mean?" *Shorty, don't leave me,* she wanted to beg him. But Johnnie Sue Rawlings begged no man. He could stomp on her heart before he'd bring her to her knees.

"I mean, right from the beginning, you've been so afraid of how this would end that you forgot to worry about keeping it alive. I've been straight with you, Johnnie Sue. I never made you any promises I couldn't keep, and I never told you any lies. I wanted to come through here and enjoy some time. I wanted you to enjoy it, too. But you're too damn scared of getting hurt to enjoy a damn thing about your life, and you're making it damn hard for me to enjoy *you!*''

He slammed the door on the way out, and Johnnie Sue shuddered right along with the thin hotel walls. She wanted to rush after him, to beg him to forgive her, to make love to her in the twenty minutes he had left.

But that would have been some other woman. Not Johnnie Sue.

Still, a moment later she found herself opening the door just as the engine of the big rig started up. She was about to call out something crusty but forgiving when a couple surreptitiously ambled by her.

She stifled a gasp of recognition as the woman looked her in the eye. The other woman gasped, too.

Johnnie Sue was certain that Fran was more surprised to see *her* at the Washburn Hotel in broad daylight than she was to see Fran. After all, Fran had probably spent more nights and afternoons here than she'd spent in her daddy's home. But now Fran would know why Johnnie Sue was here. And she would make sure that everybody else would know, too.

The sounds of Porter's communal laughter seemed to assail her; she closed her eyes and looked away. Suddenly the big rig was moving, but she couldn't bring herself to run after it. She couldn't bring herself to beg.

For several moment she couldn't think, couldn't move. Shorty was gone and Fran Bixby was right here…with a man whose arm had encircled her waist with probing fingers reaching for her breast.

Johnnie Sue had not seen his face, but she had heard his laughter. Not once, ever, had she heard Seth Rafferty laugh—and anyway why would Fran take him to a beat-up hotel when they lived together?

But she knew that laughter like the back of her own hand. It belonged to a married man. A regular.

A man whose wife meant a lot to Johnnie Sue.

CHAPTER ELEVEN

RENE DID NOT walk straight to Larry's after work, even though she knew he expected her to. He'd called earlier in the day and asked her to drop by and make a report on how things were going after she closed up the place, and she'd told him she'd be happy to.

Maxine had been at her elbow the whole time, of course, insisting that *she* should be the one to make a report to Larry. As soon as she hung up, Maxine had demanded. "Are you going to tell him yet?"

She stared at the prescription on the counter, the one with Fran's name. The small plastic bottle looked like every other bottle on the counter; the only difference was that Rene had only checked the contents of the other bottles once. On Fran's prescription, she had ordered Maxine to watch her remove the cimetidine pills from the receiving bottle, double-check the precise amount, then recount them three more times before Rene placed them in the tiny bottle. She had typed up the label four times because her jittery fingers had made typos on the first three tries. Maxine had reread it for the tiniest hint of an error, and Rene found herself glancing at it about once an hour. Once, in a flurry of nerves, she had even called Doc Swanson and spoken to him herself to make sure that the nurse hadn't made some inadvertent error.

She knew she had made no mistakes. The only question in her mind was whether or not it would have been safer to refuse to fill the prescription altogether. But Fran could have made political hay out of that, too, and Duncan's just couldn't sustain the publicity. Especially now that Larry had gotten shot and the new Pharmafix was open down the road.

"Whether I tell him will depend on what shape he's in, Maxine. The last time I saw him, he looked like hell. But he sounded clearheaded on the phone, and he wants to find out what's going on before he takes his rightful position at the helm. If he's feeling strong when I get there, I'll fill him in."

Maxine glared at her. She was a hostile ally at best.

"Don't you do anything to hurt that boy," she warned. "I'll have your hide if you do."

Rene rolled her eyes, glad that she no longer had to pretend to be nice to Maxine for Larry's sake. "Maxine, I've worked my tail feathers off ever since he got hurt, and I bet he won't even think to pay me overtime. What does it take to convince you that I'm on Larry's side?"

Maxine had no answer to that. She looked sad and sallow as she mumbled. "That boy heals real slow."

Rene wasn't sure whether she was talking about his gunshot wound or his marital heartbreak, but in either case she didn't want to go into it with Maxine. Stoutly she observed, "He's not a boy, Maxine. He's very much his own man. I'm quite sure he can take care of himself."

She wasn't so sure she could take care of herself, however, not in the mood she was in by the time she reached Larry's house. She'd gone home to shower—the humidity was about ninety percent—and put on a clean sundress. It was a white-and-blue seersucker print that made her feel fresh and feminine. Flat sandals on her smooth bare legs gave it just the right touch. If Larry had invited her over as a pharmacist—well, she was free to wear whatever she wanted after work. If he wanted to pick up where they'd left off when he'd been injured, her garb would help them both push Duncan's from their minds.

She took a deep breath and rang the doorbell, steeling herself to tell him the truth about Seth tonight. Unless he was terribly weary or in pain, she knew she had to get it over with. Especially now that Fran would be coming to Duncan's any day.

The door swung open soon after she knocked, and Rene knew instantly that Larry was okay. He was wearing a turquoise polo shirt and a matching pair of cotton shorts that showed off his tanned, muscular legs. His smile was hesitant, but radiantly warm.

"Good evening, Rene."

She swallowed hard. "Hi, Larry."

"You look like dawn."

She swallowed again. "I get pretty sticky working all day. I just took a shower."

He ran a lazy hand through his still-damp hair. "So did I."

She didn't ask why, but her heart started hammering. "Come in," he said, ushering her inside. To her surprise, he locked the door—a rare thing for anybody to do in Porter—and even slid the deadbolt. For a minute she thought that the gunshot had really frightened him, but then he crossed the room to the phone and took it off the hook, too.

He circled back to Rene, met her eyes, watched her in perfect silence.

"It seems to me," he said softly, "that the last time we were alone together, we were rudely interrupted."

A lump surged into her throat. She could feel her body swaying toward him, unfurling like a spring bloom.

"You were telling me about Sandra."

He shook his head. "No, I was finished with Sandra. I got shot while I was kissing you."

She licked her lips. He wanted her; she could see it in his eyes. Her hormones started to do tiny somersaults of anticipation. She suspected that his hormones were dancing, too.

"Do you want a report on the store before we…pick up where we left off?"

He grinned. It was a grin she'd never seen on Larry's face before. Unmasked anticipation. Open desire. "Not unless it burned down while I was gone."

Her own smile was a full confession of her priorities this evening. Seth would have to wait. She would not—could not—spoil this perfect moment.

"That's not where the fire is," she admitted.

Larry's grin widened. Then he sobered, and a tense kind of hunger stole across his face.

No foreplay could have roused her more. She felt a quivering, quiet, but intense, buildup inside her body. Tonight was going to be the night. This time, she was certain, he would not back away.

Still, he did not kiss her. He took a step closer, his eyes still on her face. He seemed to be savoring the sight of her, savoring the night to come. Slowly, as though she were made of something quite fragile, he cupped one breast.

Rene closed her eyes and stifled a whimper.

One thumb swept across her nipple. Left, right…left one more time.

She bowed her head. Her body was in flames.

"Yes?" Larry whispered.

"Oh, God, yes."

Her nipple was trapped between two deft fingers as his lips claimed hers unerringly. Rene's hands slid around his waist, down to his hips, pressing them against hers. She could feel his free hand cradling her nape; warm fingertips carved intricate designs of delight in her hair.

This kiss was not like the others they had shared. Those had been hot and hopeful; they had aroused her sensual needs but not her confidence. This time there was no hesitancy in Larry's body, no question in his touch. Only an urgent need to please her.

"Oh, Larry," she whispered against his mouth. There was so much she wanted to tell him, so much she wanted to share. But at the moment the simplest of words seemed overwhelming. Her mouth was meant to be an instrument of pleasure.

Each kiss grew more intense, each embrace more heated. Weeks of banked passion kindled and flamed.

Rene wore no slip and no hose. It took him only an instant to slide his hand under her panties, tangle those probing fingertips in her dark, hidden hair. She never knew just when he pulled off the silken fabric and lowered her to the couch. Suddenly she was on her back beneath him, naked from the waist down. Her full skirt bunched inoffensively in unimportant places. Larry's fingers worked magic between her legs.

She kissed him again, embracing him fiercely until he stifled a sharp cry. Despite her own keen arousal, Rene knew it was not a cry of pleasure. Appalled at her own selfishness, she burst out, "Oh, Larry, I didn't mean to hurt you! Are you really well enough for this?"

"I'm well enough, but I could probably be more careful," he confessed, still stroking her intimately. "This might work better if I stretched out on the bed and let you get on top."

Rene raised no objection. The only problem she had was enduring the thirty touchless seconds or so when he had to stop fondling her to walk to the bedroom. On the way he asked her about birth control; she told him she still had an IUD. Then she undressed him quickly, stopping only once when she saw the bandage still covering his chest. He told her to ignore it and concentrate on more important parts of his anatomy.

Taking the hint, she tried to give him the same rich pleasure he'd so eagerly offered her. He grew even harder as she gripped him with both warm hands, and her arousal spiraled as he teased her nipples while she stroked him.

To think I didn't always love him, some part of her mind recalled in disbelief. *To think I once thought of him as a brother.*

He pulled her closer, gripping her thighs as she straddled his torso. As he took one nipple in his mouth and lashed it with his tongue, his thumbs edged forward to part her legs with deft, electrifying strokes. Rene slid backward until his erection pressed between her legs. She was on the edge, almost beyond control, but she didn't want to rush him. Ever since they'd met, he'd held back; she'd pressed him to love her. She didn't want to be the aggressor in their lovemaking, not this time. Not until she was sure he wouldn't change his mind again tomorrow. Not until she was sure he wouldn't say she gave him little choice.

"Please, Rene!" he begged her, teasing both taut nipples with his fingers. "Please tell me you're ready. I'm not going to last."

She didn't ask him for any clarification. She angled herself just right as she slid over him and he plunged in. Instantly she was in a frenzy, a frenzy that knew only Larry's name.

His own response was just as fierce.

For a long while thereafter, conversation was out of the

question, but when Rene's heart ceased to thunder, she asked softly, "Are you sure I didn't hurt your wound?"

"I'm tougher than you think I am, Rene," he whispered against her throat. "I've got enough strength to enjoy this all night as long as you don't beat on my chest." He patted the bandage on the left side...a few inches from his heart.

It was right then—and not a second sooner—that Rene remembered Seth.

She didn't want to talk about her marriage. She didn't want to do anything to spoil this perfect night. But if she didn't take the risk now, everything could be destroyed tomorrow.

"Larry," she forced herself to begin, "I need to talk to you about some things."

"Tomorrow," he whispered, his tongue curling in the shell of her ear.

"But Larry, I really—"

"Tomorrow, and that's an order," he repeated, his lips moving down her jaw to her throat in the most incredibly delicious pathway. "I'm the boss, so don't argue with me."

For the rest of the night, he *was* the boss. Neither his wound nor his doubts nor his gentle, loving nature got in the way of his determination to give Rene every imaginable sensual pleasure...and to demand the same for himself. As he whispered the words of love she'd waited so long to hear him say, she was putty in his hands, and she made no effort to conceal it.

The only thing she wanted to conceal from Larry Duncan was the truth about the reason she'd first applied for a job in Porter. The more she yielded to her love for him, the more terrified she was that she might lose him once he knew the truth.

"HERSHELL, WE'VE GOT trouble," Maxine gushed in a half whisper over the Duncans's Cornsilk table. "I don't know how bad it is, but…Orville and I think you should know."

He was tired. He didn't want to think about trouble. After keeping a vigil by Larry's bedside for so many days, he'd brought his boy home yesterday and then gone back to his own house and slept all afternoon. By midnight, he'd been wide awake and prowling around the town. He'd knocked on Johnnie Sue's door, but she hadn't heard him. This morning she was as grumpy as a hibernating she-bear rousted from her winter nap, so he figured it was just as well he hadn't troubled her, anyway.

"What's going on, Max? Did that new girl mess things up?"

"It's not that, exactly, Hersh, though there is a problem there." She looked angry more than frightened. "But Frannie's causing trouble again. Doc Swanson prescribed her some ulcer medication."

"From Duncan's? That's crazy!"

"That's what I said, but Rene said it would be better not to make a fuss. She had me double-check the pills a couple of times to make sure she got it right. I'm not even going to mention it to Larry till Fran picks it up. That way if there's any problem, Fran can only blame it on Rene."

"Are you sure the Hamilton girl didn't make any mistakes?"

"I'm sure. I checked the prescription again after she left. Besides, she's always very careful about medication, and she seems really worried about messing up anything for Larry."

He cleared his throat. "Is she sweet on him? I mean *really* hooked?"

He hoped so. He didn't even know the girl, but he honest-to-goodness hoped so. Because Larry was lost, and

Hershell didn't think he could stand it if some floozy broke his boy's heart again.

"It's hard to tell," maintained Max. "Most of the time she's pretty cool about everything, including him. But the night he got shot, she was hysterical. And she wanted to stay with Larry. She tried to go to the hospital with him, but I made it clear that she'd just be in the way."

He didn't answer. He suspected that if anybody had asked Larry, he would have been thrilled that Rene cared enough to follow him.

"But some things have been bothering me. I mean, let's say Rene's in love with Larry. Let's say she wants to protect Duncan's from any more trouble because of him."

Hersh nodded.

"Let's say that Larry's actually babbled everything about Fran and the lawsuit to this stranger he's known less than a month, so that's why she knows where Fran lives, how awful Fran is and who Fran's living with in her daddy's house."

Hersh narrowed his eyes, getting her point at once. "Larry wouldn't tell her all of that. He probably doesn't even know her boyfriend's name."

"Exactly. But Rene knows it. And she knows he's from Des Moines."

"Lucky guess."

"The night after somebody shot at Fran I was driving past Clancy's on my way home from choir and saw Rene's little red car in the back lot. At the time I thought it needed service, especially since she walked to work the next day and she'd always driven before. But when I asked her later if Henry'd done a good job for her—just trying to be friendly, you know, 'cause Larry ordered me to—she didn't know what I was talking about. I got to thinking, why was she parked at Clancy's if he wasn't working on her car? And then I got to thinking, why was Fran parked at Clancy's the night someone shot at her if he wasn't working on *her* car? And then I got to thinking about what Fran does with anybody, and I figured out what Rene was doing, too.''

He studied her quietly, fighting a curious nudge of nausea. ''You think Rene's got somebody else.''

''I sure do.''

''And you think you know who it is.''

''I *do* know who it is.'' Her smile was triumphant. ''I got it from Johnnie Sue. She's known for a while now, but it took me some doing to worm it out of her. She's been stalling me, but last night I asked again, and she was in a terrible mood and snapped out the answer just to make me go away.''

''Johnnie Sue knows, too?'' He was wondering why nobody ever told him anything. If Max and Johnnie Sue thought he was too old to know what was going on, he really should just curl up and die.

''The night after the shooting, Frannie's boyfriend came in here. He met Rene after work.'' She paused while he absorbed the fact, then gritted his teeth when she dropped the punch line. ''He had a key to Rene's red car.''

Hershell felt sick. Truly, deeply, profoundly ill. Why hadn't Maxine told him yesterday, before Larry had invited Rene to spend the night with him? Why, oh, why had she waited until it was too late?

''I didn't want to burden you while you were worried about Larry, Hersh, and I didn't think she could do him much harm until he got well. I never dreamed that things had gone so far. I thought I'd have more time! But based on the way he came in whistling this morning, Hershell, I think I made a terrible mistake.'' She blushed. ''I'm pretty sure Rene spent last night with him.''

Hershell didn't deny it. If Larry were some other sort of man, it wouldn't matter. But the whole damn town knew that Larry didn't make love to a woman unless she owned his heart.

"When he asked me how things had gone in his absence, I just told him that Rene had done all right. I couldn't bear to tell him everything Johnnie Sue's found out, not when he looked so damn happy. She's been working on a plan to get rid of Rene, but until Larry got back on his feet, he needed her running Duncan's too much for us to risk chasing her out of town."

Hershell felt weak and old and tired and murderously angry with the Hamilton girl. "Out of all the men in Porter, why did she choose Frannie's fellow?" he demanded. "What kind of lousy luck is that?"

"Luck had nothing to do with it," Maxine snapped. "Rene didn't meet Seth Rafferty here in Porter. She *followed* him here." She leaned forward tensely as she delivered her final gut-wrenching blow. "That scheming bitch used to be married to Frannie's beau."

TO SAY THAT Larry returned to Duncan's renewed, refreshed and well on the way to recovery would be an understatement. He felt as though he were soaring. He knew that he'd burn out by mid-afternoon and need to go home and rest, but at the moment he felt terrific. Rene, on the other hand, after a week of twelve-hour work days under great stress, desperately needed to sleep in and probably get caught up on her shopping or housework or laundry. He'd left her asleep with a loving note asking her to come in to work by two or three, promising to discuss the nature of her "overtime duties" after work tonight.

He knew he looked ridiculous. No man who's just been released from the hospital ought to be walking around town positively beaming. But he truly had never felt happier in his life.

Somewhere, deep in his memory, he knew that he should be holding something back. He knew that Rene had once loved another man deeply. But she'd told him that the flame had died and the ashes were stone-cold, and after last night, he believed her. Surely no other man's name had filled her heart when she'd cried out her pleasure in his arms.

He loved her. And he finally believed she loved him.

He wished he could have shared the news with Maxine, but she spent the whole morning scowling and fussing over him. It was a mighty busy morning, anyway—it seemed like half the town had shown up just to take a look at him. He felt like putting up a sign charging admission: Local Pharmacist Shot in the Chest But Lives To Tell His Story.

By ten o'clock he'd told his tale a dozen times. He almost asked Maxine to postpone lunch so he wouldn't be left alone with the masses, but she seemed quite determined to take off at exactly twelve o'clock. Even though he was fielding several customers, he didn't try to stop her. She'd been logging extra hours during his absence, too, and she was probably as tired as Rene.

But lunch hadn't improved her spirits any. She was edgy and actually snapped at a customer or two. He wanted to ask her what was wrong and see if he could help, but business never let up. Normally he'd look upon such heavy consumer traffic as good news, but unfortunately most of his friends and neighbors were more interested in the state of his health than the state of his business.

Rene had done a good job in his absence. There didn't seem to be any big glitches. The prescriptions had been filled; the records were up-to-date. A month ago a trip to the hospital would have spelled disaster for Larry; either he would have had to let his father come back to run the place or else he would have had to shut down. And if he'd done that, half of the people who would have had to visit Pharmafix might not have bothered coming back.

It was almost two-fifteen when he spotted Fran Bixby marching in the front door. She was the last person he wanted to see this afternoon, but he refused to let the sight of her spoil his good mood. Because there had been no further trouble over Wanda Carmichael's death since Joel had recognized that Wanda herself was responsible for mixing the drugs against the advice clearly stated on the pill bottle from Duncan's, he'd stopped worrying much about Fran. Why on earth was she here now?

"Good afternoon, Fran," he greeted her as civilly as he was able.

"You're alive, I see," she said coolly.

He nodded, feeling a curious sympathy for the difficult woman. Now that he'd been shot, he had a lot better understanding of her panic on the night somebody had fired at her. "Elwood making any progress on your case?"

She shook her head. "Not a damn thing. I think the same guy tried to shoot you." She chuckled without mirth. "Actually I'm glad some joker did try to kill me first. Otherwise Elwood would probably think I'm the one that shot you."

He didn't share her sense of humor. The thought had crossed his mind that she and her boyfriend had staged a phony shooting precisely so she *could* shoot him later. After all, *he* was the one who'd had a bullet pulled out of him. Fran hadn't even been nicked.

"How can I help you today?" he asked professionally, hoping to curtail her visit.

"That damn fool doctor called in my prescription here

by mistake. I told him to call it in to Pharmafix, but I guess he forgot.''

He watched her eyes and realized that she'd never told Doc Swanson anything. Either she'd forgotten to ask for a new pharmacy after so many years of dealing with Duncan's or she'd hoped to find some new way of stirring up trouble.

"Hold on, Fran. I'm sure it's right here." As he checked the shelf behind him, he found the prescription at once. A quick glance at the label assured him that Rene had typed it with care. The dosage sounded sensible. He couldn't see the color or shape of the pills through the umber plastic, but he knew that if he opened the bottle, Fran would question him.

He decided not to risk giving the enemy ammunition. He trusted Rene.

"I bet this was called in while you were in the hospital," Fran caustically observed, foiling his hopes of subtlety. "Who took over for you here? You damn well better not have let that doddering old dad of yours fuddle my pills."

Larry felt the back of his neck flame, but he tamped down his temper. "My father hasn't worked here in some time, Fran. This prescription was handled by my assistant, Miss Hamilton. She is a highly qualified pharmacist from Des Moines. She came to me with the finest recommendations."

He hoped his very personal pride in Rene didn't show on his face. Even facing Fran, a downer if there ever was one, he still felt too full of joy to really feel depressed. He couldn't even summon up much anger with her today.

But a sudden well of fury blackened Fran's face. *No,* he corrected himself quickly, *it's not fury so much as fear.*

"You don't mean *Rene* Hamilton, do you?" It was a

whisper. It was a gasp. "Larry, for God's sake, tell me Rene Hamilton isn't *here!*"

In that instant, he knew. He didn't know the details, couldn't make the connection, couldn't imagine the pertinent facts. But every instinct in his body told him that his original doubts about how Rene had chosen Porter had been grounded in common sense. She had lied to him. She hadn't chosen Porter at random to escape big city woes. She'd come here quite deliberately for some surreptitious reason. A reason that had something to do with Fran.

A reason that might have something to do with the shootings.

How could she have deceived him after they'd shared so much? Unless they hadn't really shared it. Unless she'd faked everything right from the beginning.

Unless she'd played him for a sap.

Last night she told me she loved me, another voice cried out. *And, God help me, I believe her.*

As steadily as he could, he told Fran, "Rene Hamilton works here, Fran. And I assure you, you couldn't be in better hands pharmaceutically."

"I don't give a damn about the pills, Larry!" she hollered at him, increasing the dread in his heart. "Rene lives for her work; I know she's good at that. But there's only one reason she could possibly have come to Porter!"

He didn't want to know what reason, but he knew he had to ask. Besides, Fran was getting hysterical. Even if he'd begged for her silence, she would have told him anyway.

Trying to still his trembling, he asked, "Why do you think she's in Porter, Fran?"

"Why the hell do you think?" she shrieked. "To get her husband back!"

CHAPTER TWELVE

RENE HAD WAKENED up late, stretched like a cat and read Larry's loving note before she'd wandered home to shower and change. She'd spent most of the day enjoying Beverly Bryan's latest romance, and now she was ready to enjoy the sight of Larry's loving face. She still tingled from the night before, and she was counting the minutes till she could join him in bed again.

She left her hair loose except for a fancy clip on the side. She wore another sundress under her smock. This one was watermelon pink. She took the time to do her nails in a matching color and dig out the one pair of tiny hoop earrings that matched. Despite the sturdy nurse's shoes she had to wear to counteract her foot fatigue, she felt a little bit glamorous.

One look from Larry and she knew she'd feel absolutely beautiful.

But it didn't work out that way. When Rene strolled into the store, Maxine was handling the counter. The woman had never been friendly, but today she looked at Rene with unmistakable malevolence. "Larry's in the back. He wants to see you right away," she growled.

At first, Rene was not alarmed. If Larry had told Maxine that the two of them had finally worked out their troubles— or even if she'd guessed—it was likely that she'd pout and disapprove. Rene was certain she'd get over it in time.

But when Rene slipped into the back room—her whole

system crying out for the joy of Larry's smile—she realized in an instant that something was terribly wrong.

He was sitting at his desk, facing the doorway, but he did not raise his eyes to greet her. He looked almost comatose. He was gray.

She rushed to his side and knelt beside him. "Larry, do you need a doctor? Is it your chest? Or did you just overdo it and—"

Just as she reached out to touch his arm, he moved sharply, brushing her aside. When his eyes met hers coldly, his fury could not be denied.

"Larry?" she whispered, stepping back as though he'd hit her. "What's wrong?"

Could she have imagined that wonderful night? Those magical moments, those hours in his bed? Never, in all the time she'd known him, had she seen Larry look like this. She didn't know that he had a hard side, didn't know what had happened to bring it to light. She only hoped that whoever he was mad at, he wouldn't take it out on her.

And then, she knew. She read it in his stony visage as clearly as if it had been chiseled there. Somehow, some way, he'd found out about Seth. There could be no other explanation.

She fought the wave of nausea. Trembling, she sat down. Desperately she tried to think of something she could do.

He did not speak. He stared at her as though he'd never seen her before, never kissed her, never cuddled her in his bed. As though he'd never said "I love you," or whispered words about forever. Never brought her hope that she'd found a new home.

"Fran Bixby picked up her prescription a while ago," he said tonelessly. "It appears that she's acquainted with you."

Rene glanced down at her watermelon-pink nails. She

had to say something! But it seemed futile when Larry looked at her that way.

Beads of sweat erupted on her face. She realized she was shaking.

"I...I did come here because of Seth, Larry," she finally managed to murmur, "but I realized it was a mistake almost right away. After I fell in love with you, I realized that what had happened with him didn't matter anymore." Desperately her eyes met his. "I didn't lie when I told you he was gone from my heart, Larry. I didn't lie when I told you how much I love you."

He was looking at her, but his eyes were blank. He continued as though she had not spoken. "I'm in no condition to work full-time yet, so I'd appreciate it if you'd stay on until I can replace you. I've already sent out the word that I need help. I'll work nine to three; you work three till closing. Your work here at the pharmacy has been above reproach, so I'll give you a good recommendation if the question ever arises." For the first time a spark of feeling lit his deadened tone. "Other than that, I don't want to have anything more to do with you."

He stood up as though to leave, but Rene jumped up and blocked his retreat. "Larry, for God's sake, listen to me. I've been trying to tell you about Seth for days. The night you told me about Sandra, I meant to tell you everything. But when we started kissing I forgot all about him, and then you got shot!" Her own voice sounded strange to her, almost incoherent. She was starting to cry, which further muffled her clarity. "After that you were in no condition to hear bad news! Still, I told you in the hospital we had to talk as soon as you felt better; I told you last night again."

He looked exhausted. He looked ill. He looked utterly implacable. "Rene, you lied to me," he repeated, as though that said it all. "You came here to try to get your ex-husband back. What more do I need to know?"

He started to march out, but she still couldn't let him go. She grabbed his arm, pulled him to a full stop, swallowed the terrible tears that all but rendered her voice inaudible. Her panic was swirling out of control.

"When I found Seth with Fran, I just straightened my chin and walked out, Larry. I didn't fight for him. I never asked him for a second chance." Her voice shattered as she gave up trying to check the stream of tears. Her grip on his forearm tightened. "But I'm *begging* you."

He didn't answer. He just pulled her hand off his sleeve as though she were a leech he'd picked up by mistake in the old Porter swimming hole.

"I've read this book before, Rene. I know how it ends," he told her tonelessly. His eyes met hers as he delivered the killing blow. "I'll be damned if I'll read even one more page."

JOHNNIE SUE HAD SEEN Fran sashay into Duncan's, then storm out again. A moment later she'd ducked into Dixie's Dress Shop, about halfway between the Cornsilk and Clancy's.

So far, Larry hadn't come out of Duncan's. But Rene had sailed in.

She waited, feeling helpless as a mother hen watching a fox take her baby chick in its mouth. She'd tried to keep an eye on things for Larry. She'd found out what she could about the girl. But she'd been so rattled by the shooting that she hadn't quite figured out how to handle the situation without hurting him further. And then last night, after Shorty had roared off, all of her capacity for rational thought had just disappeared.

All night she'd stewed about him, tried to remember his

angry words. She'd told herself that he was a pretty hot-tempered guy, and God knows, she had a short fuse herself. They'd had a spat; it didn't mean anything. If she had chased him off with a knife that first time, a few harsh epithets shouldn't mean much to a man like him.

He'd promised never to leave her without saying good-bye. She'd reminded him of it once or twice since then. And she believed—she really did believe—that she mattered a little bit to him. He wouldn't leave her hanging. If he really meant to end it, he'd send her word. If he didn't, he'd be back when he cooled off and passed this way again.

He had to come back. She'd lost her damn fool heart to him.

Half an hour after she'd last seen Fran, Maxine buzzed in. Gert was right behind her, fussing, as usual, over some new problem with Julie's pregnancy. The baby had started kicking up a storm, keeping the poor girl awake all night. Johnnie Sue didn't tell her that she would have given anything to have been kept awake by a baby who'd lived long enough to kick. But she kept her eyes on Maxine, waiting for the word.

"He looks just awful," Maxine murmured as she slid into the booth, waving to Lotty as she wheeled herself through the front door. "He had more color in his face when I saw him in the hospital."

"Who looks awful?" Gert asked. "Is Larry having a relapse?"

Maxine shook her head. Johnnie Sue wanted to tell her to shut up, to give Larry a tiny drop of privacy, but she knew that Gert wouldn't let it rest. If she felt the need to root around for more information she was likely to spill the beans to somebody else.

Maxine relayed a blow-by-blow description of Larry's

falling out with Rene, supplying her own dialogue for the few words she'd failed to overhear. It was obvious that she was glad the girl had gotten her comeuppance, even though Larry was the one who was surely bleeding.

"You've had it in for Rene right from the start, Max," chided Lotty. "She's a good girl. You gals hate her because of Hershell, but she kept that place going while Larry was laid up. You got to give her credit for that. Larry's sure never had any complaints about her."

"He's in love with her, Lotty!" Maxine burst out. "He can't see the forest for the trees."

"Well, I say it's about time! He's suffered long enough. You have no call to bad-mouth the girl just because—"

"Just because she lied to him? Just because she did just what Sandra did? Came to Porter to get her husband back?"

"Sandra didn't come to Porter to get her husband back," Johnnie Sue pointed out. "Her lousy husband followed her here."

"Same difference. In fact, in Rene's case it was even worse. She pretended to love Larry just so she could keep working in Porter!"

This last comment was from Gert, and to Johnnie Sue's surprise, Maxine grudgingly defended the girl.

"Well, that's not quite true, Gertie. We were so desperate for somebody that Larry would have hired her if she'd been old and ugly and male. And he never would have fired her for not falling in love with him. From what I could tell, everything was going along fine at the store until she started chasing after him."

"See?" crowed Lotty. "Why would she chase after Larry if she wanted that other man?"

Nobody had a good answer for that, though everybody contributed a suggestion.

"So what happened when Fran said Rene used to be married to Seth? Larry just fired her like that?"

"Well, he made a few calls to Des Moines to his friends who usually dig up recruits for him. He didn't say a word about Rene. Just that he needed to have more help."

"And what did Rene have to say to that?" Gert asked.

Maxine shook her head. "I don't know. All she cared about was convincing Larry that she loved him. To hear her talk, she didn't give a damn about her job."

While Maxine opined that this was proof that she'd never cared about the job anyway, it made Johnnie Sue wonder if the poor girl really did love Larry after all. Nobody had less patience with romance than Johnnie Sue, but even *she* had been on the verge of begging her man for a second chance last night. Of course, he hadn't broken things off the way Larry had; he'd just left in a huff.

She still believed he'd be coming back. He simply had to.

"She's been cooking something up," Maxine maintained. "I didn't trust her right from the start. You remember what I told you, Gert? The night I found her hiding out in Clancy's parking lot?"

"At first you thought she was with Henry," Gert said bitterly. "I wouldn't put it past the two-bit bastard."

From Johnnie Sue it was an everyday word, but from Gert it was downright blasphemy. She didn't want to think what Gert might do if she found out that Fran was carrying on with Clancy at the Washburn Hotel. With any luck at all, Johnnie Sue could nip that in the bud before it ever got back to Julie. Even so, she was tempted to cut out his damn heart.

It was while she was thinking about Julie that she considered how any wife was likely to feel in her situation. And while the girls continued to talk, her mind began to come up with fertile notions. Julie would never have the gumption to make a man pay for his sins the way Johnnie Sue would. But Rene was another kettle of fish.

Suddenly it struck her like a gale-force wind. Maybe Rene hadn't come here to get Seth back from Fran! Maybe she'd come here for revenge! Maybe she *had* tried to shoot Fran!

No matter what she wanted, wasn't it possible that she had, at some point along the way, genuinely fallen in love with Larry? It wouldn't be hard for any normal female her age to do.

Johnnie Sue was about to play devil's advocate and drop a startling notion or two when Fran Bixby stomped in the door. She looked flushed and almost frightened. *Small wonder,* Johnnie Sue thought uncharitably. *She's just learned how the shoe feels on the other foot. And she won't have a leg to stand on if I tell Seth I saw her sneaking into a room last night with another fellow.*

She slid into a booth as far away from the other women as she could, for which Johnnie Sue was grateful. With any luck at all, she could get rid of the bitch without any of them finding out about Shorty.

And they couldn't find out. It was more important now than ever. Now that he might not be coming back.

"Excuse me, ladies," she sarcastically declared. "I have to sweep some vermin out of my establishment."

Maxine chuckled and even Lotty covered her grin. Gert mumbled, "Sally Haywood told Julie that Fran's got an ulcer. If anybody ever deserved to have her insides eaten up, it's her."

Johnnie Sue wholeheartedly concurred. But she wasn't about to indulge in any more gossip until she booted Fran out the door.

Armed with half a dozen purchases, Fran had barely

settled into the booth when Johnnie Sue marched over. She wasted no time in chitchat, no artificial smiles.

"I told you not to come back here, Frannie. Just the sight of you curls my stomach. And I don't even have an ulcer."

Fran straightened. Bright spots of color mottled her cheeks. Johnnie Sue suddenly realized that Fran's beauty was the fleeting kind, the kind that would leave with her youth. She was a hollow shell inside; once she couldn't entice men with her body, she'd grow old, ugly and alone.

"You and I have business to discuss," Fran hissed. "I came here to make you a deal. If you didn't see me last night, I didn't see you." Her eyes burned desperately into Johnnie Sue's. "Fair enough?"

If she'd been anybody else, it would have sounded square to Johnnie Sue. But from Fran Bixby, no promise was worth spit. Besides, the information about Fran's Washburn Hotel rendezvous might prove helpful to Hershell somewhere down the road. Or even to Larry, depending on what he decided to do with Rene when he calmed down.

"I don't make deals with the devil, Fran," she said softly, her voice dark with unspoken threat. "Now, I'm telling you once more—get out of my place. And don't come back."

She'd planned to stare Fran down, to wait until the other woman crawled away, but suddenly a big rig pulled up outside, just sitting there in front of the Cornsilk, miles from the main highway.

It wasn't red and white. It had no stripes. It didn't say "Big Shorty" on the side.

But when the driver—a hard but decent-looking stranger—bopped inside a moment later, she knew that he hadn't just happened to drop by.

She rushed to meet him in the doorway—half hopeful, half afraid. Whatever he had to say, she didn't want Fran or the girls to hear him. And she couldn't wait another minute to hear what he had to say.

"You run this place? You Johnnie Sue?"

His voice was crusty, indifferent, almost amused.

She nodded. It was hard to speak, but she managed to croak out, "What can I do for you?"

He shook his head. "Nothing. I just got something to say for a fella named Shorty."

Terrible claws gnawed at her stomach. She felt almost dizzy with dread.

"Said to tell you he don't owe you nothing but a message, and he's hell and gone to Florida this week. He wants you to know that he didn't forget the contract, or the deal, or whatever the hell it was between you two."

Johnnie Sue didn't really hear the rest of what he said; she was feeling faint. It was as though her head had drifted off from the rest of her body and was watching from somewhere far away. She was already miles off when he concluded, "Said to tell you sorry, but goodbye." He shrugged his shoulders, as though he had no idea he was pummeling a dead woman with a piece of pipe. "Goodbye with a capital *G*."

NOBODY HAD ASKED for Hershell's opinion. Not about Larry, not about Rene, not about Fran Bixby's beau. He had some damn creative theories, but he wasn't about to voice them yet because they seemed too farfetched.

The only good thing that could be said about this latest fiasco was that Larry had had the good sense to make it a clean break. Hershell didn't give a damn if the girl was hurting. She'd had it coming. She'd lied to his son.

But he was still troubled by *why* she had lied…and why

she had come to Porter. And he was troubled by why some-body had shot Larry and why somebody had shot at Fran. And, worse yet, he was troubled by the notion that some-body in town might get shot again.

The only thing he was sure of was that there hadn't been a shooting in Porter for six years before Rene had come to town, and Elwood had had no trouble solving the last one.

Hershell had gone to see Larry right after Maxine had told him the news. He'd volunteered to fill in until Rene could be replaced. He'd all but begged Larry to let him back into Duncan's.

Larry was sitting in an old armchair, staring blankly at a spot on the wall. "Rene knows her job. She'll do it right. I'm well enough to work at least six or seven hours a day."

"But you don't have to, son!" Hershell had insisted. "I can help you out. I could just run things up front and let the prescriptions pile up if that's the way you want it. Wouldn't you feel better if you just ran the girl out?"

It had been a mistake. In fact, until that moment, Her-shell had never fully realized how Larry felt about Rene. Oh, he knew he'd been entranced, aroused, eager to let her fill up the jagged hole that Sandra had left in his heart. But he had not understood that the woman had the power to *break* his boy. Not so completely. Not so soon. Rene had captured him in weeks. It had taken him months to fall this hard for Sandra.

"I can't just dismiss her. She's got to find another job first or it would wreck her reputation."

Hershell was astounded. "Is that your problem? She's the one who got the job under false pretenses. She's the one who chased you around the store and—"

"Don't, Dad." Two words, spoken with strength and despair.

They were the last two words Larry said for about an hour, even though Hershell made him a sandwich, served him a cold soda and reminded him to take his painkilling pills. Eventually he left him there, staring at that dirty spot on the wall, oblivious to his father's presence.

"You call me any time, son. You know I'll be up in the wee small hours if it gets too dark in here. I can come right over. Aggie won't mind if I leave her."

Larry didn't answer, so Hershell went on home.

MERCIFULLY post-injury fatigue put Larry to sleep right around dark, and he didn't wake up until nearly nine. It was as though an alarm clock went off in his head. He was groggy for a bit, but his memory came back soon enough. Nine o'clock, the time he should have been expecting Rene to join him.

Join him in bed.

He felt sick all over again. He battled the despair. He wondered if she might come over and plead with him, try to decide how he'd handle it if she dared.

In the end, he took the coward's way out. He drove out to his father's.

Hershell looked deliriously glad to see him, so glad, in fact, that Larry wondered just what he'd said or done when his dad had been at the house that afternoon. All he was sure of was that the dim light from the living room looked wondrously inviting, and he was certain that Rene would never track him there.

He didn't actually decide to spend the night. After all, sleep was out of the question. The two of them slouched in the living room—Hershell in his favorite recliner chair, Larry on the old couch—while the evening's mindless television fare blurred into late night news and a forties'

B movie. It was so forgettable that Larry forgot who was starring in it halfway through.

It put his dad to sleep around one o'clock, though, for which he was grateful. And it kept his mind just occupied enough that he was able, for maybe ten or fifteen seconds at a time, to blot the vision of Rene's tear-streaked face from his mind.

Maybe I should have let her explain. Maybe she really does love me. He tried to believe the hopeful lies, but reality always got the best of him. *It doesn't matter. It could never work. Seth will always be there, right here in Porter, right there in her heart.* She'd said it was over. Last night she'd made love to Larry as though she'd never slept with another man in her life. Could she really have faked that much feeling?

He remembered the look on her face in the hospital, the way she'd told him she loved him after she'd thought he was asleep.

Oh, hell, I might have been asleep. I might have imagined everything.

Had he imagined the way she'd screamed when he'd been shot? Or the way she'd stroked his head so tenderly and battled Maxine for the right to go with him in Clay's car? Or the way she'd looked when they'd joined for the first time—not triumphant but rejoicing and grateful? Or had he imagined that, too?

When the phone started ringing at 4:00 a.m., he assumed it was she.

He almost rushed to pick it up; yet he dreaded touching the damn thing.

He knew it would change nothing. It was over. He had to let it be.

He had a sudden vision of Rene in trouble, Rene with Seth at the bus stop. Rene, not Seth, getting shot.

She might be hurt. She might be scared and lonely. It might even be somebody else calling to report that she was hurt or scared or lonely.

I never asked him for a second chance, she'd pleaded. *But I'm begging you.*

He picked it up on the thirteenth ring, cursing himself for waiting so long…cursing himself for answering it at all.

"Hello," he snarled. He had to say it twice before the voice on the other end of the line answered. It was a woman, but it wasn't Rene. It was a voice he knew as well as he knew his own father's, yet it didn't sound like anybody he'd ever known.

"Aggie?" Johnnie Sue whispered eerily. "Is that you?"

A ghostly shiver shook him to his feet. A chill slithered up his spine. His dad talked to his mother all the time, and Larry was never quite sure whether he was speaking wishfully or whether he'd gone clear off the deep end. But Johnnie Sue never even spoke *of* Aggie, let alone *to* her. After three years, even when she mentioned her, she called her "Larry's mother" or "my old friend."

Now she was saying, "Aggie? I know it's too late, but I really need to talk to you."

Larry felt sick. Johnnie Sue was losing it. She sounded drunk, but she wasn't a drinker. Some dark pain, darker even than his own, seemed to slur her words.

"Uh, Johnnie Sue, it's Larry," he said. It sounded ridiculous. Johnnie Sue knew his voice in her sleep, and nobody in their right mind could ever have mistaken his deep male voice for his mother's. "Mom's, uh, not available right now. Is there anything I can do for you?"

Johnnie Sue giggled. It was a high-pitched, squirrelly sound, the kind of sound that Gert might make. He couldn't believe that Johnnie Sue even had the necessary vocal chords to reach those high decibels.

"I know she's gone, Larry," Johnnie Sue whispered in a ghostly tone. "But sometimes I just need to talk to her so bad...do you know what I mean?"

"Yes," he said uncertainly. "I, uh, I really miss her, too."

"Your daddy misses her. He talks to her all the time. I wish I could talk to her, too."

He felt helpless, confused. "Maybe you'd like to talk to Dad about her," he suggested. He'd loved his mother dearly, but he'd put her to rest. It seemed to him that his father might be able to relate better to Johnnie Sue in her current mood. On the other hand, his dad depended on Johnnie Sue so desperately that his own fragile foundation might be rocked if he saw her when she was falling apart at the seams.

"Is he sleeping?" Johnnie Sue asked. "He usually sleeps with me."

Larry did a double-take until she giggled again. "Oh, I don't mean he sleeps with *me*. But he sleeps here on my table, Larry. But he didn't come tonight. I waited ever since that man drove off. But Hershell didn't come and Aggie isn't there and I don't know what to do."

That's when she started crying. It shook him to the core. Larry had never been able to resist a crying female, and he always found comforting them an uncomfortable, awkward chore.

But this was different. He would have sworn in court that Johnnie Sue did not know how to cry. In all the years he'd known her—and, except for his dad, he knew her better than any man alive—he'd never seen her shed a tear. Not even when his mother had died.

"Johnnie Sue, you stay right there. Don't do anything,

don't go anywhere. I'm leaving this *instant*. You wait for me. Promise me!''

He couldn't keep the panic out of his voice. He felt the way he had when he'd first read the telegram that said Paulie was MIA. He wanted to wake up his father, but it would have taken precious moments to explain the situation, and he didn't have a second to spare.

When he heard the line go dead, he grabbed his keys and bolted out the door.

RENE PACKED the last of her suitcases and stashed it by the front door. Maybe it was cowardly to run away like this, but she knew she couldn't face Larry again. To work beside him—even in his absence, Duncan's radiated his essence—was more than she could bear. If he'd loved her enough to forgive her for the past, she could have endured Maxine's knowing glances and even the knowledge that Fran was probably having a good laugh. But he'd given her not the slightest room for hope. She supposed she should thank him for that.

She glanced at the suitcases, then—foolishly—made the bed. She'd already written a note for Lotty, thanking her for her kindness, leaving her an extra month's rent and promising to come back with a U-Haul trailer in a few days. She didn't explain why she was going; the whole town would know by tomorrow if they didn't know by now.

Larry would be surprised when Greg Finch showed up at Duncan's this afternoon, but when he understood what Rene had arranged, he'd be glad. He and Greg had a lot in common; Greg had recently suffered a serious injury, too. He didn't want to go back to work at his old job in the dangerous part of Des Moines, but he didn't have another job yet and hadn't quite decided where he wanted to go. He'd been getting a little bored and restless, anyway, and, mercifully, he understood how desperately Rene needed his help.

"I can't go back there, Greg," she'd explained on the phone. "Not even for an hour. But I can't leave this man without help. I simply cannot walk out on him unless I know my hours are covered. I can't do that to him."

"Make up your mind, Rene," Greg had replied at first. "Either this guy is an ogre or he's a saint. He can't be both."

"He's not either," she'd told him truthfully. "He's a man I desperately want to marry who's told me to get out of his life."

There had been a moment's silence. Because her heart was breaking and there was no one to help hold her up, she'd confessed the rest to him. "Seth and Fran live here, Greg. I came here for all the wrong reasons, and then I made things worse by falling in love with my boss. He loves me, too, but when he found out about Seth, he didn't...want to take a chance on me anymore."

Greg kindly put the rest of the pieces together. "I'll fill in for you for a few weeks, Rene. But I think you're being too hasty. If all this just happened—"

That's when she'd broken down. "Greg, I just can't stay!" she'd burst out, weeping. She didn't remind him that the moment she'd learned that her marriage to Seth was over, she'd taken off, too.

It was four-thirty in the morning when Rene's phone rang. It was not yet light. It couldn't be Greg! Surely he wouldn't cancel out on her. And yet, who else could it be? In the whole time she'd lived in Porter, nobody had ever called her but Larry and Maxine...and Maxine only called when Larry told her to.

Her heart was beating all too rapidly when she picked

up the receiver. "Rene Hamilton speaking," she said uneasily.

There was a pause, just long enough for her to draw a painful breath. Then Larry's beloved voice said, "Sorry to wake you up at this hour, but I need you to come on down to the Cornsilk."

Rene blinked twice. She was wide awake and already dressed—or rather, still dressed; she'd never gone to bed. But Larry was acting as though giving her phone orders in the middle of the night was an everyday thing. He'd never been so thoughtless even when they'd been close. After the way they'd parted yesterday afternoon, how could he possibly expect to snap his fingers and watch her run?

She had begged him. She remembered that. And she was willing to do almost anything to get him back.

But there was something wrong with his voice. The tension was terrible. His tone held no hope. And why was he asking her to meet him at the Cornsilk? It wasn't even open at this hour. Nobody would be there but Johnnie Sue.

"Larry, what's wrong?" she asked quickly, her love for him all twisted up with a new brand of fear. "Has something happened over there?"

The silence was longer this time, the wait more terrible. At last he said with poorly feigned calm, "Rene, remember that you once told me you were good at cutting hair? Well, Johnnie Sue would like to try a new style. Why don't you come right over and bring a pair of scissors with you?"

The tone of his voice was scary. Even though she was certain that somebody—Johnnie Sue?—was listening, his bizarre comment made no sense. She'd told him once that she'd cut Seth's hair back in the days when they couldn't afford a barber, but she'd done it very poorly. And she'd never cut a woman's hair!

She'd only seen Johnnie Sue's hair in a bun, but it was

surely very long. There were three beauty salons in this small town. And nobody, especially a fashion failure like Johnnie Sue, could possibly have decided that a haircut was a life or death affair at four o'clock in the morning.

And that's when it hit her: the only life and death affairs in Porter involved two shootings. Elwood had never come up with a single likely suspect. In the movies, a bizarrely coded call like this usually meant that somebody had been taken hostage.

"Larry," she asked as calmly as she was able, "do you want me to call Elwood? Do you want me to come armed?"

"Absolutely not," he snapped, as though she'd lost her mind. "Don't let a soul know what you're doing. *Secrecy is absolutely vital.* I called you because I need discretion, Rene. You're the only woman I know who won't blab a word of this to anybody here in town."

She hadn't believed that anybody could have made the nightmare of the last twenty-four hours any worse, but Larry had just done it. There was something terribly wrong at the Cornsilk, probably concerning Johnnie Sue. Larry was involved or trying to straighten out the mess. Rene had assumed that he'd called her because he'd realized how much she loved him. She'd assumed she was his first choice when the chips were down.

As she slipped down the stairs and started to run toward the center of town—knowing that a car's engine would alert Lotty to Larry's secret—she realized humbly that Larry had not weakened in the slightest. He had called her only as a last resort.

She also realized that if Larry's shooter was at large tonight, there would be absolutely nobody to call for help if he tried to gun her down.

CHAPTER THIRTEEN

THE FRONT DOOR to the Cornsilk was unlocked, but that didn't reassure Rene very much. The streets were silent, absolutely still. Not even the roosters had started crowing.

She felt her way through the darkened coffee shop. The booths and countertops looked strangely eerie under the distant blinking neon sign. It seemed like a scene out of a science fiction film.

Vaguely, toward the kitchen, she could see a dim light. She knew that Johnnie Sue's living quarters were back there somewhere, but to her knowledge, nobody had ever seen them. Even joining her in the kitchen was considered an honor, an invitation to the inner sanctum.

She heard a voice as she crossed the spotless kitchen. It was Larry's. His voice was gentle, low, as steady as a mantra. He seemed to be discussing the weather.

"The hottest year was '62, my mother always used to say. She'd hang out clothes on the back line and bring them in again before the washer finished with the next load. But Paul always said that the hottest year was the one he pitched for the team. The swimming hole dried up in June and he thought he'd go crazy. Do you remember?"

There was no reply before he continued his litany. "We kept the sprinklers on in the front yard and just crossed back and forth through the stream of water all the time. I kept thinking that Mom would rag on us for dripping water in the house, but by the time we got inside, there wasn't a loose drop on us anymore. Now that's got to be the hottest year, don't you think, Johnnie Sue?''

The door to the little room was open, so Rene was able to stand there for a moment to get her bearings before she went in.

The room itself was about fifteen by twenty. A twin bed scrunched against the wall in one corner; a dresser hogged another. One small bookshelf perched under the window. It was full of paperbacks. By the covers, Rene could tell that most of them were romance novels—her favorite free-time reading, but the last genre she would have expected Johnnie Sue to read.

When she spotted the portable stereo, the neat stack of folded linen and the half-dozen rifles in the rack above the bed, Rene realized, with an inward gasp, that this wasn't a bedroom in the conventional sense of the word. This was Johnnie Sue's entire home outside of the Cornsilk proper. What personal life she had existed in this small room.

Although everything in the room was tidily snugged in its proper place, there was one blaring sign that something had gone terribly awry. In half a dozen spots—on the curtain rod, on the bookshelf, on the floor—were foot-long chunks of oyster-colored hair. A Roy Rogers knife lay on the floor.

Johnnie Sue was sitting on the bed. Larry sat close beside her. His frantic eyes were on Johnnie Sue; one hand gently stroked her back. But Johnnie Sue did not seem to see him. She seemed oblivious to the condition of her bizarrely short-cropped hair. It stuck up at jagged angles all over her head as though some small demon had taken possession of a razor.

The fear that had gripped Rene all the way to the Cornsilk took on a new form of life. At the moment, she was less afraid of the mysterious shooter than she was afraid of what had happened in this room tonight. A woman hard as nails had splintered right down the center of her crusty core.

Rene made a tiny sound to alert Larry to her presence. Johnnie Sue did not seem to notice.

"Rene." One word, laden with relief.

Desperately she wished that his love for her had something to do with the gratitude, but she knew he was moved by his love for Johnnie Sue, not for her.

"I'm glad you had some time to drop by. Johnnie Sue thought she'd like a new haircut. She's a stubborn old cuss and wanted to do it by herself and save some money. But that's pretty hard to do, you know. So I was telling her how good you got at cutting Seth's hair." He said the name as though they'd discussed Seth a dozen times. "And I said, 'Why don't I call up Rene and ask her to fix you up before the Cornsilk opens in the morning? That way nobody'll ever see you looking less than your best. You'll have oodles of compliments by breakfast.'"

His eyes were pleading, *begging* Rene to understand. And she did understand, more than she'd once have thought possible. For all her coarse bravado, Johnnie Sue was a woman just like Rene. And, just like Rene, something had happened to crack her. She looked every bit as broken as Rene had the night she'd found Fran with Seth...and she probably felt as rudderless as Rene did now that Larry had tossed her out of his life.

She had no idea what had happened to Johnnie Sue, but she was sure that the devastation of her once-waist-length hair was the symptom of her despair, not the cause of it. Still, Larry was right. At the moment, nobody knew she'd gone berserk but Larry, who'd never tell a soul, and Rene, who wouldn't have a soul to tell. If they could get Johnnie Sue acting normal by daybreak, she might have a chance of holding on to her cherished role as Porter's resident termagant. If she greeted her regulars in her present condition, life would never be the same for Johnnie Sue.

"No problem, Lare," Rene declared with all the confidence she could muster. "I'm a whiz with a pair of scissors. I'll have Johnnie Sue looking like the belle of the ball in no time."

She watched his shoulders slump with relief. He took a minute to let Johnnie Sue get used to the idea—or maybe just to assimilate the fact that the posse had finally arrived—before he stood up and said gently, "Let's go out to the kitchen where you can sit in a straight-backed chair." He picked up the Roy Rogers knife lying on the floor, obviously the weapon she'd used for the massacre of her hair. When Johnnie Sue didn't move, he tugged on her hand. "Let's go, Johnnie. Time's a wastin'."

After that it was Rene who took over, Rene who chattered nonsensically while she trimmed and cut and combed the whopper-jawed strands of hair. Under the best of conditions, it would have been hard for her to cut a woman's hair. She only knew how to do one cut, and even then she'd just been cutting back growth, not changing the shape. At the moment, Johnnie Sue's hair *had* no shape.

Rene worked from the perspective that anything would be an improvement. Besides, what was important was not what style she created, but rather the illusion that Johnnie Sue *had* a style—any style—in mind. Her image was so brusque that a very short, mannish cut actually suited her. Besides, between Rene's limited skill and Johnnie Sue's limited remaining hair—some of it only an inch or two long—it was the only thing she could do.

While she cut, she talked. And when she ran out of meaningless, cheery things to say, Larry took over. When the cutting was finished, Rene hauled Johnnie Sue into the shower, insisting that the haircut would look much better after a shampoo and blow dry. Fortunately Johnnie Sue did have a dryer—an ancient one, but it worked—and her hair did look a bit fluffier once Rene was through. She wouldn't go so far as to call the cut attractive, but it did look more or less intentional. If Johnnie Sue could muster her usual panache, she could sell her regulars on it.

Deliberately she steered Johnnie Sue toward her usual jeans and bright shirt, reminding her that her new hair cut was both pert and practical. Johnnie Sue went through the motions of getting ready for work, docilely accepting her directions. But there was no sign of life in her eyes, no indication that she was ready to do what she must do.

Moments before Sam was due to arrive, Rene took Larry aside. "Maybe we should just say she's got the flu and put her to bed. Everybody gets sick sometimes. The regulars will believe it."

He considered the suggestion but dismissed it. "No. It's like walking a horse with colic. I'm afraid if we let her go down she'll never get up again." He seemed to choke on the words. "I've never seen her like this, Rene. I checked the place over. She hasn't had a drink. No drugs. This zombie you're looking at is just the result of something inside her that broke. Now we've got to find a way to tape it back together until she can start to heal."

"Maybe your dad could think of something, Larry. You've always said they were awfully close."

He shook his head. "They are, but...it's a relationship that requires her to be the stronger one. I think being strong for him might help keep her going. And I'm not sure he *can* keep going if he sees her like this."

He studied Rene for a moment, eyes full of anguish, not all of which was due to Johnnie Sue.

She heard the front door open. She heard Sam call out cheerfully, "'Mornin' Johnnie Sue."

Suddenly Larry crouched down beside her. "Sam's here, Johnnie. You've got to go out there and act like yourself. I know you can do it. You're tough as nails, remember?"

She looked at him with the forlorn hopelessness of a kitten trapped in the rain. Slowly she shook her head. "Larry, I feel like a squashed bug."

Larry looked overwhelmed by this confession, but it gave Rene hope. At least Johnnie Sue was talking. Clearly she knew what was going on around her, despite her pain. It was the best sign she'd seen in over an hour.

"Johnnie Sue, I know you're hurting like hell. And when you're ready, you know I want to hear all about it. Maybe I can make it right. Maybe—"

"You can't make it right. Nobody can make it right. I had a chance, a real chance, and I blew it. I was too scared to reach out and grab happiness with both hands."

Larry rocked back on his heels just a bit, and Rene could guess what he was thinking. After all these hours of trying to console her, Johnnie Sue was finally responding to his attention. When it was almost too late.

But Rene suddenly realized that Johnnie Sue had been assimilating the situation, slowly coming back to terms with herself. She knew that the haircut would work, knew that she almost looked like herself. In a perfect world, she would have had more time to get herself together, but Porter's world wasn't perfect. Time was running out. Johnnie Sue needed one quick jolt to get back on her feet, and Rene decided to give it to her.

She crossed the room quickly, stepping in front of Larry before he could stop her. "Sam's here, Johnnie Sue. The whole damn town will be here in a minute. You want me

to go out there and tell them all you're too much of a wimp
to face them all?''

Larry gasped.

Johnnie Sue slapped Rene in the face.

Larry gasped again.

Johnnie Sue stood up, cheeks suddenly red, chest heav-
ing. ''Damn you, girl! You'll answer to my .30/30 if you
ever call me a wimp again.''

Fiercely she elbowed Rene out of the way and stormed
out to the kitchen. ''Goddamn it, Sam, you're late!'' she
hollered, although it was just now five thirty-five. ''How
many times do I have to tell you to get your tail feathers
in here on time?''

Larry was staring at Rene—glaring at her, actually—but
his ears seemed trained on the kitchen. Then, quite suddenly, he grinned.

''You did that on purpose,'' he cheerfully accused.

''Damn right I did,'' Rene agreed, rubbing her tender
cheek. ''I sure hope it was worth it. I'm going to be bruised
for another week.''

Larry laughed, keeping his voice low so Sam couldn't
hear him. The bedroom door was half open, and a curious
man might have tried to look in.

''I don't know how to thank you, Rene,'' he said soberly. ''You probably saved her life.''

Rene thought that was probably overstating the case, but
she figured she'd made a fair contribution to Johnnie Sue's
public image. ''Do you know what happened, Larry? Did
she get some bad news from somewhere? Was she dumped
by someone?''

''Dumped?'' He looked stunned. ''As in...a *man*?''

She nodded.

''Rene, she hasn't looked twice at a man in thirty years.
And even if she did, what man would look twice at *her*?''

"My point exactly." The room began to grow strangely quiet. At last she spoke the words that had filled her heart ever since she'd arrived. "Larry, my mother always says, 'I'm a woman and I know a woman's heart.' And quite frankly, all my female instincts tell me that right now Johnnie Sue feels about the way I do."

His expression darkened. "You don't have any trouble getting men to look at you, Rene."

"That's not what I meant and you know it."

He shook his head. In the early morning light, his face looked terribly gray. Abruptly Rene remembered that he'd only been out of the hospital for a couple of days and he'd surely been up most of the night. This wasn't the time to burden him with her own problems, to beg him for one more chance.

But she knew she was going to do it, anyway. This was the last time she'd ever be alone with him.

"Larry, at the very least, please let me explain. Please let me—"

He laid one hand on her mouth. It was a caress as much as a restraint. His eyes looked terrible; his face looked gaunt. "It doesn't matter, Rene. I could never trust you. I could never be sure."

Tears filled her eyes. The strain of the night was taking its toll. "Larry, I love you desperately," she admitted, her voice breaking on the words. "You told me that you loved me. Wasn't it true?"

He slipped both hands in his pockets, as though to keep from touching her face. He studied her for an endless moment, a moment so long that fresh hope almost bloomed before he rendered it stillborn with his words.

"I'm grateful for your competent work at Duncan's. I'm grateful for your help with Johnnie Sue. As to the rest of my feelings—" his voice grew hard and his beautiful brown eyes shut her out ''—they no longer have anything to do with you.''

IT WASN'T EASY, but Larry smuggled Rene out the back door by the storage bins, then circled back in the front as he sometimes did for breakfast. He wanted to be on hand just in case Johnnie Sue needed some back up. And he wanted to keep busy so he didn't have to think about those moist green eyes that had begged him for love, for hope, for a future.

How many women, he asked himself, would have come at his call tonight? Only hours before he'd tossed Rene out of his life, and virtually fired her, and yet she'd come the instant she'd realized he needed her help. She had no call to help this tough old bird, and yet she'd done it selflessly. He owed her for that. He owed her for taking such good care of his store.

''Well, looky here. Johnnie Sue done lost her hair! Got carried away with one of them knives, Johnnie Sue?'' asked Henry Clancy as she sloshed hot coffee in his cup and some on his hairy arm.

''I'll damn well cut off your private parts if you make any cracks about my hair,'' Johnnie Sue groused with her usual aplomb. ''It was just too long. Got in the way, like some fellows I could mention.''

''I think it looks pert and practical,'' said Larry, quoting Rene as best he could.

Johnnie Sue tossed him a glare that was riddled with gratitude. ''It gets the job done.''

Johnnie Sue got the job done, too. Although there were moments when he thought she looked shaky—and once when she disappeared a bit too long in the back—she spent the next hour slinging insults and hash in her usual peppery mixture. By the time he left for the store at eight, he was reasonably certain that the worst was over. Later, he'd check back with her privately, though she might deny it had ever happened. And he'd subtly find a way to ask his dad to keep an eye on her today.

Bleary-eyed and weary, he unlocked Duncan's and slipped inside. It was daylight now—hot and steamy—and he wondered how he could possibly work through the morning until he was supposed to be relieved by Rene. She was probably as tired as he was, so he couldn't bear to ask her to come in early. And, besides, he needed to marshall his defenses before he saw her again today.

The shock and the anger were beginning to fade. Now when he looked at her—when he looked at her smock hanging by the desk—it was easier to remember the pleasure. Not just the joyfully sensual night they'd spent together, but all the tiny moments of friendship that had bloomed between them during their usual workdays. Rene subtly deflecting Gert's endless chatter; Rene smiling despite Maxine's chill. Rene in the hospital, touching his hair, confessing her love in a whisper.

Her face haunted him as he ambled through the pharmacy and sat down at his desk in the back. That's when he saw it—an envelope addressed with only his first name. He knew her writing, knew what that letter would contain. Another plea. Or even an explanation.

And then, quite suddenly, he realized that it would also be a statement of her intent to resign.

When I found him with Fran, I just walked out, she'd told him. Was it a warning? Or just a pattern he could have broken if he'd figured it out in time?

Larry tore the envelope open in a rush. He panicked at the first line: ''I know this couldn't be a worse time for you to be short staffed at Duncan's....''

"No!" He slammed his fist on the desk. "Damn it, Rene, no!"

He kept on reading, clenching and unclenching his fist. The assurances that followed the first line did little to soothe him.

I have made private arrangements to hire you a substitute. My friend Greg Finch, the one who was injured in the holdup (no, I didn't lie about that), is at loose ends right now, and I've persuaded him to bail me out of this awkward situation. He will report to you today during my assigned hours and will continue to work for you until you find a suitable replacement. I'm well acquainted with his work and I'm sure you'll have no complaints.

She went on for several paragraphs explaining details of various accounts and informal conversations with customers that she felt Larry would need to know about. He wondered why she didn't just tell him in person before she left—it would have been much easier—and then he realized, with a sudden elevator-drop to his stomach, that Rene intended this letter to serve as a last goodbye.

It may be cowardly of me to go like this, Larry, but I can't bear to rub shoulders with you every day when I see such ice in your eyes. I came to Porter for Seth, but I stayed because of you. If your love for me has vanished overnight, there is nothing for me here, and many reasons why I should go.

I have made separate arrangements with Lotty, and she will have a forwarding address for me in the event you should change your mind. I will not be too proud to come back if you can bring yourself to forgive me, and I hope to God you won't be too proud to ask.

With love for you always,
Rene

He read the note three times before he realized that he didn't give a damn about Greg Finch. The man's reputation may be top-notch, but he wasn't Rene. And Rene was the only other pharmacist he wanted at Duncan's Drugs.

She was the only woman he wanted in his life.

HERSHELL DIDN'T CARE for Johnnie Sue's hair. Not one little bit. He'd been looking at her with her hair on top of her head for twenty-odd years, and this short-cropped stuff wasn't Johnnie Sue. It made her look like a man.

Of course, she did *act* like a man, in lots of ways, but that didn't bother him any. Johnnie Sue was just…Johnnie Sue. Tough and strong. Savvy. Always there for a friend. She was more of a sister to him than Lotty, and he loved Lotty quite a lot.

There was something wrong with Johnnie Sue this morning, and he didn't think it was her hair. Her hands were edgy. Sometimes she snarled at folks, like she did when she was in a bad mood, but when she was in a bad mood, she rarely ignored a zing or two. She'd smiled tolerantly at half a dozen good-natured insults hurled her way just since Hersh had arrived at eight-fifteen.

She hadn't seemed any too pleased to see him. When he'd asked if she'd seen Larry, she glared at him and said the boy had been in for breakfast and where he spent his days and nights was none of Hershell's business. He had a sinking feeling that she knew something he didn't—like that Larry had slunk back to Rene like a dog with its tail between its legs when he'd left Hershell's house last night.

He'd found Larry's car on the street in front of Duncan's when he'd wandered into town at dawn, but that didn't mean Larry hadn't walked from the drugstore down to Lotty's place. Chances were good he'd spent the wee small hours of the morning with Rene.

Hersh had barely stuck his fork in his scrambled eggs when Larry himself bolted out of the front door of Duncan's and jogged across the street. He barely said howdy to Johnnie Sue before he slid into their regular booth.

"Dad, did you mean what you said about wanting to come back to Duncan's so much you'd even work if I didn't let you fill prescriptions?"

Hershell's eyes widened. He choked on his eggs. "I meant it," he muttered when he could talk.

"I thought I was ready to come back to work, but I'm just plain burned-out. Even before the shooting, you know how long I put in those terrible hours."

"I know," said Hershell. He didn't add that he had volunteered three million times to help ease the burden.

"I want to take a few days off right now. I need you to supervise everything while I'm gone."

Light flooded Hershell's heart. Duncan's to himself for the next few days! He wanted to jump up and run across the street and kiss the bells on the back door.

"I can do that," he promised staidly. "But you gotta tell that damn girl that I'm in charge."

Larry's lips tightened. "She won't be there. I've got a replacement coming in today. Name is Greg Finch. Good recommendations. But he doesn't know anything about our operations. I want you to keep an eye on things."

Hershell nodded. He was getting the picture. Larry needed to go off and lick his wounds for a while. That was okay. It was just a matter of time before everybody here knew what had happened. Maybe by the time he got back the subject would be put to rest.

"Now, Dad, you've got to promise me that you'll let Finch fill all the prescriptions. I mean it. I don't want you selling anything but aspirin."

Hershell made no effort to conceal the fact that he was sorely offended. "I've been running that pharmacy since before you were born, son. I'll be damned if—"

"Promise me, Dad. Look me in the eye and promise me."

He glanced down at his eggs, unpalatable now. "Larry you don't even know this young whippersnapper."

"Promise me."

"Son—"

"Promise me right now, or I won't go."

There was a strength in the command that Hershell had not heard in his boy's voice before. He wondered, as he often did these days, when his son had grown to be a man. Could it really be more than thirty years since he'd been running around in diapers?

Hershell met Larry's eyes and asked in a low tone, "Did you really think I killed Wanda? Did you add your initials to her prescription to cover for me?"

Larry did not look away. "Yes, I did, Dad."

"You thought I messed up that bad? You thought I wasn't man enough to face the music if I had?"

For a long while Larry did not answer. His eyes were grave. At last he said, "It looked like a choice between my dad and my professional reputation. There wasn't really much of a choice to make."

Tears burned Hershell's eyes. "Paulie wouldn't have done it," he said softly. It was not an accusation. It was an acknowledgement of the son who'd always stood by him the way Aggie had taught him to. "Nobody's ever given me a finer gift," he whispered.

Larry glanced around, then squeezed Hershell's bony wrist.

Hershell had to swallow hard before he promised, "I'll let Finch fill the prescriptions. They can pile up on the counter and folks can stay sick while they wait. They'll probably all go down to Pharmafix and the damn store will have to close."

When Larry released his father's wrist, his eyes welled with something Hershell hadn't seen there in a long time. Gratitude. Respect. A filial feeling much stronger than obligatory love. "Thanks, Dad," he said softly. "You better get on over there. I'm leaving right away."

Hershell didn't wait for an engraved invitation. He shot out of the seat like a missile leaving the launch pad. But Larry was faster. He was already halfway out the door.

RENE WOKE ABRUPTLY to the sound of someone pounding a few feet from her ear. She glanced at her watch and realized that it was already past eight. She'd meant to be long gone by now. But she'd been so fatigued when she'd returned from the Cornsilk that she'd curled up on the couch for just a moment to catch her breath and have a good cry. Now the sky was full of bird song, and light was streaming in.

"Dammit, Rene, let me in!" Larry shouted through the door. "I know you're here. Your car's still in the lot. I'll get a key from Lotty if I have to!"

Rene blinked twice and shoved her hair out of her eyes. She dragged herself across the room and pulled the door open. "Not everybody's up at this hour, Larry, and you're making enough noise to wake the dead," she pointed out tersely, too sleepy to care if she sounded cross. "Forgive me if I didn't rush right over to the door the minute I heard your imperial knock."

He stared at her, looking a bit chagrined. He also looked

breathless, as though he'd been running. And he looked as fatigued as she.

"You were…asleep?" he guessed.

Rene was too tired to put up any defenses. Besides, what was the point? She'd made no secret of her devastation. "It's been a long night. I got fired yesterday, the man I love told me to get the hell out of his life, and I had to give somebody who hates me a hair cut in the middle of the night. I didn't think an hour or two of shut-eye was really out of line."

Larry glanced down at her suitcases and swallowed hard. He was quite pale. In some ways he looked just as frightened as he had when he'd been trying to cope with Johnnie Sue.

"I…I'm sorry," he murmured. "It didn't occur to me that you might not be awake. I was afraid you wouldn't talk to me. When I found your note, I was afraid you were already gone."

"Logistical error," she admitted wearily. "I was getting ready to leave when you called. By the time I got back I was just too worn out to drive."

His eyes bathed her weary face, then settled somewhere in the vicinity of her throat. "Rene, may I…may I come in?"

She realized then that he was still standing in front of the door. Some of her neighbors were leaving for work or bouncing off to summer school. Whatever came next, she knew she didn't want to share this last discussion with anybody else.

She opened the door and stepped back, closing it behind him. Then she returned to the couch, perching uncertainly on the arm. Larry followed her, taking a seat in the armchair across from her. He leaned forward as he watched her, resting his elbows on his knees.

"Rene...I was so eager to catch you before you left that I really didn't think of what to say."

Her eyes lifted to meet him. She didn't dare hope he'd changed his mind. And yet, when he was so close and smelled so good, what else could she possibly hope? What could she say?

"I felt sick when I read your note," he admitted darkly. It was obvious that they were difficult words. "I can't imagine Duncan's without you. You've simply got to stay."

Rene shook her head. She closed her eyes, unable to face the pleading she read in Larry's. "I feel awful about leaving Duncan's at a time like this, but I just can't bear to be...so close." She stumbled over the word, the memories, the shattered hopes. Then she confessed, "Just the sight of you is torture."

When he didn't answer, she opened her eyes and met his with all the strength she could muster. "I know you're hurting. I know you think you mean nothing to me, that I lied to you about everything and played all sorts of games. It probably hasn't occurred to you that you're not the only one who feels like he's been run over by a herd of horses." She felt fresh tears flooding her eyes again and battled to dam them. "But I'm hurting, too, Larry. I'm dying inside. You've got three dozen people in this town who'd do anything in the world to protect you and buck you up while you're down. But I'm all alone here. I've got to go back to Des Moines."

"There's someone...special there?" he asked tensely.

Rene wanted to slap him the way she'd been slapped by Johnnie Sue. "I have a close girlfriend or two there," she snapped. "And no haunting memories of you."

His eyes met hers, met and held with a boldness she

hadn't seen in him before. "Does Seth know you're going to leave?" he asked bluntly.

"Seth's probably forgotten I'm here!" she burst out. "I only talked to him once, the night after Fran was shot, and *he* came looking for *me*. But not because he wanted me back; he just wanted to know what was going on." Now the tears were impossible to block. "I told him that I loved you, and he told me that he loved Fran. We talked about what went wrong and parted as friends. I don't ever expect to see him again." She covered her face with both hands. "I never expected to see you again, either. When I wrote that note, I never expected to get a midnight call from you."

"Rene, that couldn't be helped. I thought Johnnie Sue was going to do something crazy. I'm terribly grateful that you helped me put her back together."

She stood up, still trembling, but determined to get a grip on herself. "You already told me that, Larry. And I've already told you that I can't work for you. I'd like to be on my way now unless there's something else you came to say."

He did not rise. "There's something else I came to say."

Rene sat down.

He ran two nervous hands through his hair. Sweat pearled along his upper lip; hard choices visibly debated in his brown eyes. For a terrible moment he stayed silent. Then he reluctantly confessed, "I don't want you to leave, Rene."

She didn't know what he meant. She didn't know what to say.

"I'm not talking about Duncan's. I don't want you to leave *me*."

Rene gulped back another sob. She closed her eyes and trembled. She waited for him to touch her, to make everything all right. She waited for his explanation, but it wasn't what she wanted to hear.

"I don't feel right about what you've done. I don't trust you. I feel stupid. You played me for a sap." Each angry word was like a punch. "I'm hurt, Rene. And I'm mad as hell."

It was hardly a speech that spoke of reconciliation, but at least he was sharing his true feelings with her. And he was no longer trying to send her away.

Then he declared with ruthless honesty, "I don't feel right about giving you another chance. I think it's a mistake. I'm pretty damn sure I'm going to regret it later."

Rene's eyes flashed open. She didn't even try to conceal the desperate hope that rippled across her tear-streaked face.

"Are you—" she swallowed a terrible lump "—thinking of giving me another chance, Larry? A chance to explain?"

He glared at her. "I'm not sure it'll do any good. Truth to tell, Rene, I doubt if I'll believe you."

Her eyes met his with fresh determination. "I'll tell you anything you want to know. Anything. No matter how embarrassing or painful."

He tugged thoughtfully on his mustache. "You've already admitted that you followed your ex-husband here and he turned you down flat. How much worse can it get?"

She shook her head. He *had* to understand this point. "He didn't turn me down, Larry. I mean, not in Porter. By the time I saw him, I didn't want him anymore. By then, I—"

"I've heard this spiel before. If you've got any other nasty secrets, I want you to spill them right now."

Rene was getting angry. Maybe it wasn't worth begging Larry for another chance, not if he was always going to beat her over the head with her past sins. Love could not flower in a relationship devoid of trust. "There's nothing left to tell," she snapped. "I made a mistake. But it was only a matter between Seth and myself. It had nothing to do with you." This was one point she had to make him understand. "By the time I first hinted that I was falling in love with you, I'd already turned my back on him."

Larry was watching her closely, and she knew that his next words would be crucial. He would either send her away or take her in. Either way, the anguish of uncertainty would be over.

And then the front door swung open. "Rene?" Lotty called out as she wheeled into the apartment uninvited. "Are you okay? I got a call from one of the neighbors. Said some man was hollering at you." Suddenly spotting Larry, she glowered and glanced at her watch. "And it's only eight o'clock in the morning!"

Rene could see a line of red sneak up on the back of Larry's neck. "I'm sorry, Lotty," he mumbled. "I'm afraid I sort of lost my temper with Rene."

"Your mama raised you better," Lotty squawked.

"So she did. But my mother's got nothing to do with this. Rene and I need to talk alone, Aunt Lotty." He started to shut the door, but Lotty's wheelchair jammed him aside.

She whirled into the suitcases immediately, knocking them askew. Rene jerked upright. *Damn, it's bad enough having to face Larry. I can't bear to face Lotty, too.*

Lotty glared at the suitcases, then at Larry, then focused fiercely on Rene. "You going somewhere? You just barely moved in here, little girl."

Rene tried to speak; she tried to gesture toward the envelope with Lotty's name on it that perched so openly on her desk. She wanted to point out that she'd paid a hefty deposit and left a full month's rent. But before she could speak, Larry beat her to the punch.

"She's not moving out just yet, Lotty. She's just going away for a few days."

Rene's eyes flashed up to meet his. Was he kidding himself? Did he think he could talk her out of quitting? *Not without a clean slate between us, Larry,* her eyes warned him fiercely. *I won't be your employee if you hold me at arm's length.*

"We've both been working too hard, Lotty, so we're going to take the weekend off. I just dropped by to pick up Rene." His eyes never wavered from Rene's. "Dad's going to supervise the guy I hired to fill the prescriptions and Maxine's going to supervise Dad. We'll be home Sunday night. Rene can tell you all about it then."

Rene could not speak. She could not take her eyes from Larry's face.

"Where you going?" Lotty asked suspiciously.

"Dubuque." He said it as though it were the first city that sprang into his mind. "And we're in a hurry. I'll take Rene's bags down to my car if you'll get out of the way." Before Lotty could answer, he grabbed both suitcases and bolted down the stairs.

Lotty's shrewd eyes made it clear that she was only getting half of the story, but she didn't offer any objections to Larry's arbitrary game plan.

Neither did Rene.

CHAPTER FOURTEEN

AT THE TIME, it seemed like a lifetime while Rene tried to fob off Lotty's questions and Larry brought his truck around. She had no idea what he had in mind, but it was obvious that he didn't want to talk about their situation to Lotty and equally obvious that he didn't want Rene to leave town. Her bags were packed and Larry had them. There was no logical reason why she couldn't sail off with him wherever he wanted to go.

And many compelling reasons to do so.

When he pulled up in front of her apartment he pointedly sounded the car horn, enabling Rene to toss a quick good-bye to Lotty while she locked the door. She scurried down the steps just as Larry reached across the seat to throw open the door. He pulled away as soon as she slipped inside.

He didn't talk until they reached his house just moments later. As he braked he said gruffly, "I'd like you to make a quick call to some chain hotel in Dubuque and make reservations while I put some clothes together. Grab some sandwiches or something, too."

He started to get out of the car, but Rene stopped him with a firm hand on his wrist. She was more than willing to follow Larry's lead, but she couldn't hang in limbo for another minute. They were alone again. She simply had to know what he was thinking.

"Larry, don't you think we ought to talk this thing

through?'' she asked gently. ''Don't you think you ought to give me a clue as to what I can expect if I charge off to Dubuque with you?''

He glanced down at her hand as though it were a large, unsavory spider. Slowly he met her eyes.

''I thought you'd want to go with me.''

''I do! I mean, I want to do…whatever it takes to work things out.'' Her eyes were filling with tears again. Desperately she battled them. ''But I'm confused. You don't act like a man who's taking his ladylove on a romantic weekend for two. I feel like I've been kidnapped by somebody who'd be happy to put a bullet through my head.''

Again he studied her hand, but he did not touch her. Great sorrow lined his weary face. ''Rene,'' he finally admitted, ''I've been up all night. I'm not a hundred percent well. I'm probably going to be mad at you for quite some time. I need a hot meal and a hot shower and about twelve hours' sleep before I'll be fit company, and it may be that long before we can really have a sensible conversation.'' Bleary eyes met her own. Sadness and defeat colored his hopeless words. ''In the meantime, I don't want to lose you.''

Her fingers splayed out on his arm. Her desperate grip tightened. ''Larry,'' she whispered, ''are we going to be all right?''

He looked awful. Exhausted, angry, miserably sad. She knew that other things had contributed to the state of his countenance, but a lot of it could be laid at her door. She half wished she'd never laid eyes on this man. She'd brought him nothing but heartache.

Slowly his hand crept up to cup her face. She relished the miracle of each warm finger. She felt like a parched stalk of corn celebrating the first spring rain.

Larry tugged her toward him, bent forward until his forehead touched her own. He closed his eyes and sighed deeply. He slipped his fingers into her hair.

"Yeah," he acknowledged bleakly. "I guess we'll be okay."

She waited for the great wave of relief those words should have triggered, but she couldn't ignore the despair in his husky tone.

IT WAS FRIDAY afternoon when the Cornsilk regulars first heard about Fran, and the news was vague. A nurse at the Washburn Hospital said she'd arrived with stomach pain. Lotty had proposed the possibility of a miscarriage, assuming she'd been secretly pregnant, and Orville had voted for appendicitis.

Johnnie Sue didn't really care what was wrong with Fran, or even if she recovered. In the first place, if anybody deserved to be laid up in the hospital, it was that little tart who'd caused so much trouble for Hershell and Larry. In the second place, if the girl felt wholly rotten she wouldn't have the energy to spread rumors about Johnnie Sue.

It had been a hellish couple of days since she'd last seen Shorty at the Washburn Hotel, but Johnnie Sue was certain now that she'd survive...as long as nobody in town found out about Shorty. She was reasonably certain that Fran would protect her secret out of the most basic of human needs—self-preservation. But that security would exist only as long as she still wanted Seth. When that affair ended—and, with Fran, the end of any affair was just a matter of time—she'd have no reason not to blab about whom she'd been with at the hotel and whom she'd seen there.

Based on the way Hershell was hovering over her, Johnnie Sue figured that Larry had told him to keep an eye on her before he'd skedaddled out of town. Of course, Hershell had only been in for meals and evenings—every other minute he'd been shining at Duncan's. How he loved that store! From the moment Larry had told him it was his for the duration, he'd pranced around looking like a kid at Christmas.

Johnnie Sue had refused to rain on his parade. Besides, the worst was over now. She couldn't imagine how she'd let the whole thing with Shorty happen. Going to bed with him—well, maybe that made sense. But falling head over heels for the fellow had been just plain stupid. She knew better; she deserved what she'd gotten. The one thing she was thankful for, now that she'd returned to her senses, was that he had been a man of his word. Without that message, she might have waited for him forever. That goodbye had been a gift. A lesser man would not have bothered to give it.

Fortunately nobody else seemed to have figured out that she'd nearly lost her stuff for a while there. Not even eagle-eyed, malicious Fran, who'd been stupid enough to leave a prescription bag in her booth when she'd come by to try emotional blackmail. The next morning she'd come back and found it right where she'd left it, too stupid to realize that Johnnie Sue would have to have been in a daze to have missed seeing the thing during her nightly sweep of the Cornsilk.

She wasn't in a daze any longer. When Henry Clancy started wandering in every hour on the nose, she knew he was sniffing out news about Fran.

Henry wasn't much of a man in Johnnie Sue's eyes, but he was a regular and he was still married to poor little Julie.

"What's up, Henry? You look like something the cat dragged in," she greeted him with her own brand of sympathy when he showed up around suppertime. When he glanced up, his eyes were filled with naked pain. She was surprised. She'd always assumed that Henry's heart lay just behind his zipper. It was a surprise to discover that he actually could care about a woman so deeply.

And downright disheartening when you considered that the woman was living with somebody else and Henry himself had a wife who was eight months' pregnant and only nineteen years old. If Gert found out she'd probably shoot him through the head.

Johnnie Sue had something more subtle in mind. She'd planned to start salting his coffee today, but he looked so pathetic that she'd decided to wait until Fran was well.

"So what do you hear about Fran?" she asked a couple in the front booth who lived out near Fran's place. Their property abutted the same poorly paved road that ran past the Clancy family farm. Gert also lived on the farm in an old caretaker's cottage near the main house. Henry and Fran had pretty much grown up together, so Johnnie Sue figured that Wednesday night was hardly the first time Henry had wormed his way into Frannie's pants. "Any word on that tummy ache?"

The woman looked disturbed. "Oh, it's more than a stomachache, Johnnie Sue. We just came from the hospital, and they wouldn't even let us see her." She looked almost embarrassed to admit her concern for the town pump. "Her daddy was so good to us, don't you know," she offered by way of explanation.

Johnnie Sue decided not to go into that. Bernard Bixby had been a good ole boy, and she missed him. Most folks had not held it against him that his girl had gone astray.

"So what's the word? They fix her up all right? She gonna be okay?"

She glanced at Henry. He was hanging on every word. The man shook his head and looked Johnnie Sue right in the eye. "Don't look good for Fran, which means it don't look good for you."

Johnnie Sue was startled. Had Fran told these people what she'd seen? Left them some sort of directions or "open only if I die" letter?

She was scared to ask but couldn't help herself. "What do you mean?"

He shrugged. "Her boyfriend says she's slipping fast."

Henry gagged on his coffee. Johnnie Sue was shocked. "You mean she actually might *die?*" Granted, she hated the girl and she had it coming, but Johnnie Sue's brand of vengeance generally stopped just short of wishing people dead.

His wife nodded. "Way it looks, it's more than likely. And if she does, Doc Swanson's gonna ask for an inquest."

Now she felt her stomach churning. Elwood's piercing questions after Fran's shooting—and her own guilt about Larry's—left her rocky on her feet. "Why the hell would Doc Swanson do a thing like that?"

"Because three days ago Doc found out she had an ulcer—not real good but not real bad. He gives her a prescription to make it better. Then all the sudden she's bleeding inside like crazy and they can't make it stop. Doc says something like that probably couldn't happen without some help."

"What kind of help?" blurted Henry, not even trying to mask his concern.

"The kind that somebody could slip into her coffee or something. Poison, I guess, or something that would really aggravate an ulcer."

Henry sputtered his coffee all over the counter, giving Johnnie Sue a moment to pull her thoughts together while she cleaned up. Damn Fran Bixby! Wasn't it bad enough that she'd caused trouble for Hershell and spied on Johnnie Sue? Broken Larry's heart by revealing the truth about Rene's ex-husband? Did she have to go and die right after she'd left that damn prescription bag at the Cornsilk where anybody could have seen it?

But nobody had seen it; Johnnie Sue was pretty sure of that. She hadn't even seen it until Fran had come back.

Odd then, that Gert had asked later if Fran had been back to retrieve it. If she'd seen it on the floor during their afternoon coffee break, why hadn't she bothered to pick it up?

She wondered idly if Gert knew about Fran and Henry yet. Johnnie Sue wasn't going to tell her; Gert might not be able to keep from spilling the beans to Julie. And poor little Julie had her hands full just trying to keep herself together until the baby came. No, Johnnie Sue would nip this thing in the bud before it came to light. And if Fran had the courtesy to die, the problem would resolve itself.

The woman, enjoying the attention now, glanced brightly at Johnnie Sue. "If she dies and they call it murder, they'll start looking for a motive. Since everybody knows that you ran off Fran with a rifle," she pointed out straightforwardly, "that means they'll start with you."

IT WAS ALREADY DARK when Larry awakened. He flipped on a small bedside lamp and glanced at his watch. Nine o'clock. He'd slept ten hours, and he felt as though he could have done with ten more.

To his surprise, Rene, in bed beside him, was wide awake. She lay on her back, studying the ceiling, hands limp on the bedspread. She did not speak; had not, in fact, said much since they'd arrived here. She'd said even less in the car.

He couldn't really blame her. At best, he'd given her

lukewarm forgiveness. Actually he hadn't forgiven her at all, and she knew it. He'd just acknowledged the fact that he wanted her too much to give her up just yet. But they both knew that unless he could put the past behind them, it was just a matter of time.

They had not touched each other in the quiet cottage. Utterly exhausted, they'd both realized that they weren't likely to resolve anything until they'd gotten some sleep. His had been heavy; he still felt almost drugged. He didn't know about Rene.

He didn't ask. He just rolled on his side, half facing her, and said, "Hi."

She twisted her head in his direction, but her body remained prone. "Hello, Larry." Her tone was formal. Nothing in her expression gave any hint that they were sharing a bed, albeit platonically. Nor was there any indication they'd shared a bed much more intimately in the past. Suddenly that seemed a long time ago.

"Have you been awake awhile?"

"About an hour."

"You could have read or watched TV or something. Once I conk out, I might as well be dead."

She offered him the tiniest of smiles. "I'll keep that in mind."

He felt curiously empty. Alone. Rene looked like a small waif. She was too proud to ask him about their relationship again—he'd already told her what he could—but she wasn't a good enough actress to keep the pain from her eyes.

He reached out to take her hand. It was cold. Her answering grip was timid.

"I've hurt you terribly," he heard himself say, as though the notion had just occurred to him.

Rene closed her eyes and faced the ceiling again. "Proud of that, are you?" she said.

He drew her hand to his mouth and kissed it. He felt as though the poison had all been drained out of him. Now there was a hollow space that only Rene could fill.

"I never tried to hurt you, Rene," he told her truthfully. "Under the circumstances, it was inevitable."

She turned onto her side to look at him. "I wish you could understand that I was trying to keep from hurting you. I tried to tell you a dozen times. But when things were good between us, I just couldn't bear to take the risk that you might pull away."

He released her hand and cradled her head. Her green eyes were glistening again, but no tears slipped down her face.

"What do you want from me, Rene?" It was gently asked; he really wanted to know the answer. "Not just today, but down the road. Where do you see us going?"

She licked her lips. "The truth?"

His tone grew chilly. "There's no point in talking unless you're going to tell the truth."

She swallowed hard. Her eyes admitted defeat. "Before…before Fran came in for that damn prescription, I thought…in time…that I might want to marry you." The words were not easy for her. She almost looked ashamed.

He took a deep breath. His fingers tightened. His blunt nails stroked her scalp.

"You sound as though you've changed your mind."

She edged infinitesimally closer to him. "I'm afraid it's too late. If you can't bring yourself to trust me, a relationship between us can never work out."

He wanted to kiss her, but it would have seemed abrupt. "Maybe you're asking for too much, too soon," he suggested kindly. "Your…betrayal…has been a major blow. Maybe all we need is time."

Her eyes met his with fresh tension. "I did *not* betray you, Larry. When you were a stranger, I wasn't honest about my plans or my motives, but I didn't deceive you about my qualifications for the job. At the time, my personal life was none of your business. By the time you had a right to know my secrets, they were all part of the past. My reasons for coming to Porter didn't matter anymore." Her voice was low, hungry with the need to be believed. "You never shared my heart with Seth. You pushed him out on your way in."

It was nothing she hadn't said before, but now—in the quiet hotel room, after a decent rest and time to assimilate all that had happened—it sounded like a scenario he could forgive. For the first time since Fran had told him the awful truth, he began to believe that they really might find a way to heal the rift.

"I believe you," he said simply. He did. It didn't help all that much, and it didn't mean that he might not have a hard time forgiving her completely. But he did believe that she loved him…and that she really didn't want Seth anymore. "I know that I wouldn't have reacted so wildly if it weren't for what I'd been through with Sandra. I wouldn't even have been so upset if we lived in some other town. Everybody's bound to make the obvious comparison."

She looked only slightly less relieved. "I know that, Larry, and there's really nothing I can do about it. Fran and Seth aren't going to leave Porter. Seth will hold my secret for his sake as well as my own. But with Fran's mouth…"

She didn't need to say the obvious. Neither did he.

To his surprise, a smile suddenly sprang between them. The situation wasn't funny, but he was warmed by a sudden sense of camaraderie, anyway. Fran or no Fran, he and Rene were on the same side in this battle. They would face Porter hand in hand.

"Can you live with the gossip?" Rene asked gently.

Larry pondered the question for a moment, then gave her the same honesty he'd demanded of her. "Better than I can live without you."

Suddenly she was close beside him, her hands cupping his face. Their lips met in sweet relief and the tenderest of healing gestures. He wrapped his arms around her and held her close.

"I'm so sorry, Larry," she whispered. "Sorry for everything. But if I hadn't come to Porter looking for Seth we never would have met. Isn't that worth something?"

He pulled her closer and kissed her again. "It's worth everything," he confessed, feeling foolish and yet strangely joyful. "Promise me that if I ever go nuts again and tell you to get out of my life, you won't leave."

She buried her face in his shoulder, and he could feel the moisture of fresh tears. "I can't go through this again, Larry. You just tore me to shreds inside."

He hugged her, hard, then kissed her temple fiercely. "Rene, I'm sorry. I never thought about how it might be affecting you, not until today. All I could see was the egg on my own face. I felt like such a chump when I found out you'd lied to me."

"If you love me, Larry, please let it be for now. I can't bear to talk about it anymore."

And just that simply, he realized that their fight was over. It was time to let it rest.

He kissed her ear and then the side of her neck. It took him some serious nuzzling before she turned and found his lips again.

As he cradled her tenderly and waited for the tears to

dry, he became aware of the thinness of her summer cotton nightie, not to mention the fact that it had ridden up around her waist. Since he was sleeping in nothing but his black briefs, a full-bodied hug quickly brought them skin to skin. His flat, solid chest against her enticingly soft and curved one.

Slowly the mood of healing began to change. He felt his arousal creep up on him, a need for bonding and reassurance that went beyond the sensual need Rene always triggered within him. His body slowly tightened as his kisses dropped a little lower. His lips laved the valley of her throat just as one firm breast seemed to roll into his waiting hand.

To his surprise, she tightened. He'd thought the shift in mood was mutual, but he suddenly realized it wasn't what she wanted at all.

"No?" he murmured with some confusion, unable to release her just yet.

She didn't answer right away. Sending off mixed messages, she wriggled closer. "Larry, I just want to be sure."

He didn't move his hand from her breast, but he didn't stroke it, either. "Sure of what?" he asked as a sudden gust of panic filled him. Surely she wasn't speaking of Seth!

Her mouth found his again. She kissed him longingly, but her body was still tense. "I want to be sure that we're making love because we're us again. Not just a man and a woman in a hotel room having sex."

There was nothing she could have said to convince him more fully that she was the woman he wanted her to be. "Oh, Rene," he whispered from the depths of his soul, "I love you so very much."

Her mouth opened in a silent O of surprise, then closed as his lips found hers again. But this time there was no hesitation in her kiss, no tension in the body that had lain so rigidly at his side. She pressed toward him eagerly, one knee brushing over his own. Her hand seized his elbow, then slid down the taut strength of his arm. When she touched the hand that covered her breast, she pressed his fingers. Hard.

The smooth blunt end of his thumbnail skidded ever so softly across the stiff nipple tip. Rene gasped against Larry's mouth. Her knee slid farther, clear across his midriff, until his leg parted her thighs.

A moment later his mouth replaced the hand on her breast and his fingers slid down her flat stomach to the place just claimed by his leg. She pressed against him as he stroked the dense fur, whimpering as one searching finger parted it and slipped inside.

The first night they'd made love, Larry had been in such bad shape that Rene had had to do all the work, and this time he was determined that it would not turn out that way. When she reached for him, he firmly grabbed both wrists with his free hand and pinned them to the pillow above her head. There would be time for his own pleasure later. Right now, he wanted to concentrate fully on pleasing Rene.

With her arms up and back, her breasts rose to him, their rigid hunger vivid even in the dim light of the room. She squirmed and whimpered; he reveled in the pleading tone as she cried his name.

Maybe she'd once cried for Seth that way, but it had been a long, long time ago. Now he was the only one in her heart; he could see it in her eyes. Rene Hamilton belonged to him with every inch of her soul.

"Larry, please!" she begged him as his fingertips found the tiny hub of her woman's desire. Slowly he stroked it, with one fingertip after another—each starting at the top and sliding all the way down. Desperately she pressed against him with her lower body. She tried to free her arms from his grip, too, but that was just for show.

"Let me touch you," she begged him. "Let me make you feel this good."

"Later," he ordered, his lips and tongue plundering her other breast. "This time is my gift to you."

A moment later her hands broke free. She dug both hands deeply into his hair, crying out as she pushed his head down lower. He knew what she wanted. He slid both hands up to deftly twist her nipples while his tongue slid down to silence the throbbing between her open thighs.

She cried. She screamed. She almost pulled out a chunk of Larry's hair. In a matter of moments he was so aroused he thought he'd climb the ceiling. He didn't want to rush Rene, but he was desperate for his own release.

She did not make him wait.

IT WAS SATURDAY afternoon when Elwood showed up at Duncan's. Hershell thought nothing of it at first. Elwood was as regular a customer as anybody else in town, though his wife did most of the shopping for him. Maybe he just wanted to see how Hersh was doing since Larry was out of town.

He grimaced at the thought. Poor Larry was suffering like hell, no doubt, trying to come to grips with the web that Hamilton girl had spun for him. It was going to be a grim weekend for the poor boy any way you looked at it. But for Hershell, these two days were like being reborn. His only regret was that Duncan's was closed on Sunday.

He also regretted that Larry hadn't confided in him as to the nature of what was wrong with Johnnie Sue. His directions on that subject had been terse and brief. "Just stay close. Be alert. Give her lots of attention and don't ask any questions. She'd be mad as hell if she knew I said anything to you.''

Actually Hersh was the one who was mad as hell. How could Johnnie Sue have confided in Larry and not in him? Oh, the boy said he'd just sort of stumbled in when she was at a weak moment, but that didn't wash. Johnnie Sue didn't *have* weak moments. Granted, she'd been acting pretty strange lately, but that didn't mean she needed any special attention. Larry had probably just come up with the notion to give his doddering old dad something to do.

Of course, he'd given him Duncan's for the weekend, and that was more than enough. It was everything. And everything had gone perfectly, too; he couldn't complain. He and Max had worked together, just like the old days. The new fellow, Finch, was nice enough, and he'd offered no complaints or rude questions when Hershell had explained that he had to fill all the prescriptions, no matter what. Hersh kept a close eye on him, but the guy never stepped out of line.

All in all, Hersh was feeling pretty damn proud of himself until Elwood showed up. He felt so good, in fact, that it took him a while to realize that Elwood's mood was black as tar.

"Afternoon, Hersh. Didn't expect to find you here."

"Larry's out of town," Hersh answered brightly. "Left me in charge. So, anything you want—"

"I didn't come to shop, Hersh," he cut him off. "I'm here on official business, I'm sorry to say."

Bile charged into Hershell's throat. Beside him, he felt Maxine freeze. "Has something happened to Larry?" he asked with a gasp.

Elwood shook his head quickly. "No, Hersh, nothing like that."

"Paulie? You've heard some word?"

With Elwood's second head shake, the worst of the nausea subsided. If his boys were still alive—and until he got confirmation about Paulie's death he'd wait for him forever—he could bear anything else. Still, he begged miserably, "Don't tell me somebody else is dead."

This time Elwood nodded. "I'm sorry, Hersh. Fran Bixby died about three hours ago."

Hershell blinked. He'd heard that Fran was in the hospital for ulcers, but he hadn't paid much attention to the details. Unless she was causing him trouble, Fran Bixby was not at the top of his list of concerns.

"I…reckon that's too bad, Elwood, on general principles," he said, thinking Aggie would want him to show some sympathy. "I mean, as a Christian I guess I've got to say that, but I can't tell you it'll wreck my sleep. In fact, I can't for the life of me figure out why you dropped by here to tell me."

Then he remembered the cimetidine prescription that Rene had filled. His stomach heaved as he realized that Elwood must believe she'd made a mistake.

Elwood studied him carefully. "Fran didn't just up and die, Hersh. She had a little help."

"Help?" He choked on the word.

"The autopsy won't be complete until tomorrow, but they found some pills in her purse that could have done it. Something called piroxicam."

"Couldn't be piroxicam," countered Hershell. "Way I heard it, she was hospitalized for a bleeding ulcer. Least that's what I heard from Johnnie Sue. Piroxicam's what you use for arthritis. Safe enough for most people—a damn fine drug when you come right down to it—but not if you've got stomach trouble. Even if Doc Swanson slipped up and forgot to check that out, any competent pharmacist would have mentioned it to her. Standard procedure. It'd even be on the label.''

Elwood fiddled with the holster of his gun. ''It didn't say piroxicam on the label. It said cimetidine. And that's what Doc Swanson prescribed for her.''

Behind him, he heard Maxine squeak, ''And that's what we gave her, Elwood. Rene Hamilton filled the prescription and had me check it twice. Lotty's taken piroxicam for years, and believe me, I know what it looks like.'' She puffed herself up proudly. ''Nobody at Duncan's would make a mistake like that.''

Elwood's eyes narrowed. ''You say Rene Hamilton filled the prescription? And she had you check it twice? Is that standard procedure?''

Maxine flushed.

Greg Finch, who'd started looking jittery at the sound of Rene's name, quickly spoke up. ''Rene Hamilton is a first-rate pharmacist, Sheriff,'' he told Elwood. ''There's no way she could confuse piroxicam with cimetidine and give it to a patient suffering from ulcers.''

''I believe you're right about that,'' Elwood said darkly. ''I don't believe she could make such a grave error. Which makes me wonder why she bothered to ask you to check her work, Maxine...just this once.''

Maxine's hands were trembling. ''We didn't want any more trouble with Fran after the shootings and all. We talked about refusing to fill the prescription, and we finally decided that Fran would cause more trouble if we didn't fill it than if we did.''

''You made this decision on your own? You and Miss Hamilton?''

''We had no choice! Larry was in no condition for us to bother him, and he'd given us strict orders not to bother his father.''

Hersh slumped. He felt old and tired and foolish. Even if no Duncan had put those pills in the bottle, Duncan's Drugs was still responsible for a customer dying from an incorrectly filled prescription. It would all start up again. Even dead, Fran Bixby would still haunt him.

Oh, Aggie, what am I going to do? he asked.

There was no answer. She couldn't speak to him with others in the room.

"But you checked the prescription, Maxine?" Elwood persisted. "I know you're not a pharmacist, but you know your stuff. If you checked the pills yourself and you're sure they were cimetidine—when you last looked at them— that's good enough for me."

Maxine nodded. "I checked. I was sure."

"After that, was Rene ever alone in the store?"

Finch broke in, "Now wait a minute, Sheriff! I—"

"She had her own key, Elwood. She could have come back anytime. Now that I think about it..."

"Think about what?"

"Well, the connection, you know. I knew Rene was up to something, but I didn't think it had anything to do with Duncan's. I knew she met some fellow after work once, but I figured it was a sex thing or blackmail or something because she never tried to steal the drugs."

"She was meeting somebody?" queried Elwood, tugging out a tiny notepad. He looked deadly serious now. "I thought she was dating Larry. Way I heard it, he got sweet on her pretty damn soon after she came to town."

"He did," explained Maxine, her voice dropping harshly, "and she pretended she liked him, too. But it was a setup all along. The guy she really wanted to get close to was her ex-husband. The same old thing as Sandra. Rene's ex moved here after their divorce. It's the reason she came to town."

Hershell wasn't hearing anything he didn't know—poor Larry had sketched him an outline of the situation when he'd morosely camped out at his house—but hearing it laid out so starkly for Elwood, he wondered how Larry could possibly have tried to forget it all and patch things up with Rene this weekend. The way Lotty told it, he'd all but ordered the girl to go away with him. But what good would it do? She was bound to tear his half-healed heart to shreds.

And then, as Maxine piped up with her last bit of information, he realized that Rene's alleged romance with another fellow was the least of Larry's troubles.

"You're telling me that Rene Hamilton came to Porter to track down her ex-husband? That she might even have gotten this job to set up this pill mix-up?"

Maxine nodded. "I think it's possible, Hersh, especially when you consider that Seth left Rene for Fran."

Elwood stared at Maxine in disbelief for almost fifteen seconds. It took Hershell twice as long to accept the truth, as clear as sunshine after a thunder shower.

The girl his boy loved had used Duncan's to stage a murder.

IT WAS NOT QUITE nine on Sunday night when Larry brought her home. They pulled into Lotty's parking lot in silence, the three-day glow serving as words between them.

When she'd hopped into his car on Friday morning, Rene had not believed that there had been any real hope for their future. She had not imagined that the knots in their relationship could truly be worked out. She would have sworn in a court of law that they would not have been discussing wedding dates on the ride home from Dubuque.

It was Larry's opinion that there would be less gossip if they just got married quietly and presented it to the town as a fact before Fran had time to sling much mud. Intellectually Rene agreed, but she also knew that neither she nor Larry were really ready to take such a step. They'd just survived their first fight, and though at the moment they both felt joyfully serene, she wasn't about to lay any bets on how deep Larry's forgiveness truly ran. It wouldn't take much for him to doubt her again. She never intended to do anything that he could view as a betrayal, but if something came up—some rumor, some unfounded flutter of Porter gossip—she had no protection but the truth. And if such rumors ever involved another man—especially Seth—Rene knew that the truth would be an inadequate weapon against Larry's accusatory grief.

Besides, his father still seemed to consider her the enemy. She had to find some favorable way to meet him…and some way to convince him she would be good for his son.

Larry studied her face in the glow from the streetlight, then leaned over to kiss her cheek. "I'm glad we went," he told her, then grinned at his understatement. "I love you, Rene. Everything's going to be okay."

She put her arms around him and held him close. They kissed deeply before she pulled away. "You want me at work tomorrow?"

"If you don't mind. I'm going to be pretty beat after all the exercise I got this weekend—" his grin was enough to make her pant "—and I suspect I'll need to rest up for tomorrow night."

"Tomorrow night?" she teased.

He nibbled her ear. "I'm planning to seduce one of my employees."

Rene laughed, a happy, erotic sound deep in her throat. "If you're going to send Greg back home, I guess that means one of the high school girls, Maxine or me."

She felt his deep male chuckle vibrate her chest as his hands slid through her hair. "They're too young and she's too old."

"Should I be flattered that I won by default?"

He kissed her soundly. "I don't know if you're flattered by my love for you or not. But don't you ever doubt that you've won it."

His eyes bathed her with tenderness. She hugged him with all her might.

"I love you, Larry. Don't ever question it again."

He kissed her once more, but he did not answer. "See you tomorrow, sweetheart," he said softly. It was the first time he'd ever used that endearment, and it shook her to the core.

The kiss deepened. After a moment she got lost in it. Larry turned off the ignition. Manly arms pulled her close.

"Rene," he whispered against her hair as the mood totally engulfed her, "why don't you just come on home with me?"

Rene didn't argue. She just gripped his knee, nails lightly digging in, as he revved up the motor and drove three more blocks to his house.

They slipped inside in silence, not bothering with their bags. Larry's cool sheets awaited them, welcomed them, as Larry tenderly covered Rene's eager body with his own.

As he spun a web of pleasure that held her captive, she felt secure, beloved, profoundly happy. For the first time since she'd come to Porter, she felt as though she had a home.

It was a cruel illusion, though, snatched from her only half an hour later when she was brutally awakened by the sound of shouting while a fist pounded on Larry's front door.

"Son? Let me in! We got trouble! That girl you hired to take my place just up and murdered Fran!"

CHAPTER FIFTEEN

RENE FROZE. So did Larry. His hand, still on her breast, shrank away slowly. Passion, so richly shared just moments ago, vanished from her heart.

"Damn it, Larry, wake up!" Hershell hollered. "Lotty heard your car pull in but by the time she got down to the lot you'd left and that girl had flown the coop! Elwood's gonna be here any time. He already came poking around Duncan's to see if we had anything to do with it!"

By this time Larry was on his feet, hair askew, tugging on his jeans. He scrambled to the front of the house, leaving the bedroom door ajar. Rene pulled the blankets up to cover herself, but she could not bring herself to move.

From her vantage point she could see the tightly bulged muscles in Larry's still-bandaged side as he jerked open the door and literally dragged his father in. "For pity's sake, Dad," he growled. "You don't have to tell the whole damn town."

"The whole damn town already knows, son. And if you'd left a phone number in Dubuque you'd know, too. Elwood would have sent a posse over there, but I swore on a stack of Bibles that you wouldn't run off with some outsider who'd just killed somebody if you'd known. You're not *that* smitten with the girl."

There was a terrible, dull silence in the living room. If cossacks had been about to invade the house, Rene could not have moved.

She hated Fran. Fran was dead. And while she couldn't feel profoundly sorry, nobody that vibrant and young should have to die.

In spite of everything, she felt true grief for Seth. Frannie's death would crush him, and he had nobody to hold his hand.

Vaguely she heard Hershell's loquacious recitation of the facts: Rene had come to Porter to get even with Fran; Rene had filled Fran's prescription; Rene had substituted piroxicam for cimetidine. It was not proposed as theory. In the old man's mind, it was obviously fact.

But Rene didn't care about what was in Hershell's mind. It was Larry's thoughts that troubled her. From her spot in bed, she could not see his face. But she could read the terrible tension in his half-naked body as he faced his father, absorbing the hammer blows of Rene's situation.

In rising panic, she began to realize just how perilous that situation was. Hershell was mumbling about "motive, means and opportunity," and she knew that he was right about that. Lots of people in Porter had had it in for Fran, but nobody had easy access to piroxicam and Fran's prescription and the knowledge that would allow a murderer to think of the deadly switch. Only a pharmacist was likely to know that. Or maybe a pharmacist's bookkeeper and clerk.

But worse than the likelihood that she might be framed for something she'd never even thought of was the strong possibility of losing Larry. Even if he didn't buy the theory that she'd committed such a heartless murder, the ensuing furor was bound to unearth all the doubts he had so tentatively overcome.

Trembling mightily, she rose from the bed and began to dress out of sight of the doorway. She was numb. She was about to be railroaded by a small town into serving time for murder. If Larry didn't believe her, she didn't have a chance.

"You've got to call Elwood right now and tell him you didn't know a thing about it. You've got to give him any clues you can about where she might have gone."

Before Larry could answer, Rene marched through the doorway, her very best mask in place. It was not easy, under the circumstances, to present a good front. She could not conceal the fact that Hershell had interrupted them in bed, nor could she do much about her disheveled appearance. Her purse was by the front door where she'd dropped it on the way in and the rest of her things were still in Larry's car. Worse yet, she knew she was white-faced with panic.

She also knew she had no time to waste.

"I haven't gone anywhere, Mr. Duncan," she said as calmly as she was able. "I'm not running away from anybody. I didn't kill Fran. I'm not guilty of anything but loving your son."

Hershell's basset-hound face wrinkled in shock. His panicked old eyes glanced to Larry, then back to Rene.

She could tell he was debating the propriety of offering some apology for interrupting them, but it was obvious that in this crisis, the normal rules of etiquette did not apply.

Slowly—ever so slowly—Larry turned to face her. Rene met his eyes. It took all the willpower she possessed.

For a moment she just stood there—terrified, defeated, outraged.

Larry looked bleak, almost broken. He did not speak.

"Larry," she said softly, "you know I had nothing to do with this. Whatever else you're thinking—and that's pretty plain to see—you know I didn't waltz off to Dubuque with you and leave Fran Bixby to die."

"She wasn't planning to go to Dubuque when she

switched the pills," Hershell snapped. "But she was all packed up and ready to go."

"I was leaving because you told me you didn't want me anymore," she answered stoutly. She was speaking to Larry; she did not face his father.

But that didn't keep the old man from talking. "Don't you see how clever she is, son? You already know she hoodwinked you into hiring her so she'd be in town right handy. Maybe she didn't know about Fran's ulcer then; first off she tried to shoot her. But she was waiting for an opportunity, and when this one just fell in her lap, she decided to take it and run."

Rene was done trying to defend herself. The facts were all against her. Her only hope lay in Larry's championship. If she couldn't count on him, she might as well surrender.

"Please help me, Larry. You know I don't stand a chance on my own."

To her surprise, Larry's eyes suddenly flashed in anger. He had been almost motionless since the start of his father's harangue. She had assumed that he'd been assessing the case against her, constructing evidence of his own. Now, abruptly, she realized that he'd been simply dumbstruck.

"Are you trying to convince me that you're innocent, Rene?" he demanded. "Is that what you're trying to tell me?"

In that moment, Rene gave up. She gave up Larry. She gave up all hope for happiness in this life. Everything light and good inside her seemed to curl up and die.

"For three days we've been together, healing all our old scars, planning our new life. A half hour ago, we were in that bed together while you showed me how you love me." He pointed furiously toward the bedroom. "And now you're pleading with me to save you from being railroaded for a murder?''

She would have cried, but the pain was too deep. She would have defended herself, but she found no words. She sank slowly to the couch because her legs would no longer hold her.

Just before her back met the fabric, Larry bolted across the room and seized her.

''My God, Rene, did you think it was all a game? Did you really think I was that faithless, that shallow? I told you I loved you. I asked you to be my wife! Did you think I'd toss everything we have out the window at the first hint of trouble?''

Benumbed, Rene realized that Larry wasn't talking about believing her. He wasn't hammering her with guilt. He was outraged that she'd doubted him! He was yelling at her out of love.

She felt his firm, warm grip on her fingers, saw the determination in his face. For the first time since his father had started banging on the door, she felt a glimmer of hope.

Her trembling escalated into bone-jarring shakes that were beyond her control. The banked tears exploded now. She felt like a very small leaf in a very big tornado. If Larry hadn't been gripping her hands, she would have collapsed at his feet.

''Damn it, Rene! We've got a first-rate crisis on our hands! We've got to figure out who killed Frannie because Elwood sure as hell isn't going to if he's convinced he's got the killer. Any other suspect is somebody local, and he'd much rather believe it was you.''

Despite his orders, Rene started sobbing. Only now that she knew she had an ally could she admit to herself the depth of her terror. Only now that she knew Larry still loved her could she dare to believe she wasn't going to be alone.

"Rene!" Larry shouted, as though to shock her senses. She closed her eyes and collapsed on the couch.

At once his anger vanished. He dropped to his knees beside her and lifted one hand to her face.

For a moment she just leaned against him, savoring the life-giving hope of that touch.

"Oh, Larry," she whispered brokenly. "I was so certain I had lost you."

She felt his loving fingers cradling her head. He dropped a kiss on her temple. "Sweetheart, my love for you is not at issue here. That's a given."

She cried even harder.

"But we don't have time for romantic interludes or histrionics right now. We've got to figure out what happened. We've got to put our heads together and work out a game plan." He kissed her lips just once, a gentle reminder of his passion. "We've got to give Elwood a killer on a silver platter before he has time to arrest you."

Nodding, she swallowed hard. She wiped her tear-flooded face with one of the sofa's throw pillows. She clung tightly to Larry's hand as he rose to face his father.

As though he had never heard a word of Hershell's accusations, he said tensely, "Dad, Rene is family now."

There was a long, terrible silence. Rene found the courage to meet the old man's eyes. She tried to remember that Larry loved him; that he had more reason to love Larry than to hate her.

He looked stiff and unforgiving. In fact, he looked as if he thought Larry were quite mad. She expected him to turn around and storm out of the house hurling more accusations, but he stood his ground.

At last he grumbled, "If that's how it's gonna be, son,

I guess we better get crackin'. Your little missy is in trouble up to her eyeballs.'' His tone held a nearly mute hint of sympathy. "It's gonna take a heap of doing to bail her out.''

JOHNNIE SUE was sitting at her table, sipping dully from her coffee mug, when she heard the front door open. She was not surprised. It was nearly ten. She'd been expecting him.

"Take a load off, Lare," she said calmly. It wasn't easy, but she lifted her eyes to face him. "How was your trip to Dubuque?''

He pulled out a chair and straddled it. His eyes were haunted, angry, questioning.

"Forget Dubuque, Johnnie Sue. Elwood thinks Rene killed Fran.''

She nodded, sipped again. "All the evidence seems to point in that direction.''

He shook his head. "None of it points in that direction. Not if you know Rene like I do.''

She lifted one eyebrow in disdain. "Still addled, are you? I figured by now you'd know the truth.''

She'd hurt him. He visibly flinched. Johnnie Sue wasn't sure why she'd needed to do that. Maybe to prove to herself that he was as vulnerable as she was. Maybe to make herself feel sorry for him. Sorry enough to do what she had to do.

"I'm going to marry Rene. I'm absolutely certain that she's innocent. But that won't do her much good unless we unravel this mess before the real killer gets away.'' He swallowed hard and looked Johnnie Sue right in the eye. "She thinks you did it.''

The mug came down on the table hard—harder than Johnnie Sue meant it to. She was not surprised that Rene thought she'd murdered Fran—she'd been mulling over the evidence that could draw any skeptical person to that conclusion—but she was stunned that Larry suggested it with such vehemence.

"My God, boy, has she turned you against me, too?"

He took her hand. He squeezed it hard. "Never. You know better." Love mingled with the anger in his eyes. "But she's got a good point I want you to think about. She says it takes a lot more brass to make somebody suffer for three days bleeding inside than to shoot somebody outright. She doesn't think anybody else could tough it out but you."

Johnnie Sue wasn't certain she liked the backhanded compliment. "So what's your point?"

"If somebody's been acting shaky the last few days, you'd know it. And if somebody who ought to hang around in here hasn't been in since Thursday, you'd know that, too."

She nodded, trying to think about who she'd seen and who she hadn't. Henry Clancy had sure been acting like a bear with a sore paw. But before Johnnie Sue could mention that, Larry said, "Dad says you haven't been telling Elwood everything, Johnnie. I don't know what you're trying to hide, but you've got to come clean with me. Rene's counting on me, and I'm counting on you."

For a long moment she just stared at him. The blankness of the night she'd cut her hair started to settle over her once more. There was a bulldozer crushing the Cornsilk, with her heart inside it, and there didn't seem to be anything she could do.

She told him about Shorty and the night Fran was shot. She told him about Seth coming to meet Rene. She told him about seeing Fran at the Washburn Hotel with Henry Clancy the night before she'd called to speak to Aggie.

"So you think Seth did it? In sort of a jealous rage?"

She could tell he rather liked the idea. She liked it, too. It made sense—except for the fact that Frannie's boyfriend had struck her as too wimpy to pull off such a feat—and it meant that she could ignore the fact that there was somebody else she hadn't seen in several days.

"I can see him trying to kill Fran or Henry the night those shots were fired in Henry's back lot. But why would he try to kill me?" His eyes darkened. "Does he feel some sort of leftover jealousy about Rene?"

She glanced down at her mug. *Dear God, I don't want to tell him,* she prayed. But Larry's hand closed over hers. "Whatever it is, Johnnie Sue, I've got to know. Just tell me."

She still couldn't look at him. "I told you I saw Seth get into her car."

"Yes." The word was tense, anguished, as though he dreaded what she might say next.

"The next night I was waiting for him with my rifle." Her eyes flashed up. "Just to wing him. To scare him off. I'd already started checking out Rene and I knew she'd been married to him. I just wanted to protect you, Larry. I wanted to get her out of town without breaking your heart."

He didn't get it yet. She saw confusion in his eyes.

"It was dark when she left the back way with a man. They walked like lovers. I was sure it was Seth."

For a long moment no dawning registered on his earnest face. Then, abruptly, he turned gray. "My God," he whispered.

She started to cry. She felt her world slip away. "I only meant to wing him, Larry. You know I'm a dead-eye shot." She tried to smother a sob. "I had to do something to make her go away."

He was silent. He looked deathly pale.

"There was something about the way your head moved when you kissed her—I don't know—but suddenly I knew. I was already squeezing the trigger. When I tried to stop, it threw off my aim."

She couldn't say anything else, not with Larry looking at her—looking *through* her—like that. He put one hand over his chest and slowly rubbed the wound. Johnnie Sue covered her face. In thirty years she'd never let anybody see her cry, and here was Larry watching her bawl like a baby for the second time in five days.

"Is that why you snapped?" he asked. "The night Rene came here?"

She shook her head. Oh, it was part of it, part of the dismal gloom. But by then Larry had been home from the hospital, feeling fine. Happy as a lark about Rene.

"I got a message from Shorty," she whispered, as though the kitchen walls had ears. "He wanted me to know it was really over."

Her eyes met his bleakly, admitted the still aching depth of the pain.

"Oh, Johnnie Sue," he soothed her, reaching once more for her hand. "Why didn't you tell me all this right from the start? Dad and I could have...well, I don't know just what we could have done, but we would have been there for you." He squeezed her icy fingers. "We're family, Johnnie Sue."

For a moment she just lost it all together, cracked and wept and felt her seams unravel. Larry held her hand, crooned quiet words of comfort, and didn't say a word about Rene until she was spent, silent, almost feeling better.

Then he asked straightforwardly, "Do you know who killed her?"

She shook her head. "My vote's on the boyfriend. He could have shot at Fran just like I shot at you. Just to scare her, shake her up. They never found any bullets. He could have been certain not to hurt her."

"If he didn't want to kill her, why did he switch the pills?"

"Maybe he lost patience. Maybe he didn't know about Henry for sure in the beginning. Maybe he still hoped she'd give Henry up."

"Maybe." Larry thought about it a minute. "As desperately as I'd like to hang it on him, I can't see him blubbering all over her bedside for three days without spilling the beans. Shooting a false lover in a fit of rage makes sense. Watching her die like that...Rene says he doesn't have it in him. He's not a very strong person."

Johnnie Sue was forced to agree with him. "He struck me as a marshmallow."

They sat there facing each other in the silence of the Cornsilk. She didn't want to hear his next question, but she knew there was no way to stop it.

"Who's been acting squirrelly lately?"

"Clancy's falling apart at the seams," she hedged. "Broke right down in here the day we heard she died."

"Did he ever go to the hospital?"

"Not that I know of. But I don't know who'd be around to find out. Probably just the boyfriend."

"I better call Rene and have her ask him."

She was incredulous. "Rene is with Seth?"

He nodded. He didn't look happy about it, but he didn't look nearly as disturbed as she'd have expected. "We mapped out a game plan. She's the only one he's likely to talk to. Dad's grilling Maxine."

"You suspect her, too? Don't be an idiot. I'd sooner suspect Julie Clancy."

"If she weren't such a sweetie, she'd be a good bet. Henry's always treated her like garbage. She deserves so damn much better."

Johnnie Sue couldn't argue that. She'd always liked little Julie, who was so much sharper than Gert. Gert had scrimped and saved all those years to get that girl to college! Larry had been so pleased with her work for him. But youthful folly had defeated her potential. And now that poor girl was barely nineteen, pregnant, with the most indifferent husband in the world. It was enough to make her wish she *had* killed Fran...or maybe Henry Clancy

"Johnnie Sue, I can't believe Maxine would do something like this, but then again, who else could? She hated Fran and she'd do anything to protect Dad from more trouble. You know that. And on the day that prescription was filled, only three pharmacists were in this town, and none of us did it. Nobody but Maxine had access to that prescription before it left Duncan's. That is, nobody who'd know what to do."

"What do you mean? I don't know beans about medication, and even I know what piroxicam does to a stomach ulcer."

"How'd you find that out?"

She shrugged. "Maxine was telling us about it one day in here. Not blabbing any state secrets, mind you, just warning Lotty about taking piroxicam."

"Lotty's on piroxicam," Larry stated bleakly. "Does that mean we have to consider *her?*"

Johnnie Sue shook her head. "Lots of people in this town have arthritis. It probably wouldn't be that hard to get inside and take some pills from a bathroom cabinet if you knew what you were looking for."

"According to you, anybody who was in the Cornsilk

on the day Maxine talked might have known what to look for.''

''Not anybody. Just Lotty and Gert and me.''

Suddenly he froze. His eyes narrowed on her face.

Slowly she continued. ''Somebody who had access to other people's homes—say, a housekeeper—wouldn't have much trouble getting piroxicam if she knew where to look. And if she were in the habit of filling friends' prescriptions, she might even know which ones had piroxicam.''

He was fighting it; she could see. He didn't want to believe it any more than she did. But he hadn't discounted it outright yet, and that was a bad sign. And he didn't know the half of it.

''She'd have to know Fran had a stomach ulcer.''

''Gert went to school with Super Mouth Sally.''

''She'd have to have access to the prescription. I can't see her sneaking into Duncan's to make the switch. And even if she did, how would she know Fran was coming in?''

''Sally again.''

Larry closed his eyes. ''Tell me why this is crazy, Johnnie Sue. Tell me why it couldn't be Gert.''

She did not answer. She let him get used to the idea that had been gnawing at the back of her brain ever since he'd asked who'd been missing for the past few days. She wasn't used to it yet.

''Larry, the day Fran picked up that prescription, she left the damn thing in here. I found it under the table when I was closing up.''

''What the hell was she doing here?''

Johnnie Sue was feeling sick again. ''Trying to buy my silence about Henry by threatening to expose my affair. She was carrying a whole bunch of stuff. The prescription bag fell under the booth table. She didn't come back for it until the next morning.''

Larry's eyes widened. "If Elwood finds out about that, you could be in real trouble, Johnnie Sue.''

"But nobody knows, Larry. Unless somebody found it, carted it off to make the switch, then smuggled it back in here.''

He was staring at her strangely. "You know everybody, Johnnie Sue. It would have to be somebody who hangs around here every day.''

Ever so slowly, she nodded.

"Somebody who's been acting fidgety since then. Or might be feeling so fidgety he's even stayed away.''

She nodded again.

"Any ideas?''

For the third time, she nodded, hating to finger a friend. But the Duncans were family, and family came first.

"Johnnie Sue?''

She swallowed hard and told him the last tiny piece of information she'd hoarded to her chest. "Henry says Gert's been home with the flu. I don't know about that. All I'm sure of is that the day you took off to Dubuque, she asked me if Fran had come back for her prescription. I said yes, and I haven't seen her since.''

HERSHELL HATED like hell to question Maxine, but he was proud as punch that his boy trusted him to do something so crucial, so delicate, so god-awful. It was a wild hunch, a long shot, but they both felt that Maxine might know something she hadn't told Elwood, something Orville might not even know. Something that would strengthen Rene's case and point the blame toward someone else.

In his gut he still wasn't sure that Rene was innocent, but he believed in Larry, and Larry believed in her. It would take some doing to get used to thinking of Rene as family, but if that's the way his son wanted it, that's the way it was going to be.

Hershell marched into the Kensler house rather briskly, looming over Maxine even when she asked him to sit down. He knew she'd worshipped him for thirty years, and he cared deeply for her. He'd never abused their relationship, never taken advantage of her fierce loyalty. But—for Larry's sake—he had to put her on the spot.

"Maxine," he said firmly, "I need you with me one hundred percent. I need you to lay it on the line."

She seemed to understand at once. Tears welled in her eyes. "Don't make me hurt anybody, Hershell. Don't make it any worse than it is."

"A woman's dead. Another woman may go to jail for it. If that happens, my boy will never be the same."

She started to cry. "If it doesn't happen, somebody else's child will never be the same! Besides, I really think Rene did it!"

He leaned over her, tossing aside the defeat of old age like a tattered cloak he'd grown weary of. He moved his mouth inches from her face. "You want to believe she did it. So did I. But if she didn't, then we're living tooth-by-jowl with the real killer, Max."

She stared at him, openmouthed, then suddenly melted in unabashed hurt. "Hershell, you think *I* did it?" she gasped.

He studied her thoughtfully, tried to objectively study this woman who'd been like a part of him for years.

"No," he finally told her, wondering if he were as blind as his son. "But I think you just might know who did."

She shook her head. "I don't know anything, Hershell. Just what I told Elwood."

"But you've got a hunch."

Slowly she lowered her eyes.

"Woman's intuition."

She covered her face with her hands. "You're never wrong about things like this, Maxine. Tell me what you're thinking."

She couldn't face him, but somehow she got the words out. "Last week I was coming down with a cold and I took off from choir early. I happened to see Henry Clancy kissing Frannie goodbye at the station on my way home."

The information was new to him, but he was not surprised. Fran probably had wives and girlfriends who wanted to gun her down from coast to coast. But not little Julie. She'd never learned how to fight her own battles. Her mother fought all of them for her.

"I tried to keep it to myself, but I just couldn't."

"You told Julie?" he asked, wondering how she could be so cruel.

Maxine shook her head and started to cry. "Of course not. I told Gert."

IT WAS ALREADY nearly eleven when Rene left Seth and drove to the Clancy farm. She knew it was much too late to call, but she had to figure out who'd killed Fran Bixby, and she had to know tonight.

Seth had been glad to see her; not another soul in town had offered him any comfort or advice. He was appalled that Rene had been accused and revealed that the sheriff seemed quite suspicious of him, too. In a broken voice he'd told her the whole story of Fran's anguished dying, his guilt over firing blanks near Clancy's just to scare her into breaking off the affair, his further agony when Henry Clancy had burst into the hospital just hours before Fran died.

He was certain that Henry hadn't done it, but he didn't

think they should discount his teenaged wife. Just because a woman *looked* sweet and helpless didn't mean she couldn't find some inner strength.

Rene didn't believe that Julie Clancy was capable of murder, but she also knew that finding your man with Fran Bixby was enough to bring out the worst in any woman. And though she didn't know Julie nearly as well as Larry did, she had a hunch that she might be able to use an "I know how you feel" woman-to-woman talk to get information. Besides, the Clancys lived only a few farms over from Seth on the same two-lane road. She could swing by and still meet Larry and Hersh at the Cornsilk by midnight as they'd planned.

She still found it hard to believe that Larry was standing by her. He'd even suggested that she go to see Seth! He had told her once that he didn't know how to give his heart to a woman halfway, she was overjoyed to discover that that was the case.

His father would take some winning over. It was obvious that he still did not approve. But the love he felt for his son was unmistakable, and any man who'd go out on a limb for a woman he disliked and distrusted just to support his son had to be worth getting to know.

She's family, Dad, Larry had proclaimed. And just like that, Hershell had taken her in.

She'd never felt that kind of love from anybody before—unconditional loyalty. It was obviously what Hershell felt for Larry. It was what Larry felt for *her*. That knowledge went a long way toward stilling her terror.

But it couldn't erase the dread in her heart.

Rene wondered what kind of family poor Julie Clancy had. Her mother, of course, was loyal to the bone, but Henry couldn't be much of a husband. Nobody had ever mentioned in-laws in her presence, but that didn't mean that Julie didn't have some.

Rene knocked gingerly on the door, hoping that Julie was still up. The girl answered almost at once. She was dressed in a bright blue smock and matching maternity pants, yet her face revealed she was very upset.

"Julie, I'm really sorry to trouble you, but—"

"Is it Henry? Is he okay?"

She shrugged helplessly. "I don't know, Julie. I just got back into town and I haven't seen him. I just got the word about Fran."

Julie opened the door and ambled disconsolately back into the house. "*Fran.* That's all I've heard about for the last three days. Poor Fran is dying. Poor Fran is dead." She looked ashamed as she mumbled, "Poor Fran got what she deserved. I'm almost glad she's dead."

For a moment she glared defiantly at Rene, then she collapsed. "Oh, I know that's just an awful thing to say," she got out between her tears. "But how would you feel if you found out your husband was carrying on with *her* behind your back?"

Rene sat down and gingerly took the girl's arm. She'd come here for information, but her genuine sympathy could not be denied. "Julie, I did find out my husband was carrying on with Fran. For six years I was married to Seth Rafferty."

Her mouth fell open and her eyes mirrored shock. "You knew her before? You knew him, too?"

Rene nodded. "Yes, I did. And that's why I can really feel for you."

Suddenly Julie's blue eyes narrowed. "Did you ever want to just...just *kill* her, Rene?"

Under the circumstances, Rene decided that this was a

confession she'd better not make. "I was terribly hurt, Julie. I was furious."

"So was I!" She began to sob. "And the worst thing was, here was Henry blubbering like a baby, asking me to comfort him! I couldn't say anything nice, not then, so he just roared off to the hospital. I felt so guilty when I heard she died!"

"Guilty?" Rene probed gently.

"Yes! When he admitted he'd been seeing her, I actually prayed for her to die!" She shuddered, her blue eyes huge. "It's wrong to feel like that. It's just not *Christian*."

Rene nodded, not quite certain what to do. She'd expected to grill Julie for some information, and the girl's naive honesty made her feel ashamed. Julie had no secrets. Only gaping wounds.

"Where is Henry now, Julie? May I talk to him?"

She started to sob. "I don't know. He came in late last night half drunk, and said, 'She's dead. Are you happy now?' like it was my fault. I got mad and told him I had nothing to do with it. I've been so sick since I've been pregnant and he's been so...so...*awful!* He just yelled at me for a while about how great Fran was compared to me and—" She broke off as the tears shook her into jelly. "Then he just took off! I haven't seen him since then!"

"Oh, Julie," she said gently, knowing how deep ran the hurt and how long would burn the scars. "I wish I could do more to help you."

She sobbed a while longer. "The worst part of it is, my mom's been sick and she hasn't been much help at all. I called her last night, and she just said not to worry, that everything would be okay now that Fran was dead. She didn't sound at all surprised to hear that Henry had been sleeping with her."

"I'm sorry, Julie," Rene said gently. "I'm glad you've

been so honest with me. And now I want to be honest with you. Elwood thinks I may have killed Fran to get back at her for stealing my husband.''

"You didn't, did you?"

"No, of course not. My point is that if Elwood stops suspecting me long enough to consider the possibility that Fran had stolen another wife's husband more recently, he might get around to suspecting you.''

Rene regretted the words the moment they left her mouth. Julie needed to be warned, but not at this hour, not when she was all alone.

Sheer terror snaked across the young girl's face as she sprung up and rushed toward the phone. "I don't mean to be rude, Rene, but maybe you ought to go home now. I've got to call my mom and ask her what to do!''

She was spilling out the gist of their conversation into the receiver by the time Rene reached the door. She drove off feeling profoundly sorry for the girl and furious with Henry. He was even worse than Seth.

And then, despite her pain and anguish, Rene felt a tiny gust of joy nudge her heart. She finally had a man who was not like those two male jellyfish. She had a man who was long on integrity and who placed importance on trust. She was still frightened and worried, but she did not feel alone. At last, she was absolutely sure of Larry.

But Larry wasn't there to help her when a pickup truck lurched out of a side road about ten minutes later. Trucks were a dime a dozen in this part of the state, but most of them moseyed along with all the speed of grazing cattle. This one was bearing down on her quite rapidly. Maybe teenagers, hot-rodding?

But the truck didn't move in a blaze of glory. It jerked and bolted, behind Rene, as though the driver were having some difficulty keeping control. Rene decided that it would be smart to give the erratic vehicle some leeway, especially since a semi was barreling toward her from the other direction on the narrow two-lane road.

To get away, Rene drove fast. But the pickup kept coming faster.

LARRY DIDN'T WANT Rene to think he was checking up on her, but he had to find out if Henry had gone to the hospital before he confronted Gert. If he'd just been a grieving lover, he might have gone to confess that he loved her. If he'd tried to kill her, he might have deliberately stayed away until she'd died.

His conversation with Seth was short and awkward. Neither man volunteered any personal information.

"This is Larry Duncan. May I speak to Rene?"

"She just left. She's on her way to the Clancys'."

"Clancys'? At this time of night?"

"She wants to talk to Julie, woman-to-woman. She seems to think they have something in common."

He didn't say what, and Larry didn't press it. "I need to know if Henry ever came to the hospital to see Fran before she died."

There was a long, dark silence. "What difference does that make?"

"If he killed her, it could make a lot of difference."

Seth unleashed a harsh expletive. "Believe me, Duncan, I'd be thrilled if the cops could hang this on Clancy. I'd cheer at his execution. But when he showed up in Frannie's room, he blubbered like a baby. They weren't alone—everybody was trying to save her. Nurses, doctors, techs—all of them trying to get him out of the room. He went berserk. Believe me, if he'd had anything to confess, he would have blurted it out for everyone to hear. He was out of control."

For a long moment Larry was silent. If it wasn't Henry and it wasn't Maxine and it wasn't Gert—and he just couldn't believe it was Gert—then it *had* to be Seth.

"I guess you were mad as hell when you found out about Clancy," he probed.

Seth swore again. "Damn right, and let me save you the trouble of trying to get me to confess that I did it. I was mad enough to kill, but believe me, if I'd had the gumption, I would have killed Clancy, not Fran." He paused for a moment, then added darkly, "I might do it yet."

Larry knew by his tone that he was just grousing. He also knew—with a confidence that warmed him—that the man who'd once owned Rene's heart was no longer any threat to his heart. It was obvious that Rene was the last thing on his mind.

"How long ago did Rene leave there?" Larry asked.

"About twenty minutes ago. She ought to be—" he broke off, then said in some surprise "—she just whizzed by my kitchen window. I've never seen her drive that fast."

Larry didn't like the quiet urgency in the other man's tone. If Rene was driving fast, she was probably upset. Or else she had information she needed to get to him in a hurry.

"Thanks for your help, Rafferty," he said as magnanimously as he was able. "Rene'll probably get back to you if—"

"There's a truck trying to force her off the road, Duncan!" Seth burst out in a tone that echoed disbelief and shock. "Get Elwood or Clay out here fast!"

AFTER THE CRASH, the kaleidoscopic clash of colors and sounds rocked Rene and heightened her muzzy confusion. A red light above her kept whirling around, and off to her left, two others did likewise. She felt the pressure of a gathering crowd, heard the screams, the silence, the confusion. Somewhere nearby, a familiar voice was crying.

"Mama? You can't be dead. You can't just leave me!" And then the same young voice, between gulping sobs, "When she found out that Fran was seeing my Henry, she swore she'd fix her wagon, but I swear I never knew what she was going to do! When I called her to tell her what Rene said she just went crazy and said she had to stop her before she figured it out and told you. She'd been acting so skittish all weekend, and then she just...snapped."

Another voice indistinguishable from the hubbub of the crowd crooned to the girl, promised to take care of her. It was a woman's voice, not Julie's husband's.

Hands touched Rene's neck, her face, her back. Competent hands but unfamiliar ones.

"Brace her neck before you move her," she heard Seth command.

She knew she was alive. She hurt like hell and she was dizzy, but she was certain that she would be all right.

Someone else said, "They know what they're doing, son." Elwood's voice. At a distance. "Damn girl shouldn't have been trying to play private eye."

Anger in the words, but not at her. She could feel regret and self-accusation in the tone.

They were all around her. She knew, in the haze of pain and inner turbulence, that Gert had been the killer; Julie had called Gert in tears; Gert had tried to run down Rene. She recalled being jounced four or five times from the rear before the Datsun had finally swerved off into a cornfield. Gert's truck had swerved, too, in the other direction. Into the path of the oncoming semi.

She heard them all. Efficient paramedics, the heartbroken daughter, policemen espousing regret. But she didn't hear the voice she longed for. Couldn't see the beloved face.

"Sir, you'll have to step aside so we can put her in," directed the ambulance driver.

"I'm going with her," Larry said.

She closed her eyes, fought back tears of joy and fresh-born hope, tried to reach out to him. But either her arms were tied down or else she couldn't move them, and she couldn't seem to focus on him. She tried to cry out, "Larry, I'll love you forever. If you died tomorrow, I'd never go back to him."

But she could not speak, could not move. She was slipping from consciousness again.

"This is an emergency, sir. We can't allow any passengers unless they're family."

Family. For years she'd had no one to fill that role. It was the reason she'd married Seth; the reason he'd come to her graduation in June. And now she was going to the hospital with nobody beside her. Even if Seth had offered, she did not want to be with him.

"I'm not leaving her, not for an instant," Larry vowed to the paramedic, his voice low but unshakably firm. And then Rene felt his hand in her hair—tender, possessive, permanent. "I *am* her next of kin."

EPILOGUE

LARRY AND RENE got back from Dubuque on a Tuesday morning in August. It seemed like a prosaic spot for a honeymoon to Johnnie Sue, but they seemed to feel that a certain room in a certain chain hotel had some sort of sentimental value. In any event, any fool could see that the trip had gone well. They'd been sitting in the Duncans's booth holding hands and spooning for the last half hour, and Johnnie Sue had a hunch that when they went home to Larry's, the door would be locked and the phone would be taken off the hook long before nightfall.

Rene looked terrific. She was beaming, and her hair, splayed loosely over her shoulders, positively glowed. It was hard to believe that she'd been released from the hospital just a month ago. But her injuries, though painful, had not been severe, and the young heal fast.

Larry himself looked proud as punch. It felt good to see him so happy, and even better to see the pride Hershell took at working at Duncan's again. Larry still wouldn't let him fill prescriptions, but he waited on customers and gave free advice, grinning like a Cheshire cat. Now that he spent more time talking to real live people, he didn't spend nearly so much time talking to Aggie.

So life went on for Johnnie Sue. She'd convinced herself that she was more or less over Shorty. After all, even when a man doesn't say that he won't be coming back, there comes a time when you've got to accept the fact that he's not coming. And if he bothers to send you a message that leaves no room for doubt, there sure as hell isn't much point in pretending he'll change his mind. Especially if he's a stubborn old cuss like Shorty.

Henry Clancy hadn't changed his mind about Julie. He'd sort of gone nuts when he'd figured out how Fran had died. He'd sold the gas station to some nice new fellow who'd wanted to escape the hustle and bustle of Des Moines, but poor little Julie hadn't received hide nor hair of alimony once he'd disappeared.

Johnnie Sue had fixed her up an extra room in the back. She wasn't all that thrilled about taking on a young girl and a baby, but on the other hand, she was fond of Julie and she felt a hell of a lot better knowing she was doing something for poor Gert. And she knew sure as shooting that it was what Aggie would have wanted her to do.

Larry and Rene were just leaving when the big rig pulled up just beyond the front door where everybody in town could see it half blocking Main Street. It was red with white stripes and it said "Big Shorty" bright as blue blazes on the side.

Johnnie Sue started shaking. She wanted to run outside, to drag him in—or tell him it was much too late. She could only endure one heartbreak in a blue moon.

Then she thought about all the good times and all the bad with this gruffly loving man. She thought about what she'd freely given him...and what she'd fearfully denied him. He'd come back to claim her publicly, and publicly she'd have to tell him yes or no.

She slipped back into the kitchen and filled a mug with coffee—two sugars, one drop of cream—and set it on her private table.

She reached the swinging doors just as Shorty filled up the restaurant with his virile presence, stomping toward her till he stood dead center in the room. He reared back a pace when he saw her hair, then his eyes narrowed while he waited to see if she had the courage to acknowledge him.

For a long moment he was silent. She could hear nothing but the galloping of her pulse. Most of the folks kept on eating, but Larry stared at Shorty as though he knew.

Shorty looked like hell. Sunken-cheeked, haggard, like he'd been hurting, too. She wanted to run to him, to put her arms around him and beg him not to leave her again. But that would have been some other woman. Not Big Shorty's Johnnie Sue.

"I dropped by for a cup of coffee," he proclaimed belligerently. His voice could be heard by everyone in the room. To make his point—in case anybody in Porter had yet missed it—he tacked on pointedly, "I want you to serve me in the kitchen, Johnnie Sue."

Oh, he'd given her a second chance, all right, but he'd left her with only two choices. She could throw him out on his ear or take him back into her heart. She knew she didn't have the strength to throw him out, but if she served him in the kitchen every damned soul would know her most cherished secrets. They'd chuckle and tease her all the time and laugh themselves silly if he left her again.

She thought of the Cornsilk, of the happiness it brought her and the loneliness if failed to stave. She remembered the moments of laughter and joy in Big Shorty's bed...and read the unspoken plea that now called to her from his unsmiling eyes. Johnnie Sue could see that he was hurting as much as she was, but she knew that if she gave him one iota less than he demanded, he'd climb back in that big rig and storm off, anyway.

She didn't waste time debating with herself. She thrust both hands on her hips and brayed, "Well, get the hell in here before the damn stuff gets cold, Shorty. I don't have all day.''

The tiniest of smiles lit the darkness in his face, but he didn't say a word as he marched across the room. He had at least two yards of room to maneuver as he elbowed his way past Johnnie Sue's breasts, but his biceps brushed one, anyway.

Even though she knew the whole damn restaurant was watching, Johnnie Sue reached for his hand.

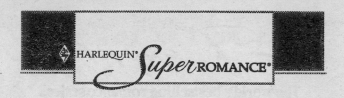
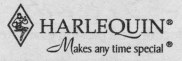

HARLEQUIN®
INTRIGUE

WE'LL LEAVE YOU BREATHLESS!

If you've been looking for thrilling tales of
contemporary passion and sensuous love stories
with taut, edge-of-the-seat suspense—then
you'll love Harlequin Intrigue!

Every month, you'll meet four new heroes
who are guaranteed to make your spine tingle
and your pulse pound. With them you'll enter
into the exciting world of Harlequin Intrigue—
where your life is on the line
and so is your heart!

THAT'S INTRIGUE—
ROMANTIC SUSPENSE
AT ITS BEST!

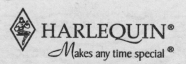

Harlequin®
Historical

From rugged lawmen and
valiant knights to defiant heiresses
and spirited frontierswomen,
Harlequin Historicals will
capture your imagination with
their dramatic scope, passion
and adventure.

Harlequin Historicals . . .
they're too good to miss!

HARLEQUIN®
Makes any time special®